Sign up for our newsletter to hear
about new and upcoming releases.

www.ylva-publishing.com

FROM FAN
TO
FOREVER

Tiana Warner

Acknowledgments

Thank you Laurel Greer and Chris Zett for beta reading, Stephanie Warner for being my sounding board, Alissa McGowan for being such an amazing and careful editor, my Crit Coven for all the years of feedback and moral support, and my family for the unconditional love and encouragement. Thank you as well to Astrid, Jenny, and the rest of the Ylva pack for all of your hard work and for believing in me and my stories.

Chapter 1
Dragging Home a Moose Floatie

I'VE BEEN AWAY FOR ONE night, and in that time, my street has turned into a movie set.

Easing my car to a stop behind an orange-and-white-striped barricade, I gape at the crowds, white tents, and trailers filling the intersection in front of my apartment. A metal fence surrounds the area like a crime scene.

My gut twists and I tighten my grip on the steering wheel. On any other day, this would be exciting, but all I want right now are my bathtub, bed, and painkillers. Today is supposed to be a blissful day off before I have to start my master's thesis research, not a daring crusade to get to my front door.

A crane lifts a camera high into the air, where ropes and wires crisscross above the set. Is that a zip-line leading into my favorite pizza place? What kind of over-the-top action flick is this?

My third-floor balcony is visible from here, with its two wooden patio chairs and the wilted hydrangeas that Abby and I never remember to water. In the window beside it, my dark bedroom curtains are shut, as always.

Staying home to spy on the set would have been more fun than that stupid-ass camping trip, but here I am, sweaty and hungover.

Scowling, I back up my rusty, old SUV and circle the block, searching for a way into the parkade.

In the rearview, my reflection is waxy and pale, and my short, sandy hair is so greasy that it's a shade darker, like I've just come out of the shower. Self-loathing has sucked the confidence from my posture.

Yeah, I was an idiot, but in my defense, Julia was flirting with me and totally into it.

"'Ooh, Rachel, let's get naked in the lake together,'" I say to the windshield, mimicking her sultry tone.

It's hard to believe that the unspoken thing between us is over—late-night study sessions, hanging out after class, inside jokes, our shared suffering as we both go after master's degrees in medical physics. She'd quickly become a good friend, and after she found out I'm a lesbian, she started asking questions about my love life and wanting to hang out more—like she was curious. Like maybe she thought she wasn't straight and wanted to explore some things.

Months of anticipation, over in one night, leaving me hollow.

This camping trip was supposed to be a big end-of-term celebration for our department. For Julia and me, it was a culmination, an excuse to get drunk and spend a couple of nights together.

The tension between us was ready to snap, and it did—so hard that it gave me whiplash.

I rub my temple, weaving through the streets and trying to get to my parkade. The movie set takes up way more space than it has any right to, forcing me to make a wide perimeter. As soon as I figure out how to get to my apartment, I'm filling the bathtub and dropping in a glittery bath bomb. Since I left yesterday morning, I've swum in a lake, gotten sweaty, been briefly rained on, and walked through a lot of spiderwebs, so I need a good scrub. My skin is so sticky that my shirt is plastered to my back.

After circling for ten minutes, I resign myself to parking three blocks away. I drag my camping gear down the road—the bag of damp clothes, the cooler of food I never ate, and a mostly deflated moose floatie. The early summer heat wave adds more sweat to what's already dried to my skin. I'd better not run into any neighbors in the elevator, or they'll be in for a treat when they get a whiff of me.

I swipe my fob to get inside, and before I open the door, laughter erupts behind me.

I whirl around, ready to tell off whoever is laughing at me for dragging camping gear down the street, but the sound is coming from the movie set.

A metal fence separates me from the set—they have to keep us peasants out, obviously—and white tents block most of my view beyond it. Between two tents is a gap that tunnels my vision to a point.

My heart does a wild, out-of-control flip, knocking me off balance so that I have to grab the door handle to stay standing.

Cate Whitney is on the other side of the fence, talking to a tattooed guy with a boom mic.

Cate. Whitney.

I forget how to breathe.

In her early forties and well-established on the A-list, she carries herself with easy confidence. She's rocking a badass black and brown steampunk outfit, including a corset, thigh-high fishnet stockings, a frilly skirt that exposes her thighs in front and hangs calf-length in the back, and a top hat with goggles resting on the brim. Her shoulder-length blond hair is in soft curls, and her white skin has a warm glow, like she's been in the tropics. She's wearing her signature mischievous smirk, her makeup drawing attention to her sharp cheekbones and ice-blue eyes.

How is it possible for anyone to be so attractive? I guess that's why she ended up in Hollywood. She's the type of woman who can rock a tux better than any man and a Valentino dress better than a runway model.

Seeing her in person sparks memories of pivotal moments in my life, making my chest flutter.

When I saw her kiss a woman in a 2000s historical drama, that was the moment I knew. Though the movie was fiction and the actors were straight, their love felt so real, sending butterflies through me. I wanted what those women had—their passion for each other, the connection that reached beyond friendship, the purity of their love.

I asked out my crush after seeing it, and she said yes.

On our fourth date, we watched that same movie together, and I made out with a girl for the first time.

So I'm not being dramatic when I say that Cate Whitney changed my life.

Now, standing with the poise of a goddess, that woman is ten feet away. She's deep in conversation with the guy with the boom mic, but that doesn't stop her from looking past him and meeting my eye.

Why? Why does she have to see me when I look like I climbed out of a dumpster?

Reflexively, I offer an awkward half-smile, which she returns.

My insides flip. This is either the greatest thing ever to happen to me or the worst, depending on whether she can smell me from this distance.

Regaining feeling in my legs, I whip open the door of my building and hurtle myself inside, then grab my camping gear and drag it in after me. The moose floatie smacks the door frame on the way in.

Cate freaking Whitney is feet away from me, filming a movie.

I hyperventilate my way up to my apartment and unlock the door with trembling hands. The familiar smell of home hits my nose—sweet-orange essential oil diffusing on the kitchen island, woven with layers of shampoo, burnt toast, and cheap coffee. Abby must be up.

I dump my camping gear and rush through the kitchen and living room toward the balcony. The apartment is as I left it, cluttered and full of low-maintenance plants. My laptop, heap of textbooks, and blanket nest are untouched on my side of the couch. Trinkets from travels, books, and pictures of friends and family take up every surface. It's disorganized—Abby prefers the term *eclectic*—but it's home.

I slide open the patio door and burst through to spy on the movie set.

The view is awe-inspiring. They've built a clockwork storefront over my favorite coffee shop. White tents and trailers, the back of wooden structures, and a lot of expensive film equipment clutter the intersection.

From the depths of the apartment, footsteps pad closer, and Abby says, "You smell like worn-off deodorant and sunscreen. I thought you weren't coming home until tomorrow."

"Cate Whitney is down there," I whisper-shout, scanning the dozens of people milling about the set.

"Fuck off!" Abby screams, rushing beside me to peer over the balcony.

I clap a hand over her mouth. "Shh!"

Abby pries my hand off. "You *saw* her?"

"Right as I was coming inside." I wrack my brain for the last headline I saw about Cate Whitney. "She must be filming *Clockwork Curie.*"

There she is. She's with a group of people behind the cameras, pointing at a monitor and nodding. She's easy to spot because of the outfit but also because of that abnormally attractive Hollywood look. What is *with* that?

"Clockwork what?" Abby says.

"It's a steampunk movie about Marie Curie," I whisper. "The scientist. We were talking about it in class not long ago."

As if a high-budget movie about science hero Marie Curie isn't awesome enough, they had to go and cast Cate Whitney as the lead. Excuse me while I cry feminist tears.

"Abby, she was, like, ten feet away from me," I say, making sure she understands the situation.

I peel my gaze away from the set. Abby is wearing a smart navy blazer and no pants. Her thick, dark hair is styled to emphasize its natural waves, she's wearing makeup, and her oversized glasses are unusually free of smudges.

"What's up with you?" I ask.

"Virtual job interview."

"What company?"

"Enough about me. Are you going to try and meet Cate?"

My heart jumps at the question like I've just been dive-bombed by an angry crow. "What? No. She's working."

"Girl, you've been obsessed with her since before you knew you were a lesbian. Remember the magazine pictures taped to your high school locker?"

"Shh!" I say, dragging Abby inside. I slam the patio door and round on her. "I can't just walk up to her!"

"Sure you can. Rachel, this is the universe bringing you an opportunity," she says, picking lint off her blazer. "Seize it."

I rub my tired eyes. Cate Whitney really is a queer icon. Between her film roles, her wardrobe, and being an outspoken ally, I'm positive that if someone were to poll all of the lesbians and ask them to rank their top celebrity crushes, she would win the popular vote.

I guess I could try to say hi to my hero. The prospect sends a nervous thrill through my chest. "What would I even say?"

Abby opens the bamboo privacy screen we use as a backdrop during video calls, which conveniently masks the surrounding disaster. "I don't know. *Big fan of your work?*"

"Ugh, that's so normal."

"If you want her to remember you for something abnormal, fine, but I think you're better off sticking with something average here."

"Fair enough." I hesitate, heart thumping. Then I shake my head firmly. "No, I can't. It's too awkward."

"You have to!"

Carefully, she places her laptop in front of the dirty dishes and unfolded laundry on the kitchen table.

"You just want me out of the apartment during your interview," I say.

"Well, yes, but I also want you to seize the day. Do it. I'm not letting you back in until you say at least one word to her."

"Excuse me?" I say, laughing.

"You heard me, Rachel Henrietta Janssen," she says severely. "I'm shoving you out the door and bolting it until you succeed."

"What if I'm not allowed on se—"

"I double dare you," she says in a girly tone reminiscent of our high school slumber parties.

"Oh, shut it."

She makes chicken noises and I throw a tissue box at her. It bounces off her chest.

"Did Amelia Earhart let people stop her from achieving her goals?" she asks, waving her arms.

"Amelia Earhart died while achieving her goal, Abby."

"Beside the point. You'll thank me later."

I chew my lip. As uncomfortable as it would be to approach a celebrity, I would live my life in deep regret if I didn't do it. Cate Whitney is more than a celebrity crush. She's a legend, an icon who helped me discover my sexuality and come out.

"It's not like you're the only one. I saw a couple of girls leaning over the fence to get pics with the actors last night," Abby says, a wry smile on her lips, like she knows I'm at my tipping point.

I can't help it—my face breaks into a grin. "Dare accepted. I'll ask her to sign the back of my phone."

I grab a permanent marker from the jar on the counter.

"An autograph? What kind of person in this day and age—" Abby stops, probably remembering that the alternative is to ask for a selfie, and I hate having my picture taken. "I guess having Cate Whitney's signature on the back of your phone would be cool."

"Hell yeah, it would. Do I have time to shower before your interview?"

"Yes!" Abby squeals in excitement. She opens her laptop and settles into a chair, checking the position of the privacy screen. "You've got twenty-four minutes to get out of here. Why are you back early, anyway? How was camping?"

"Good luck with your interview," I shout, racing to the bathroom.

My attempt to dodge her question doesn't work, and she chases after me.

"How was camping, Rachel?"

"Fine!"

"Liar."

Ugh, she's too perceptive.

Before I can shut the door, she wedges her hand between it and the frame.

"What happened with Julia, Rachel?"

Chapter 2
Bringing My A-Game

I OPEN MY MOUTH TO tell Abby it's nothing, but she gives me a stern look. I'll feel better when I talk about it, and we both know it.

"Fine. You were right about her."

Abby's face falls. "Oh. Shit."

"Give me one sec," I say, shutting the door.

She gives me a minute to get into the shower. I pop some painkillers, strip down, and step under the lukewarm stream with a groan. I don't think a shower has ever felt so good.

The moment I shut the curtain, Abby comes into the bathroom and sits on the counter. "Okay, go."

I sigh, squeezing shampoo into my palm.

"So we're all drinking around the fire and playing beer pong," I say, my voice amplified by the bathroom's acoustics, "and she keeps catching my eye—or maybe we're catching each other's. Either way, it's hard to misinterpret the way she's looking at me. It's that sultry, through-the-lashes look, you know?"

"Oh, yeah. Definitely flirty."

I lather my hair, eyes closed. "We end up standing beside each other at the drinks table, and we're both getting fall-down drunk, like we're using alcohol for courage. And she keeps grabbing my shoulder *for balance*."

"Mm. I've used that ruse many a time."

"Exactly. So I tested the waters with a flirty tequila shot—that move where you put the lime in your mouth so the other person has to bite it from your lips."

Abby squeaks. "And she did it?"

"She lingered as our lips brushed."

A pause. "Okay, that's more than flirty."

I rinse my hair, stomach twisting in anticipation of what comes next. "So I'm like, 'Hey, want to get in our bikinis and jump in the lake?' And you know what she says?"

"What?"

I crack open the curtain to see her face. "She says, 'Who needs bikinis?' and runs into the lake naked."

Abby gasps, her eyes enormous as she drinks in this juicy story. "You skinny-dipped?"

I nod, vividly recalling the swoop that went through me, like the moths around the lanterns had gotten trapped in my chest.

I tug the curtain closed and grab the conditioner.

"Where was everyone else?" Abby says.

"Drunk and occupied. Nobody noticed us running off together."

The glassy lake was out of sight and sound of the campers, leaving the two of us alone in the pristine wilderness. The bright streak of the Milky Way crossed overhead, and the BC rainforest loomed thick and high on all sides, like we were at the center of a snow globe.

The moonlight was bright enough to see her blazing-hot gaze, her pale, glistening shoulders and chest, and her nipples playing peek-a-boo at the surface. After months of falling for her, of smiling when she smiled, wanting to make her laugh, wanting her to think about me when we weren't together, I finally had her alone—ready to follow through on what we'd been silently promising each other.

When she drifted closer, laughing in her usual adorable way, heat tingled between my legs. This gorgeous woman had told me she wanted to try kissing me, and there was no questioning what was going to happen.

"So we're in the water," I say, scrubbing down, "and she tells me my tattoo is sexy and uses it as an excuse to touch me."

"God, that tattoo has been such a sex-starter for you."

"I know, right?" Who knew a ribcage tattoo would have that effect? Women love the glimpse of it when I wear muscle shirts. "Anyway, I asked if she was still curious, and she nodded, and…"

9

And beneath the water, her skin was achingly soft and warm in the cool lake. I ran my palms over her curves, up to her breasts, and her breath hitched, smelling like tequila and lime as it tickled my face.

Our lips met. Her hands brushed over my breasts, gently, and then with confidence as our tongues explored each other's mouths. Heat spread through me, a tingling rushing lower.

Her fingers traveled down my neck, over my back, and down to my hips, where she pulled me against her. She moaned as I teased her with my tongue, playing with her lips.

Then her hand moved lower, lower…

"And stuff started happening." I turn off the water and reach through the curtain. Abby passes me my towel. "And then…"

I wrap the towel around me and step out of the shower, solemn. Abby's covering her mouth, like she's afraid of what's coming.

"Her boyfriend found us," I say, my self-loathing at an all-time high.

Found us, shouted at us, drove a crack into that perfect snow globe.

"Boyfriend?" Abby shrieks. "She didn't tell you that she has a *boyfriend*?"

"Oh, I knew about Andrew," I say, heat rising in my face. "But she barely ever talked about him, and when she did, it was to complain about him. She spent more time with me than him last night."

"Ah."

"So, yeah, I'm an idiot…" I tug open a drawer and absentmindedly rummage. "But also, she's clearly not into him anymore and just stringing him along! So I don't know which of us is the worse person here."

"You're probably both awful," Abby says helpfully.

I sigh. "So she starts defending herself. 'We were just having fun, Andrew. I told you I wanted to experiment, Andrew.'"

Abby jumps off the counter. "Fuck off. She didn't."

"For fun. An experiment. No real feelings."

My eyes burn, and I turn away under the pretense of reaching for the hairdryer. It gives me the few seconds I need to pull myself together.

"So I left them to fight it out on the shoreline and went for a walk," I say, relieved to hear cool indifference in my voice.

My walk lasted until sunrise and sobriety. Because that's what I do when I'm stressed or confused or too drunk to make good decisions—I find a nice path, and I walk.

It probably wasn't smart to walk alone in the forest at night, where the cougar and bear populations are famously high, but I'm alive, aren't I?

Alive and fine.

Sort of.

"Oh, Rachel," Abby says. She lifts her arms, then drops them, like she was about to wrap me in a hug before realizing it would get her shirt wet before her interview. "Babe, you deserve better than that. You shouldn't be anyone's experiment or *just for fun*. You're someone's soulmate."

"Thanks," I say, blinking before my burning eyes betray me.

Abby's been warning me not to get attached to Julia for months, and she was absolutely right. Julia didn't want a girlfriend. She was experimenting with her sexuality, and I was the test subject.

But my last serious girlfriend was shy, guarded, and desperate to keep me a secret, so Julia's free spirit lured me in. Her boldness was hot, and I let my heart take hold of me.

Why did my brain have to run off and imagine a relationship with her? Bringing her home to meet my family, flying to exciting destinations together, walking the beach hand-in-hand? This physically hurts, like a stab wound in my chest.

"I'll get over it," I say, forcing a smile. "It's her fault that blew up. Right?"

"Oh, for sure. She came onto you, and now she and her pissed-off boyfriend can work that out."

I don't know if Abby is just being loyal, but it makes my smile come easier.

"You can just, like, avoid Julia on campus forevermore," she adds.

I grimace. "I absolutely will be doing that. Anyway, I'll get out of here so you can do your interview."

Abby hesitates, and I feel her stare.

"I'm fine, Abby. Really. Meeting my lesbian awakening will cheer me up."

She smiles. "That's the spirit."

"How long do I have?"

Abby checks her phone. "Twelve minutes."

"I'll be out in eleven." I race to my bedroom, which is basically a cave because I never open the curtains and only have one bedside lamp. I put on black Bermuda shorts and a white collared shirt, then quickly do my hair and makeup. If I'm going to meet an actor I have a massive crush on, I should bring my A-game. I dry and spray my hair, sweeping it to one side, then put on dark eyeliner and touch up my eyebrows.

I check out my reflection in the dusty mirror that I haven't had time to clean in months. My undercut needs attention, but I have no time for that right now.

"Confidence," I whisper, trying to summon it.

I'm more nervous than if I had to do a presentation, but this is a once-in-a-lifetime opportunity, and I'll kick myself if I miss the chance to meet Cate Whitney. If it's totally awkward, I'm sure her memory of me will blend in with the thousands of other fans who have approached her.

And if I'm not allowed to meet her…well, I'll have to try harder. Fangirling aside, Abby dared me, and I probably won't be allowed back into the apartment until I do it. We take Truth or Dare very seriously.

I put my phone, key, and the permanent marker in my pockets.

"Good luck," I whisper, slipping out the door as Abby settles in front of her laptop, still pantsless.

She gives me a two-finger salute. "Same to you."

On the street, I let out a slow breath. I feel better after pouring my heartache onto Abby, but the hole in my chest is going to take time to heal. I haven't had a serious relationship in five years—not since Sarah and I broke up in grade twelve. I've been telling myself I'm not in the right mental state, and that university makes it hard to find time for it—but this tells me I'm ready to be fully invested in someone again.

I guess it just won't be with Julia.

Ugh, she wasn't even my girlfriend, and it still feels like I got dumped.

Walking the perimeter of the set, I find a gap in the metal fence where people with badges walk in and out.

I address the security guard blocking it. "Are there any meet-and-greets with the actors?"

He laughs like I'm cute for asking. "Sorry, love. The actors are pretty busy."

I figured as much. I'll have to see if I can spot Cate over the fence—or else sneak inside, if I'm feeling especially daring.

I pretend to give up and walk the perimeter again, testing for weaknesses like a clever velociraptor trying to escape her enclosure.

The fence reaches all the way around the set, and the only break is at the back of one of the white tents—but that's no good because the tent is blocking the way in.

I pause.

Unless…

There's a gap between the ground and the base of the tent. What if I could lift it and slip under?

If Abby were here, she would be pushing me toward the gap right now.

I don't know what possesses me to do it. Maybe I'm too tired to realize it's a terrible idea on all levels. Maybe I'm feeling reckless after such a catastrophic weekend. Maybe I'm so desperate for a small win in my life that I'm willing to do something drastic to get it. I wait until the street is empty, then drop to my hands and knees and lift the bottom of the tent.

It's stiff, made of some kind of thick, ruthless polyester. I have to tug hard to fit under it, and even then, I'm lying on the pavement with my boobs pressed flat.

Panting, I claw my way under and pop out on the other side with a gasp.

I try to stand—and my head smashes into something.

"Ow!"

I brace on all fours, dizzy. Why the hell didn't I check whether I ended up underneath anything?

Beside me, several trays hit the floor, and fruit and sandwiches scatter across the pavement.

"Fuck," I say, crawling out from under the table. My hand smears a mustard-covered croissant across the ground.

Apparently, I have arrived in the craft services tent.

"Oh, you scared me," a smooth voice says.

I lift my gaze and meet a pair of ice-blue eyes. Everything inside me melts. I'm about to become a puddle on the pavement.

I did not think this would work.

I honestly expected to be kicked out or to wander the set for five minutes before panicking and leaving, so that I could tell Abby I tried.

Cate is standing there, holding a script in one hand and a strawberry in the other. She's cool and charming in her steampunk outfit and professional makeup—and I'm on the ground with mustard on my hands.

Chapter 3
Big Dyke Energy

Cate Whitney stares at me in a way I never, ever wanted her to stare at me—a mix of confusion, horror, and pity. She lowers the script, which she must have been reviewing.

I jump to my feet, wiping my mustardy palms on the back of my shorts. "B-big fan of your work," I blurt.

Dammit, why did Abby have to suggest I say that? I sound like an idiot.

I guess it's better than saying, *Hi, you were my lesbian awakening and I've seen your movies multiple times and find you incredibly attractive.*

My face is absolutely on fire. I definitely look like a shiny tomato right now.

Cate tilts her head, perplexed. "Are you…working on set?"

Her smooth, husky voice brings to mind the number of villains she's played. My insides tingle.

Then the meaning of her words sinks in.

Crap. She's onto me.

"No, I don't work here," I admit. "I was wondering if—" I stop, like my throat has sealed shut. If I tell her I snuck in to ask for an autograph, she's going to think I'm a stalker. I don't want to be responsible for giving her the feeling that she isn't safe from rabid fans.

Am I being a rabid fan? *Dammit, Abby.*

No, it's not like I keep track of where she is and what she's doing. I respect her privacy and avoid tabloids and paparazzi shots. I just admire her. And I'm torn between wanting to be her and wanting to kiss her.

Fuck. I'm being weird.

"I was wondering if the producer is accepting applications," I say, shoving the marker deeper into my back pocket to preserve my last shred of self-respect. "For a—science—consultant."

"Oh?" She raises an eyebrow.

I stand taller. "Yeah. I'm a graduate medical physics student specializing in Marie Curie's work."

The Marie Curie part is a stretch, but I've taken radiotherapy physics, so it's not a *total* lie.

Her lips curve upward, almost imperceptibly, and I'm pretty sure she doesn't believe for a second that I'm here for a job application. But she doesn't call security or tell me to leave.

"You probably understand this role better than I do," she says, holding up the script. "Any tips? I know Marie Curie discovered radium and coined the term *radioactive*, but I don't get what it all means or how she discovered it. Any research I've tried to do has taken me too far down a physics rabbit hole."

"She invented a technique for isolating radioactive isotopes. She discovered polonium, too." I'm about to say more, but I shut my mouth when Cate's brow furrows. This gibberish must be supremely unhelpful.

"Radioactive isotopes," she says, tasting the words. "But how does someone just *discover* a new element?"

"She extracted them from a mineral called pitchblende."

Cate's gaze is fixed on me, making my face heat up. She chews her lip, looks at the script, then points across the set. "We might be able to use a consultant. I have to get ready for my next scene, but are you okay going to find a producer?"

"Sure," I say, having absolutely no intention of making a further fool of myself in front of this film crew.

Cate eats the strawberry she was holding before I crawled into her life. The way her gaze is fixed on me while she sucks on it is enough to make me forget how to breathe.

I always thought her gay vibes were part of her acting talent, but the energy is real. It's something about the way she carries herself, or maybe the intense eye contact. If we were in a club, I'd be offering to buy her a drink right now.

I walk past her to where she pointed because it's the only thing to do. The permanent marker presses against my butt.

I knew I would be starstruck, but this is ridiculous. I can barely string my thoughts together.

Before leaving the tent, I turn and say, "I'm sorry I ruined the food table."

She casts a gorgeous half-smile that makes me sway. "I won't tell a soul it was you. Good luck with the job application."

Did I just swoon?

"Thanks," I say.

And my big moment meeting Cate Whitney is over. I open my mouth to ask for a signature, remember my last shred of dignity, and close it again.

Why can't I be cool? Why do I have to be covered in mustard and croissant flakes right now?

"Hold on," she says, striding toward me. She reaches out and plucks something from my hair.

A tingle runs down my neck.

A cobweb is pinched between her fingers. She lets it flutter away.

"Must be dirty under the table. We can't have you going for your job application with that in your hair."

From this close, she smells sweet and summery.

"No," I say, breathless. "Thank you, Cate."

"You're welcome…" She pauses, and it takes me a moment to realize she's waiting for me to fill in the gap.

"Rachel," I say. "Rachel Janssen."

A guy my age rushes over and shoves a granola bar into Cate's hands. "You got a call from your publicist about the gala. Also, you need protein."

He has the poise of a dancer and every inch of him is well put together, from his buzzed black hair to his purple suit to his platform shoes. His deep brown skin is flawlessly contoured with shimmery makeup.

"They'll be ready to block the scene in a few minutes," he adds, typing frantically on his phone.

Cate doesn't take her eyes off me, apparently immune to having this guy fuss over her while she's in the middle of something.

"Rachel," she says. "Hope I see you around."

The guy shoots me a suspicious look, like he didn't notice me until now.

I give an awkward nod and leave the tent, stomach doing flips.

I spoke to Cate Whitney. She touched my hair. She told me she hopes to see me around. My name came out of her lips.

Except she definitely thinks I'm weird.

And I am. Weird, awkward, and mortified.

Why did I sneak onto the set like this? I blame Abby.

I leave the tent behind, torn between wanting to crawl into a hole and wanting to fist-pump. It's sweet that Cate wished me luck and made me feel worthy about applying for a job I would never get. I guess her kind reputation is true.

I slip through the exit, earning a double-take from the security guard who turned me away minutes earlier.

Oh well. I'm leaving, not arriving, so he can't do much now.

I don't want to interrupt Abby's interview, so I walk up and down the beach until my gay panic subsides. Around me, people and their dogs are scattered across the shore, enjoying the heat. The sun glints off the gentle waves, where boaters, kayakers, and paddleboarders coast by. The air smells like barbecue, and seagulls are trying to ambush people and steal their food like a noisy sky gang.

I cover my face as I walk behind a couple taking a selfie. All of this activity is nice, but living by the beach is better in the off-season when there are fewer people around.

As I walk back and forth, Cate's energy clings to me like steam in a sauna. I can't get over her touching my hair.

She was way too nice to me. In her position, I probably would have called security.

My stomach growls, and I head for my favorite sandwich shop—which has, apparently, been converted into a steampunk storefront for the movie set. A sign on the metal fence tells me that all shops in the area are closed for the summer.

I groan and keep walking. There's a crêpe place up the road that'll do fine.

It's busy inside, probably because all of the would-be-customers of the other shops have been displaced. The best spots to eat have been absorbed by the movie set.

After ordering a spinach and feta crêpe and a coffee, I grab the last, lonely seat on the patio. If I were smarter, I would have brought my laptop. The nagging feeling that I should be working is a permanent fixture in my life, and I could be using this precious time to do thesis research.

I pull out my phone and look up the machine learning program I've been eyeing. There might be a gold nugget in this program if I can use it to analyze medical imagery, and I can read about it until Abby tells me it's safe to come home.

But after a few minutes of poking around the internet, it's clear that I don't have the mental capacity for this today. First, I'm hungover and haven't slept. Second, it's not easy to concentrate on deep-learning algorithms when I've just come face-to-face with one of the most talented and attractive women in the world.

Third, my heart is still dust after getting crushed by a woman who I secretly thought would turn gay for me.

I guess you could say I'm not in the right headspace for thesis research right now.

A text from Abby pops up, sparing me from my listless scrolling and crêpe-eating.

Interview went well, and they want another with the team leads in 10 mins. Are you okay to hang out for a bit? I can text you when I'm done.

Her news lifts my mood a little. It's a nice day, so I'm fine to stay out of the apartment.

Yay for rocking the interview! No problem. I'm just eating and hanging out.

Awesome. Thanks, bestie. Any luck meeting Cate?

My mouth twists into a smile.

I met her. Didn't get the chance to ask for a signature, but we said actual words to each other. My heart is still recovering.

What?!!! Is she as amazing in person?

It was like talking to a goddess. She doesn't need to know the details.

You're my hero. Text you soon.

An hour later, I've managed to absorb a few tidbits of research and am still waiting to hear from Abby. The interview must be going well if it's gone on for this long.

Programming interviews sound awful. I can't imagine having a prospective employer stare at me while I write code for several hours.

Then again, to a lot of people, everything I study in medical physics sounds awful. Maybe a six-hour interview is better than taking courses in quantum mechanics, nuclear medicine, and radiotherapy. Abby seems to think so.

I'm hungry again, so I go inside to order another crêpe. The cool air is a relief after spending a couple of hours on the patio. All four tables inside are still occupied, and two people stand waiting for their orders.

As I scan the chalkboard menu on the wall, it reminds me of the last time I had crêpes, with Julia during a study session. The ache of losing her is getting worse, like I haven't fully processed it yet. She and I had a fun thing going, even if it was doomed to end in an angry boyfriend.

I guess I thought the camping trip would end in me asking her out properly.

"What can I get you?" the teenage girl behind the counter asks, clearly waiting for me to hurry up and decide what I want.

In the mood for sweet instead of savory this time, I order the chocolate-strawberry crêpe.

I'm reaching for my wallet when the air shifts around me and murmurs meet my ears.

Heads turn toward the door. Everyone whispers, leans into each other, and points.

A tall woman walks into the café, her presence lighting up the whole place. Smiling, apparently immune to the stir she's causing, she takes off her sunglasses and looks up at the chalkboard menu.

I catch a glimpse of her steampunk costume under a jacket that's too warm for this weather. Cate Whitney must be on a break from filming.

Chapter 4
Radioactive Isotopes

Even if I hadn't known who she was, something about Cate Whitney's presence makes it obvious that she's a celebrity—maybe the designer jacket draped over her shoulders, or maybe her aura. Famous people definitely have an aura.

Beyond the glass café door, a huge, muscled guy with a samurai bun stands with his arms crossed like a bouncer.

Hot damn, is that her personal bodyguard?

By the time Cate walks up to stand behind me, my face is burning and my heart is racing.

Holy crap. I'm about to say words to her again.

We meet each other's gaze, and recognition crosses her face.

"Rachel, right?"

"Yes. That's me. Hi."

"How did the job application go?" she asks with a wry smile.

It takes me a second to realize she's not talking about Abby's interview but my fake science consultant application. The teasing note in her voice makes my face burn.

Ugh, she's totally onto me. I'm not sure how to recover from this.

"I didn't find the right person," I say, continuing my pathetic act. "So… um, I left. It's fine. I'm in the middle of getting my master's, so it's probably for the best."

Mercifully, the girl behind the counter hands me the credit card machine, demanding my attention. I fumble with my card and tap it on the machine.

"What do you recommend here?" Cate says, studying the chalkboard menu.

Her sweet coconut scent meets my nose, making me think of tropical vacations and happiness.

"Everything is good. I got the chocolate-strawberry, but um—" The memory of her lips around the strawberry in the craft services tent returns. I swallow hard. "The savory ones are a better choice for lunch."

Cate orders a West Coast, which has Pacific smoked salmon, local cream cheese, and comes with Canadian maple syrup. She smiles at me. "When in Rome."

"Good choice."

While she takes the machine from the starstruck cashier, she says to me, "I usually eat lunch at craft services, but something happened to the sandwiches."

I may die. "Oh my God, I'm so—"

"It's okay," she says, laughing. "I'm happy to support a local café."

"I'm still sorry." And more embarrassed than I've ever been in my life. Which is saying something, considering I was naked in a lake with somebody's girlfriend last night.

"I appreciate your help earlier," Cate says. "Researching for this role has been a chore. What was the term you used? Radioactive isotopes?"

I nod. "It's radiotherapy jargon. Just remember radium and polonium."

"Even that's over my head. But I need to know about these things if I'm going to play a convincing Marie Curie."

"Don't worry. I think Marie Curie's work is over most people's heads."

The girl behind the counter directs us to stand at the far end to wait for our orders.

As we shuffle along, Cate says, "Maybe. But I failed my science classes at UCLA, so this doesn't bode well, Rachel."

My heart thrums at the sound of my name on her lips. Everything that comes out of her mouth sounds like she's whispering in my ear.

"I'm sure nobody's going to judge you for failing a science class."

She grimaces. "I haven't actually told that to anyone involved in the film. And now I've told a stranger. God, please don't run to the press with that."

I'm not sure whether to laugh or swear my allegiance, so I do both. "I won't," I say with a smile. "You went to UCLA?"

"For one year because my parents didn't want me to go straight into acting. It was abysmal. Waste of their money. And now you're probably thinking poorly of me for being a bad student."

"I am not," I say, laughing. "Though I admit, I was probably the type of kid you copied your homework from."

She gasps. "How did you know about that?"

"It happens to nerds everywhere."

"Oh, stop. You're not a nerd." She nudges me gently, and her touch sends a jolt of electricity through me.

"I graduated top of my class," I confess.

"That doesn't make you a nerd."

"I play video games in my spare time and once built my own computer."

She laughs, and I grin apologetically.

"Okay, you win." She raises her hands in surrender.

Her gaze lingers on me for long enough that my cheeks burn. There's something curious behind her eyes.

"Cate!" a guy across the café says.

Cate doesn't turn, but I do. He's standing, phone up and ready to snap a photo, while his date giggles and blushes.

Automatically, I put a hand over my forehead like the brim of a hat, hiding my face from his camera.

Ignoring him, Cate says to me, "I wonder if I could ask you—"

"Just a smile, Cate," the guy says, waiting for her to oblige.

I drop my hand. "You're being rude," I say, snappier than I intended. "Sit down and eat your chicken strips, dumbass."

His date looks like she can't decide whether to laugh or be mortified. She covers a giggle, her face reddening as Chicken Strips glares at me. What kind of man-child orders chicken strips in a crêpe restaurant?

Despite my tough face, my heart thumps and sweat prickles on the back of my neck. The sight of this guy taking a photo without Cate's consent triggers a memory that I try not to think about.

I huff and focus on Cate, stepping sideways so she can put her back to the guy. "You were saying?"

Cate is wearing a little smirk, eyebrow raised.

I swear, if she keeps looking at me with such blazing intensity, I'm going to melt like a milkshake in this heat wave.

Chicken Strips unlocked something in the café. Though he's given up on asking Cate to smile for a picture, a few others seem emboldened, and there are more phones out than ever.

I'm light-headed at the sight of all the cameras facing us.

The café door swings open, and several noisy people push inside—along with Cate's bodyguard.

"Cate, can I have your autograph?" a breathless woman says.

"Hey, everybody, give her space," the bodyguard says, closing his large hands over peoples' shoulders.

"It's okay, Ken," Cate says.

I want to scream at these people. Cate was about to ask me something. Astonishingly, she seemed interested in me and my career.

As people swarm Cate, taking pictures and asking for autographs, someone shoves me back a step. Her bodyguard, Ken, forces people to stay civil.

"Chocolate-strawberry for Rachel," a guy behind the counter shouts.

I grab my order and back away from the crowd, silently cursing everyone in here.

"Autograph," a man with a thick accent says, shoving a photo of Cate and a pen close to her face.

As much as I'd like to punch everyone, it looks like it's time to get the hell out of here and go enjoy my crêpe on the beach.

"Rachel, wait."

Cate pushes over, breathless.

She holds up the pen that the guy passed her for an autograph. "I have to be back on set soon, but send me a text. I'd like to talk more about radioactive isotopes, if that suits you."

She winks, which would have made me keel backward if she hadn't been holding my hand. I'm in a dream as she writes her phone number on my palm.

"Yes. Of course. I'd love to," I say, struggling for air. When I look up from my palm, she's turned her attention to the people swarming her, smiling with a lot more grace than I would have in her situation.

"What's your name?" she asks the man kindly, a pen poised over the paper.

"No name, just signature," he says.

I'm bitter on Cate's behalf. *Asshole's going to turn around and sell her autograph on eBay.*

But she keeps smiling and autographing, pausing for photos, and asking people how their days are going—and it's clear that she's a much better person than I will ever be. She doesn't protest when people raise their phones like they're entitled to a picture, and she doesn't tell them to step back when they pose with their arms around her and their cheeks pressed together.

I look back at my palm, heart jumping.

My lesbian awakening just gave me her number.

When I tell Abby as much, she screams and throws her arms around me. "I told you! I told you it was worth going down to the set! Wow, aren't you glad you took that radio-whatever-it-was class last term?"

I laugh, looking at the digits on my palm like it's a winning lottery number.

"I have good news too," Abby says, breathless. "I got the job."

We scream some more, and our hug turns into a jumping embrace.

"What's the company called?" I ask after we've calmed down.

"Triple-X POV."

"Triple-X? Like, porn?"

She adjusts her glasses, which slipped down her nose when we jump-hugged. "Yeah. It's web development for a point-of-view porn site. They get twenty million hits a day and are one of the fastest growing adult websites. I get full benefits, six weeks of vacation, a wellness subsidy, and a six-figure salary."

"Shit," I say, putting a hand over my heart. "That is good."

She does a jig. She's shed her blazer and is in a gray tank top and underwear—her favorite summer outfit. "So, when are you going to text Cate Whitney?"

A bolt of stress strikes me, elevating my pulse. "Tonight. I'll wait a few hours."

While Abby opens a celebratory bottle of wine, I add Cate's number carefully to my contacts.

Her composure was impressive while all of those people were taking pictures and demanding her time and space. Then again, she probably doesn't have high school trauma to trigger her.

Stop thinking about that. I've been getting on fine in spite of it for years.

I dive into thesis research, forcing myself to focus.

I find a slew of papers related to my topic: using deep-learning algorithms to detect tumors. It's clear that applying machine learning to MRI scans helps to identify tumors more quickly and accurately. As for the best algorithm? That remains to be seen. I'm planning to use software that was intended for international defense and intelligence—it's the best in the world at identifying subtleties in satellite images, and I think this will translate well if I feed it MRI scans and train it to recognize tumor borders instead of patterns in a landscape.

But as I try to read papers, I keep gazing numbly into space, and I'm a fraction as productive as I should be.

At six o'clock, I can't wait any longer.

I grab my phone and open a new text.

Hi Cate, it's Rachel Janssen. My schedule is open if you'd like to meet up some time to talk about Marie Curie.

I hover over the *Send* button for so long that Abby yells from across the room, "Hurry up and send it, you disaster."

I tap the button and my message goes out into space.

I stare at our brand-new text exchange, my heart thumping, until the screen dims and goes black.

Of course she won't reply right away. She could still be filming or out for dinner with her costars or meeting with producers. I have no idea what an actor's life is like.

Or she changed her mind and regrets giving me her number.

While Abby "studies for her new job" (there's a lot of moaning and *oh-yes-mmm* noises coming from her laptop), I make dinner, distracting myself with a complicated eggplant lasagna recipe.

My phone beeps two hours later as I'm washing dishes, and I lunge for it so fast that I smack the back of my hand on the counter. I roar in pain, cradling my hand while leaning over to look at the phone screen.

The name on the message isn't Cate. It's Julia.

Hey. We're back from camping. Rachel, I am so, so sorry for how awkward that was…and for leading you into that situation. I won't blame being drunk because I was using alcohol to build courage to do that.

Awkwardness floods back to me so intensely that my face burns and my skin prickles beneath my shirt.

I shouldn't feel this guilty. She led me on. She was building courage, which means she was planning a kiss while sober.

I type a reply.

Thanks for the apology. I'm sorry for kissing you. I should've thought about Andrew.

I hope you're not too sorry for kissing me.

I blink at the words. Too sorry? Like, she doesn't want me to regret it?

Andrew and I broke up. We agreed it wasn't working.

My heart leaps as an unwanted ray of hope shines through me. I grit my teeth and smother it. Even if Julia is single, she still sees me as "for fun."

Sorry to hear that. And sorry for my involvement. You okay?

Yeah, thanks. It's a relief to let go of him, actually. I need to figure some things out.

I'm not sure what to say to that. I might be a science student, but this is not the type of experimenting I find fun.

The dots appear again to tell me she's typing. They're there for a long time. I keep staring, heart thumping.

The dots go away. Appear again. My heart beats faster.

I want to finish what we started. I want a real experience with a woman. I'm curious what it's like to taste a woman and to have her go down on me. ;)

I cross my legs to tame the tingling down there. Fuck, Julia. *There's* the flirting she's been dishing out for the last several months. She's not shy about talking dirty, and it's such a turn-on.

I'd love to give her the pleasure. I'd give her every trick my tongue and fingers know, teasing her clit, playing with her nipples, running my fingers over her G-spot. I'd build her up and give her the best orgasm of her life, leaving her a panting, disheveled mess on the bedsheets.

But she said it right there: *a* woman. She's not interested in me, just in experimenting with a generic woman. I'm a test subject—an interchangeable lesbian who can give her the experience she's after.

Maybe this sort of arrangement would work for some people, but I want to be with someone who wants to date *me*, not someone who sees me as a generic sex partner. I need an emotional connection.

I had fun with you, Julia, but I'm afraid of putting my heart through this. I know you want to experiment with women, but for me, it's about more than that. I want it to lead to a relationship.

The pause is long enough that my screen turns off before she replies.

I get that. I can't promise that I'll want a relationship.

That's all she says. Again, she's direct.
My heart aches like someone is squeezing it with both hands.

Thanks for being honest. Hey, if you realize you're super queer and want me as your girlfriend, hit me up. You're really cool, and I've had fun with you.

I've had fun with you too. :)

I leave it there. I don't want to end this conversation with a promise that we'll hang out, but I also don't want to be finite and say, *See you in the fall*. Maybe we'll hang out as friends, or maybe not.

For now, I let the conversation drop—and my heart is miraculously still beating, even though it feels completely shattered.

Dammit, why did I do this to myself?

I sit on the couch, too drained to finish the dishes.

It's been five years since I was in a serious relationship, and I thought I'd finally found someone. How naive is that? It's so obvious, now that I think about it, that she was more into the idea of me than actually dating me.

My phone beeps, and I take a minute before returning to it. I'm not ready to keep talking to Julia. I need to forget about her for a while.

But when I look at my phone, a wild flutter soars through my midsection.

Hi, Rachel. Thanks for getting back to me. Filming goes late most nights, but are you free to come to the set tomorrow around noon? I'd love to talk to you between takes.

The breath leaves my lungs.

Cate Whitney replied to me. She invited me to come onto the movie set with her. Holy crap.

Hi Cate. Yes, I would be happy to come to the set tomorrow.

Perfect. When you get to the gate, text my assistant and he'll come get you.

She sends through a contact for someone named Sean Richards.

That's it. That's the end of our text exchange. I'm breathless, wanting more, but there's nothing else to say.

I save Sean into my phone, hoping he isn't the guy who shot me a suspicious look when I stumbled onto set.

My pulse is racing with excitement. Tomorrow, I'm going to be Cate Whitney's guest on the set of *Clockwork Curie*.

CHAPTER 5
CLOCKWORK

CATE'S ASSISTANT IS, OF COURSE, the suspicious guy from yesterday.

Thankfully, she seems to have given her blessing because Sean strides over and hugs me like we're besties who haven't seen each other in weeks.

"Rachel! It's lovely to meet you. Here's your guest badge." He drapes a lanyard over my neck like it's a lei and I've just arrived in Hawaii.

"Thanks," I say, smug as we walk past the security guy who shooed me away yesterday.

The weather is mild and overcast. I don't know much about moviemaking, but I think this makes it a good day for filming.

"Cate is still in rehearsal," Sean says. "Can I give you a tour?"

"I'd love one!"

I would also love some time to stop being so nervous before I say hi to Cate. I spent half the morning brushing up on Marie Curie, afraid of disappointing Cate by not knowing as much as she expected. The whole point of my being here today is to help her, and I'd better be able to. I spent the other half of the morning stressing over looking nice—doing my makeup, trimming my hair and notching fresh razor lines into my undercut, and then pulling everything I own from my closet. After peering down at the set and realizing that nobody was dressed particularly fashionably, I calmed down and settled on a cream crop top and jeans—cute and casual. I'm a different person from the disaster who left the campsite yesterday morning.

Sean is in a gold, ruffled blouse and skintight black jeans, looking like he belongs on a runway and making me doubt my choices all over again.

"So, Rachel, Miss Smarty-Pants," he says, playfully swatting my shoulder. "I hear you're a science expert."

I'm flattered by the description, but it's not exactly true. "That depends on your definition of *expert*. I'm still working on my master's."

"Oh? What's your focus?"

"I'm planning to write my thesis about accurate tumor modeling for radiation therapy," I say with a twinge of guilt because I should be working on that right now. But I can catch up later. "I want to use computer algorithms to pinpoint the borders of a tumor so that radiation therapy does minimal damage to the surrounding healthy tissue. I found artificial intelligence software that looks like it has potential."

Sean gapes at me. "I get why Cate wants your advice."

I grin. Hopefully, I can make as good of an impression on Cate today.

Sean faces the bustle ahead and smooths his blouse. "Okay, so those tired-looking people are tech…and those sprightly kids with hope in their eyes are production assistants…anyone abnormally attractive is probably an actor…"

As we walk through the set and Sean points out the crew and equipment, I try to act like I belong. I study everyone we pass, trying to figure out who the important people are. I see what he means about the actors, but among the crew, it's hard to tell. There are lots of young, enthusiastic ones who probably haven't been in the business long. Others look grumpy and ready to drop dead—they've probably been doing this for longer. Half of the crew are frantic and purposeful, and the other half are bored and waiting, with nothing in between. All of them, right down to the youngest production assistant, carry themselves with a sense of importance. Working on a movie is cool and they know it.

"Everything seems to run pretty smoothly," I say, sticking close to Sean and making myself small so I don't get in anyone's way.

"That's what everyone wants you to think. Everyone acts like they're the most important person here—they all want to be the star in some way or another. I guarantee you everyone here has secretly practiced an award acceptance speech."

"You included?"

He laughs. "I won't deny it."

"How long have you worked for Cate?"

30

"Seven years. I was fresh out of high school when we met. I used to work for Phil Niles too, but Cate won custody of me in the divorce." He winks.

It takes a second for the name to register.

Right, Cate's ex.

Her nasty divorce from Phil Niles was trending everywhere a few months ago. I wonder what else they had to divvy up when they separated, and if an assistant was the worst of it.

A golf cart overflowing with people zooms past us, and I dive out of the way.

"You have to be important for one of those," Sean says. "Peons like us get to walk."

"Quiet on set!" someone shouts nearby, and Sean hurries on.

"Come on. They're getting ready to shoot."

A flutter of excitement goes through me as we stride over to the steampunk storefronts. The set design is impressive, like something from a theme park, and there's even a camera on a track that moves along the street. A couple of guys huddle over a smoke machine that's letting out soft puffs. A scruffy guy who must be the director sits behind the camera wearing a baseball cap, surrounded by crew.

Cate is there in her steampunk costume and full makeup, looking like an absolute goddess. My heart leaps like I've jumped off a cliff. She catches my eye and waves, and I wave back, giddy.

A sequence of shouts comes from the crew behind the cameras, like birds calling to each other from trees.

"Roll sound!"

"Sound is speeding."

"Camera ready!"

"Rolling."

"Marker."

"Scene twenty-two bravo, take one."

"Frame."

"Action!"

The shouts and the clap of the slate happen smoothly, and the actors jump into the moment.

My heart thumps as Cate delivers her lines. I've seen plays loads of times—I go to the Shakespeare festival every summer—but this is different. This is Cate Whitney filming a real, high-budget movie, and I'm surrounded by people who are connected to all kinds of celebrities.

In the scene, two women my age flank Cate as she chases down and threatens a man in the street, telling him to release the research or people are going to die. They're dressed in tattered versions of Cate's outfit and are carrying oversized weapons, more like henchwomen than lab assistants.

I'm sure Marie Curie's scientific endeavors were a lot less dramatic, but it'll make for good cinema.

As the actors speak to each other in low tones, it strikes me how weirdly showy all of this is. I imagine this scene will come across as a discreet conversation, but from here, at least three dozen people are staring at them, and it's hard to imagine the result. I guess that's why I'm not a director.

The takes move quickly, with hair and makeup rushing in every few minutes. Even the tiniest details of their outfits are given attention.

After a ridiculous number of takes of the same scene, the director yells, "Print, moving on!"

Everyone bustles around, and Cate walks toward me. My heart beats faster.

"Thanks for suffering through that, Rachel. I'm sorry it took so long."

"That was awesome! I'm in shock over how much effort goes into a scene."

"It's excessive," Cate says, looking skyward. "And this hasn't even reached post-production yet, where rooms full of engineers and editors will agonize over every frame."

Sean passes her a bottle of coconut water and the script, which he apparently pulled out of nowhere.

"Thanks, love," Cate says and gulps down half of the drink. The day is warming, and there's a sheen of sweat on her chest.

"Do you still get nervous performing in front of all of these people?" I ask.

She waves the hand holding the script. "Not in a scene like this, but don't get me started on filming scenes that are supposed to be intimate. Try pretending to have a good time in bed while forty people watch."

I imagine the scenes she's talking about, and heat creeps into my face.

"Let's find somewhere to talk," Cate says.

Nerves coil in my stomach. Time to answer her questions and hope I'm useful enough that she doesn't regret inviting me here.

She leads me away from everyone, and the second we come within sight of the metal fence surrounding the set, screams erupt beyond it.

A horde of fans waves and jumps, leaning against the fence.

"Cate! Can I have a picture?"

"I love you, queen!"

Cate waves and offers a smile before turning around and striding in the opposite direction. "On second thought, let's go into my trailer."

We head to one of several white trailers, and she opens the door to let me in.

It's like a luxury RV inside, complete with a white leather couch, boudoir, television, kitchen unit, bed, and bathroom. It's quiet and cozy after being outside on the bustling set for so long.

Cate sits on the couch and groans, letting the script hit the floor. "Help yourself to a drink."

She motions to the mini fridge.

"Thanks." I go for a pomegranate-flavored fizzy water.

Do I sit beside her? I guess it's the only spot, other than the bed.

At my hesitation, Cate smiles and motions at the space next to her on the couch.

I sit, the closeness making my stomach twist. I can't believe I'm perched next to Cate, just the two of us, at her invitation.

"Ready to impart your wisdom?" she asks in that smooth voice that feels like a whisper on my neck.

"One sec." I pop open my drink and wet my suddenly dry throat. "Okay, hit me."

She leans back and crosses her legs, contemplating. "I'm embarrassed by this question, but can you explain radioactivity to me?"

Phew, an easy one. I've got this.

"Radioactivity—" I fiddle with the tab on my drink, then force my hands to settle. "—is when an atom's nucleus is unstable, so it spontaneously decomposes into a more stable form. A radioactive element keeps decaying until it becomes stable. When it decays, it emits radiation as energy or subatomic particles."

Her gaze x-rays me, something unreadable glimmering in her eyes. "So something is unstable, and it self-destructs until it feels stable—and during its journey to stabilization, it releases energy that harms everything around it."

"That's a poetic way of looking at it."

Her lips quirk. "Marie Curie was a bittersweet tragedy, don't you think?"

"What do you mean?"

"First woman to win a Nobel prize, the only person to win two in separate fields of science… She won so many awards and refused them, even donating the prize money back to science. She never patented her discovery so that others could continue her work. She provided X-rays for field hospitals during World War I, and her work is lifesaving. She was such an incredible person, never corrupted by fame. Yet she faced so much hardship, losing her husband to an accident, living through war, and dying from radiation exposure."

"I've never thought of it like that," I say. "And you were lying about not knowing much about Marie Curie."

"I know about her life, not her work."

I return her little smile. "Her life was bittersweet, yes. But she had a meaningful existence and a daughter who carried on her legacy. She's a hero whose work is still saving lives. So I hope it's more sweet than bitter."

Cate's gaze lingers, and my cheeks heat up again. I wish I didn't blush so much around her, but she's so stunning that it's like being in the presence of the actual sun.

She gulps down the rest of her coconut water and sets it on the kitchenette.

I try not to stare at her hands, which are irresistibly attractive as they wrap around the bottle. I recall the feel of them as she wrote her number on my palm.

"The research you've done is probably more useful than what I can tell you," I say. "Her life story. I only know what she contributed to science."

"That's an important part of who she is. I need to understand what she did."

I nod, contemplating what else I can tell her. "The discovery you mentioned, the one she never patented, was for radium isolation. She worked for years to isolate radium from pitchblende."

"What did that involve?"

"A lot of work refining several tons of the mineral before she could isolate even a tiny amount of radium chloride. It took years before she was able to isolate pure radium. That's when she got the second Nobel prize."

"A quest for isolation," Cate says.

I can't help smiling. What a fascinating woman.

"Interesting how career paths make people see the world so differently," I say. "What I see as spontaneously changing elements, you see as a story, a journey from one state to another."

"True."

"Like, my dad builds houses, and he sees a yard with a beautiful willow tree and says, 'Those roots will destroy the foundation.'"

"Imagine seeing the negative in a willow tree," Cate says with a wry grin.

"To be honest, I look at one and think about spiders falling on my head."

Cate laughs, eyes glinting in the daylight shining through the window. "And I see a perfect place to read a book—or mark up a script."

I sip my pomegranate water, feeling her gaze on me. I hope all of this science talk is helpful.

"If your dad builds houses," she says, "did you get your love of DIY projects from him?"

"Yes," I say, surprised that she remembered my nerdy confession.

"What else have you built?"

"Oh, where to start?" I ask. "When I was a kid, we built a go-kart, a sensor to automatically let the dog outside, an arcade cabinet…"

She laughs. "It sounds like you had a fun childhood."

"It set me up for being an overachiever, anyway."

She searches my face, and I wish I knew what she was thinking. She uncrosses her legs and puts an arm over the back of the couch, the movement bringing her closer.

"Do you like university?" she asks, and her tone has changed to something softer, more relaxed.

"It's stressful but fun. The people are cool. Some classes are better than others."

"Hm." Cate plays with her perfectly styled hair, her finger spiraling around a rigid blond lock. "Sometimes, I wonder what I missed by dropping out."

"I don't think you've missed out on much," I say, finding it hard to believe someone of her status would want to change anything.

"Everyone misses out on something. There's no such thing as having everything."

I chew my lip, considering her words. "And if you could have something more, what would it be?"

She holds my gaze, brow furrowed, lips parted. There's a lot going on behind her eyes. She either doesn't know because she's never considered it, or she does know and isn't sure if she wants to say it.

Someone knocks on the trailer door, startling me. Cate just looks calmly at the door like she expected this.

"Cate?" Sean shouts.

She stands. "Come in."

The door flies open, and Sean holds out a granola bar. "Protein. You're up soon."

My insides sink. Couldn't we have a couple more minutes?

Cate steps forward and takes the bar. She looks back at me with something like regret in her eyes.

"If—if you think of any questions as you go through the script, feel free to text me," I say, hoping she thinks of something. I'm not ready for our conversation to end.

"Thanks." Cate hesitates. A flush rises in her cheeks. "Listen, I'd like to meet up with you again, if you're up for it. You've been a huge help. Can I buy you drinks on Sunday night?"

A balloon seems to inflate in my chest.

Drinks with Cate Whitney? Holy crap.

"Yes," I say, breathless. "I'd love to."

Her face brightens into a wide smile. "Good. I'll let you pick the spot."

I don't know what I did to deserve this. Maybe I should be grateful that we veered off topic. It left her with unanswered questions, and that means I get to see her again.

Frantically, I do a mental scan of every patio in the vicinity. We need somewhere a little bit upscale, with a view of the water where we can watch the sunset but without being by a footpath so that every passing pedestrian stares at her.

I settle on a restaurant that has a second-floor patio, making it more private.

"Oceanfront Grill has a covered patio with a good view."

"Sounds nice. Meet you there at seven-thirty on Sunday?"

I nod, having trouble breathing. "See you then."

Chapter 6
Moscow Mules and Other Spicy Things

I have never in my life been this nervous for anything. No job interview or first-date jitters have ever compared to the absolute chaos going on inside me right now.

Abby's cross-legged on my bed, offering opinions on each outfit I present as I rummage through my closet. She and I pretty much haven't stopped screaming since Cate asked me to meet up again.

"Going on set to talk about her job was one thing," I say in a cold sweat, "but this is just the two of us, sitting across from each other, and she didn't even specify what she wants to talk about. What does she want out of this?"

I clutch a shirt to my chest, breathing quickly.

"Stop it," Abby says, gathering her hair into a messy bun. She's in an oversized tee and no pants, like she's ready for bed. "She's a normal person, and you'll talk about normal things."

I breathe deeply. Cate is just grateful that I answered her sciencey questions, and she wants to treat me to drinks. That's it.

"Pretend you're on a date with someone you met on an app," Abby says. "Those types of questions."

"I can't pretend I'm on a date with Cate Whitney!" I shout. "That makes this even worse!"

"Inhale and count to four," Abby says, breathing with me.

We eventually settle on high-waisted black pants and a loose white tank that shows off my tattoo and a glimpse of side-boob. While Abby moves to the couch to play video games, I style my hair and trim a few stray locks, then spend a ridiculous amount of time on my makeup. I apply contouring, eyeshadow, lipstick, the whole works.

"Not bad." I give the mirror finger guns, trying to summon confidence.

"Get it, girl," Abby says with her mouth full of chips.

When I arrive at the restaurant, stomach fluttering, Cate is smiling for a selfie with the host. She's wearing a summery peach suit, and I think my knees are going to give out. Diamond earrings and a solitaire diamond necklace catch the sunlight. Her blond hair is styled in beachy waves, and her makeup is subtle and rosy.

Ken stands behind her, wearing a serious expression beneath dark sunglasses.

"Right this way, Miss Whitney," the host says, blushing and stumbling over his feet.

Before following, Cate's gaze traces over me, down to my side-boob, and back to my face. Her lips pull into a smile and a light, floating sensation fills me. I've seen people give me that sort of *hot damn* look before, and on her, I like it a lot.

"We'll be okay, Ken," she says.

He scans the area, obviously checking for anything sketchy, then says, "I'll wait in the car."

Cate nods, and he stays behind while we follow the host.

God, she's cool. What would it be like to have a personal bodyguard who does whatever you ask? No wonder some celebrities turn into divas.

Over my shoulder, Ken shakes hands with one of the servers and points to us. The guy nods, standing taller.

Cate and I weave through tables, whose occupants stare before leaning in to whisper excitedly to each other. It must have taken years for her to get used to living under a magnifying glass like this.

We pull out our chairs and I pause. "Here, swap seats with me. Better view of the ocean, and you can face away from…" I glance discreetly toward the gawking couple at the table beside us.

Cate blinks at me.

I motion to the chair I pulled out.

"Thank you," she says, her tone surprised.

As we sit with our chairs angled toward the water, her gaze lingers on me, and I compose myself while pretending to adjust my seat.

The sun is on its way down, the evening cool and clear. The salty scent of the ocean drifts toward us on a breeze. Below, muffled and out of sight, pedestrians stroll by on the seawall. I silently congratulate myself on the restaurant choice.

Cate orders a Moscow Mule, and I order the same, too flustered to read the menu.

"Really?" she asks, raising an eyebrow.

"It's a nice summer drink," I say.

"I tell myself the ginger makes it healthy. Like a cleanse. But with vodka."

I laugh.

She takes off her peach jacket and hangs it on the back of her chair. Underneath is a lacy white camisole and defined, sun-kissed shoulders.

"Has filming been going okay?" I ask, tamping down the fluttering in my stomach.

"It's the usual torture. Twelve-hour days that tend to bloat into fifteen, catnaps in uncomfortable places, too many bold personalities in one place and not enough alone time…"

"But you love it?"

"I love it," she says, a gleam in her eyes.

There's a pause, and I wait for her to ask me something. She must have an agenda for this meetup, right? Does she want to ask more Marie Curie questions?

But she doesn't. She gazes out at the ocean, where a stripe of sunlight connects the beach to the horizon. The reflection bathes her smooth skin in a way that makes her glow.

I want to know more about her, but I'm nervous to ask. Would personal questions be unwelcome? Would she think I'm fishing for information about her private life?

"Are you happy living here?" she asks.

The question is so blunt that it takes me a moment to process. Am I happy? Yes, with layers. Is Vancouver a good place to live? Yes, also with layers. Her question is probably more about the latter.

I nod. "I'm in the apartments beside the movie set and have a tiny view of the ocean. It's a beautiful place to live, and there's a lot to do, especially if you're outdoorsy." I pause, wondering whether she's the hiking type.

"Summer outdoorsy, yes," she says, answering my unspoken question. "Winter, not so much."

"Same. I feel guilty telling people I don't like hurtling down a snowy mountain with sticks strapped to my feet."

She laughs and lets out a breath. "Good to know I'm not alone in this."

I grin. "Anyway, it's a good place. The downsides are the ridiculous cost of living and the traffic problems. Also, it doesn't stop raining between September and June, and for the summer months, everything is on fire. But those things discounted, it's great."

Cate lets out a genuine laugh, and the sound sends a rush of pleasure to my fingers and toes. "I can relate to a few of those problems, being from LA."

Our drinks come and we thank the server. Cate doesn't take her eyes off me as she accepts her Moscow Mule.

"Cheers," she says.

I raise my copper mug and we clink them together. She smiles and we both take a sip. As the cold, spicy drink slides down my throat, my heart thumps so loudly that she can probably hear it. Why does she have to make me so nervous?

I clear my throat. "Make sure you take in the mountains while you're here, even just by driving east along the highway on a clear day. The mountain range is my favorite thing about living here."

She nods. "I'm glad you didn't recommend that I visit the Capilano Suspension Bridge. Everyone keeps telling me to go, but nobody pauses to find out that I'm afraid of heights."

A memory crops up and I stifle a laugh.

"Are you laughing at my misery?" she asks with a smile.

"No, I get it. My roommate doesn't like heights either, and she found out while we were in the middle of the bridge. I had to drag her to safety by pulling her hands, so she slid across half the bridge on her butt."

Cate laughs. "You're a loyal friend. Are you and your roommate close?"

"Best friends since high school."

The breeze picks up, making the whispering waves more noticeable. Cate lifts her hand to tame a lock of golden hair.

Something passes behind her eyes, like a hint of sadness. Was it the mention of a best friend?

"Do you miss home?" I ask, taking a guess.

"Not really. I'm a little tired of LA, to be honest. But I do miss my sister. She's the person I would trust to rescue me from a suspension bridge by dragging me on my butt."

I smile. There's more beneath her answer, but I won't pry.

Movement behind us makes me glance back. The server Ken shook hands with is firmly blocking two girls from walking toward us. They talk in low tones before the girls walk away, sulking.

It hits me that Ken probably slipped the server money to make sure people don't bother us.

"Have you been to Vancouver before?" I ask Cate, hoping she didn't see. I know she must deal with things like that all the time, but it makes me embarrassed to see people from my hometown acting this way.

"I came up here once to visit Whistler with my ex-husband. Beautiful place, even if he ruined the fun we could've had. We didn't even hit a pub because we spent the whole trip fighting."

Okay, she volunteered that personal information. Maybe I'm okay to ask her questions.

"Sorry to hear that," I say, angry on her behalf that she had her trip ruined.

She lifts a shoulder in a half-shrug. "You know how men are. They're so sensitive about everything. I got tired of having to stroke his ego all the time."

I tilt my head. "Can't say I have a whole lot of experience with men."

"Other genders?" she asks without pause.

"Mostly women."

She nods, holding me with those piercing eyes.

Wait, did she just fish for me to tell her I'm a lesbian?

"Are you in a relationship?" Her gaze flicks to my hand, where a ring would be.

"Single."

Um, what is happening with this line of questions?

Cate nods—and what was that quirk of her lips? Was I imagining that? Why did she ask about my relationship status?

If we were in a bar, I would swear she was flirting. But she's not, because she's a celebrity, and she's just being gregarious.

We sip our drinks, the murmur of passing pedestrians and diners at nearby tables filling the silence. My heart hasn't stopped fluttering.

"It's nice to do a shoot away from home," Cate says. "I think we all end up where we need to be, you know?"

"You don't think everything's just luck?"

"Oh, I'm convinced that everything happens by chance—but I also believe we have more influence than we think. Like, this opportunity came up, and I took it, even though there were others. Life always seems to align to give us what we need."

Maybe there's some truth to her words. "I actually wasn't supposed to be home the day I, um, awkwardly bumped into you on set. I was supposed to be camping. Maybe I was meant to come home early."

She raises her eyebrows. "What happened?"

Crap. How much do I share? I don't want to dump my problems onto Cate, and I don't want to share the extent of my bad decisions. "The trip was…a bust. The woman I was there for wasn't into me. But if that hadn't happened, we might not be sitting here right now. So…I guess I'm glad I had my heart smashed." And I mean it. I'll take drinks with Cate over chasing Julia. At least Cate wants to spend time with me.

My insides dance at the realization. *Cate Whitney wants to spend time with me.*

Cate smiles. "I'm glad you think so. And for the record, whoever didn't reciprocate your feelings is an idiot."

"That's nice of you to say." I run my fingers up and down the cold condensation on my copper mug, flustered. "I think the problem was that she and I wanted different things. I mean, I knew what I wanted, but she didn't exactly know yet, so she was trying to figure that out. With me."

Cate inclines her head like she gets where I'm going with this. "That's harsh. You deserve someone who knows what they want."

"That's the problem. Seems like everyone my age is floundering. It's hard to find people in their early twenties who are confident in who they are and what they want."

Cate searches my face. There's an unreadable gleam in her eyes. Her question about whether I'm single is still swirling around in my brain.

She opens her mouth, but before she can speak, the server comes back and asks how we're doing. We tear our gazes away from each other and up to him.

"I'll have another," Cate says, raising her near-empty drink. "Rachel?"

"Sure."

A pleasant tingle goes through me. If she were in a rush to leave, she wouldn't have asked for a second drink.

As the server leaves, Cate says, "Sean is having the same problem in the dating world."

I nod, wondering if this was what she was about to say before the server came. "Sean seems nice. He told me he's been working for you for a long time."

"Quite a few years. He's a good friend. I sort of poached him off my ex-husband, to be honest."

"Oh?" I wasn't digging for information on her divorce, but I have to admit I'm curious.

"I kept Sean as my assistant, but Phil got Waffles."

"Waffles?"

"Our cat. The bastard knows how much I love that cat."

"Oh, God, I'm sorry. That would be awful. I had a dog growing up, and I can't imagine—"

She waves a hand and leans in. "Don't repeat this, but my sister stole him back for me. She left a window open so Phil would think he ran away. Waffles lives with her now, and I see him all the time."

I gasp. "You didn't!"

She blushes and makes an adorably mischievous expression. "Anyway, I'm sure you saw the Phil Niles debacle everywhere."

"It was a hot topic for a while," I say with a grimace.

The server brings our second round, and Cate waits until he's gone before speaking.

"When I was a kid and my parents divorced, our extended family picked sides, making a private ordeal way bigger than it ever needed to be. So when Phil and I split, it was like living a nightmare, going through that all over again—and instead of just the family involved, it's thousands of fans too."

"That sounds shitty."

"It was. All of that piled on top of all the regular divorce pain. After so many years together, I lost friends, half my belongings, the role in the movie we were working on together, not to mention my ability to enjoy a few songs and TV shows—and yet, like I said, everything in life takes a person to where they need to be. If none of that had happened, I might not have gotten this role in *Clockwork Curie*. I wouldn't have learned who my real friends are. And I wouldn't be sitting here with you right now."

This is true. And for all the power luck has had in getting me to this patio with Cate, I'm grateful.

"Are you doing okay?" I ask.

She pauses. "I'm…better."

"Better is good," I say. "Better is progress."

"True." She hesitates. "And thank you for asking."

Her words make me wonder how many people check how she's doing. It's hard to imagine what her life is like, having so many people care about her private affairs for the wrong reasons. I'm honored that she feels comfortable enough to talk about her life with me.

Her gaze traces over me. She seems to spend a lot of time in her own head—maybe a learned behavior, like a survival mechanism for someone whose life is so public.

We finish our drinks as the sun crosses the horizon.

"Shall we?" she asks, flagging down the server.

She pays despite my feeble arguments that she doesn't have to.

When we get up, she motions for me to go ahead of her, and as I do, her hand comes to rest on the small of my back. A wave of pleasure rushes through my middle. Her palm is warm through my thin shirt as she guides us past a cluster of people.

"I'll text Ken," she says as we land on the busy sidewalk. "Can we drop you off at home?"

"Sure," I say, even though my place is an easy walk from here.

My head is cloudy, more from the feel of her palm than the Moscow Mules.

"Cate!" a man shouts from somewhere far away.

Cate closes her eyes and inhales deeply through her nose.

Across the street, two men with expensive cameras point them at us, snapping photos.

Something expands in my chest, panic threatening to bubble up. I've never seen paparazzi in real life and didn't think they were much of a thing in Vancouver.

Automatically, I cover my face and turn away, my airway constricting until it's hard to breathe.

Fuck. I should have known there would be a risk of this if I met up with Cate.

She touches my arm. "How fast can you run?"

Before I can answer, she casts me that signature Cate Whitney mischievous grin and takes off, running down the sidewalk with her stilettos in hand.

Chapter 7
Witchy Trinkets

I race after Cate, leaving the two men with cameras to shout after us from the other side of the street.

A car honks and tires screech. They must be running across traffic to follow us.

Did they get a picture of my face? Where will it show up, and what story will they tell about Cate and me?

I'm struggling for breath as I sprint after her, and there's no time to consider. The paparazzi shout behind us, following like we're game and it's hunting season.

I catch up to Cate, my Vans easier to run in than her bare feet.

"There's a shop coming up," I say, panting. "The door with the wind chimes. Go inside."

She does, skirting around two women in yoga pants and disappearing beyond the door. I follow without slowing.

The wind chimes clatter obnoxiously as we enter the silent shop. Incense attacks my nostrils and I cough. The woman behind the counter looks offended at our abrupt entrance.

"Sorry. Emergency," I say, grabbing Cate's hand and pulling her through the aisles. "If two men with cameras come inside, please tell them we aren't here. I'll buy something, I promise."

The woman blinks. I have no time to convince her further.

I've been in this shop once, and it's overflowing with trinkets and clothes, which makes it a perfect place to hide. It's spiritual but more witchy than religious. The aisles hold essential oils, glass beads, crystals, gemstones, woven baskets, wood carvings of faces and animals, fountains, and books about chakras. Abby and I bought a bundle of sage here once after she swore on her life that she saw a ghost pass through our living room.

Ducking, I pull Cate through a rack of long skirts and harem pants, the hangers squealing on the metal rod as we pass.

"Changerooms," I say. "Quick."

The wind chimes tinkle as the shop door opens, and the place fills with heaving breaths.

I open the curtain of a changeroom just enough to slip through, and we duck inside. The shop obviously had a new shipment come in because the space is filled with boxes. The open one on top reveals a stack of books about smashing the patriarchy and some T-shirts that say *Ask me about my agenda.*

This bodes well for what I asked of the shopkeeper.

Sure enough, the woman says sharply, "Can I help you?"

"Did Cate Whitney come in here?" a man says, the breath roaring from his lungs.

"No, she did not," the woman says, her tone firm and challenging. "And no photos are allowed in my store. The sign is right there."

Squeezed between the boxes and the wall, Cate and I have our hands over our mouths, struggling to catch our breath as quietly as possible.

Please don't find us.

Aside from the threat of having this evening ruined, I don't want to have a camera-triggered meltdown in front of Cate Whitney.

Cate shifts, and my belly gives a fierce swoop as I realize how close together we're standing. There's no room between the boxes and the wall, so our fronts are pressed together, my thigh literally between her legs.

Neither of us moves.

Footsteps thump through the aisles. Something clatters.

"Can I help you find what you're looking for?" the woman says.

The men ignore her. There's another tinkle of something falling.

"If you're going to keep destroying my shop, I'm going to have to ask you to leave," the woman says, using the sort of teacher-like tone that strikes fear into the hearts of people everywhere.

"Okay, okay," one of the men says.

Cate's chest heaves against me. Her arm grazes mine, and a pleasant shiver ripples through me.

She's looking at me. I'm drowning in the details of her eyes. That sweet, summery perfume is intoxicating.

Thank you, she mouths.

I nod, her presence helping to calm my jitters about being bombarded by cameras.

The wind chimes tinkle, the sound of traffic wafts in, and then the door closes.

Silence.

Cate and I breathe hard, faces tantalizingly close together, gazes locked. Whatever is passing between us seems to be sparking actual fire low inside me. I have the absurd urge to close the distance.

"I'd hide for another few minutes if I were you, ladies," the woman calls out. "I don't know if they believed me."

Cate starts, like she's forgotten where we are.

"Thank you so much," she calls back. Her breath tickles my lips, sweet from the Moscow Mules.

"Is that a regular occurrence for you?" I murmur.

She nods. "If you think that was bad, you should see the way it is in LA. It's gotten worse since my divorce. I'm fine with photos I consented to—promotional tours, red carpets—but I'm tired of them documenting my personal life. I never asked to have my photo taken while I'm out enjoying a patio, a sunset, and you."

We're so close that her murmurs vibrate through me. It's hard to breathe.

She bends to put on her stilettos, her hair brushing my bare shoulder. "Anyway, I'm sorry you had to be part of that."

"Don't apologize. It's awful how they treat you. That's why I try not to look at paparazzi photos."

I hope she can tell I'm being earnest. I can empathize for more reasons than I'm willing to let on right now.

"You're a kind person, Rachel."

"Kind? Does respecting your privacy count as kindness, or is that just basic decency?"

Cate's phone buzzes inside her bag, but she ignores it. "You'd be surprised. My privacy and secrets are worth money. I, um—" She hesitates, like she's debating whether to continue. "I lost my best friend because she sold details about my divorce to the tabloids. They offered her money, and she came to me asking for a counteroffer. I got mad and refused to pay her, so she went back and told them everything."

"Shit. I'm so sorry that happened to you," I say, my words empty after what she must have gone through.

"It's not like I didn't give her anything. I bought her a car last year, for God's sake." Her eyes get glossy and she blinks a few times. "Sorry. I don't know why I'm—"

"You didn't owe her a thing," I say, anger licking through me. "She should've laughed in the tabloids' faces. She was a bad friend. Even if you'd paid her off like she asked, she ruined your friendship the second she asked you for hush money."

How could anyone do that to Cate? This must be the reason behind that hint of sadness when I said the words "best friend" earlier.

Cate draws a deep breath. "All of that to say, sometimes it's hard to tell who likes you as a person and who prefers money. When you hit success, trust can be elusive."

"Maybe you just haven't met the right people yet," I say.

Cate's mouth twists in an almost-smile that she doesn't quite manage.

My insides haven't stopped fluttering, like there's a butterfly trapped in my intestines. This is so much more than a fangirly celebrity crush. After meeting Cate and talking to her tonight, I've crossed into the realm of actual crush.

Help.

She searches my face, like she's trying to read me. "You're trembling. Are you okay?"

Shit. I am trembling.

I consider telling her how having pictures and videos taken of me makes my chest tighten, and how I haven't posted a thing on social media since high school—but I can't unload that on someone I just met, and especially not on Cate Whitney.

"I'm fine," I say with a smile. "I just haven't experienced anything like that before."

I can't tell if she believes me, but she nods.

Her phone buzzes again, and she sighs and pulls it out of her bag. "That'll be Ken."

"Panicking that I've lured you away?"

"I'm sure." She types a reply, then grabs the curtain and peeks out. "I think they're gone. He'll come get us out front."

Cautiously, we step out of the changeroom.

"Oh gosh, I shouldn't have worn heels," Cate says, wincing.

She lifts her foot and reaches for her stiletto—and rather than brace on the wall beside her, she puts a hand on my shoulder. Her warm palm and fingers are gentle, confident.

A lick of fire trickles from her hand into my body.

Um, did she just do the classic thing where she made an excuse to touch me?

Stop it. You're misinterpreting this.

She's an actor, which means she's more outgoing and friendly than an average person. They're always touchy-feely during interviews and red-carpet events.

Or is she flirting?

What if she *is* queer? She was married to a man, but that's not to say she isn't interested in women.

She finishes fixing her shoe while I frantically try to see if there's anything actually wrong with it.

I can't tell.

Either I'm reading way too much into a legitimately uncomfortable shoe situation or she really did make an excuse to touch me.

And what about when she put a hand on my back while leaving the restaurant?

I need Abby's opinion on this.

We buy several bags worth of stuff from the witchy store, including harem pants and sunhats that we use as disguises. The woman at the counter, whose name is Rainbow, can't hide her excitement as Cate takes a photo with her and leaves a signed thank-you note.

We step outside into the cool twilight and slip into the safety of a black SUV with tinted windows.

"Urge to go shopping?" Ken asks.

"Always," Cate says casually, cramming our bags of stuff on the floor.

My shoulders relax and I let out a breath. We're okay. The cameras are gone.

"We'll bring you home first," Cate says, slipping off a shoe and massaging her foot. "My hotel is twenty minutes away."

There's a chance I'm misinterpreting her body language, like I'm such a hopeless fangirl that I'm seeing flirting where there isn't any.

Or I'm discounting what is obviously flirting because I'm assuming Cate Whitney would never, ever be interested in me.

Which is it? Am I misinterpreting kindness or being modest?

Even in everyday life, it can be hard to tell if a woman is flirting because straight women can be confusingly affectionate. But this is not the time for uncertainty. I need to know right now if Cate Whitney is flirting with me.

If she isn't, fine. If she is…*holy fuck.* I might need time to process that.

On the four-minute ride to my place, we laugh about buying so much from Rainbow's shop.

"I might incorporate these pants into my everyday wardrobe," Cate says, plucking at the crotch, which comes down to her knees.

"At least you look cute," I say. "I just look like a weird hippie."

She laughs as the car stops in front of my apartment building, and for the first time ever, I wish my place was further from the beach.

As unwelcome as a bucket of ice water is the realization that my time with Cate is up. I helped her learn about Marie Curie and then she took me for drinks to thank me and now we're done. The evening is over.

My insides hollow out as Ken opens the door and I slide out of the SUV. That was possibly the best time I've ever had getting drinks with someone.

Ken is about to shut the car door when words spill from my mouth, unstoppable. "I'd like to meet up again. If you have more science questions, I mean, or if you want a tour of Vancouver. Not the suspension bridge, of course."

The words are out, and I'm blushing. But I couldn't leave without saying them. I had to take a shot.

I hold my breath while she considers me. The pause is agonizing.

"I would like that very much," she says, smiling.

I let out my breath. "Good. Okay. Let's text, then."

"Good."

Ken is about to shut the door for the second time when Cate puts a hand on it and says, "One last thing."

My heart leaps. *You can have a million more things, Cate.*

"Were you really interested in being a consultant for *Clockwork Curie?*"

Okay, I can crawl into a hole and die now. I struggle for an acceptable answer, the heat in my face intensifying during the long pause.

"I'm just really into Marie Curie," I say.

Her face breaks into the most radiant, beautiful smile. "I thought it might be something like that."

Does she see right through me? Does she care either way?

"Have a nice ride back to your hotel, Cate."

She smooths her new pants and tips her new sunhat. "It'll be lonely, I'm sure. Good night, Rachel."

Chapter 8
For Science

ABBY AND I SPEND so long screaming over my evening with Cate Whitney that my usual bedtime comes and goes and I'm still too hyped to sleep. So is she, apparently, because we play video games until two in the morning.

When I get up the nerve to tell Abby that I was getting mixed signals and that Cate touched my lower back and shoulder, she puts down her controller in mid-game.

"Back the fuck up for a second," she says. "You think she might have been flirting with you?"

"I don't know," I say, watching both of our characters die on the screen. "It came up that I'm a lesbian because she asked if I was in a relationship—"

"She *asked* if you were in a relationship?"

"Yes. But she could have been asking normal, friendly questions and touching me in normal, friendly ways. Right?"

Abby bites her lip. "If she was a regular person, I would smack you upside the head, but… A lot of celebs seem outgoing and flirty, so it's possible that Cate was just being a charming socialite."

"Exactly. I can't ask her out or come on strong because that would make things weird if she was just being friendly. Also, I want to show her that I respect her, and asking her if she's flirting with me might come across…" I hesitate, grimacing. "I'm sure she's dealt with a lot of unwanted advances in her life, being who she is."

"You think she'll pull away if you're too forward?"

I fidget with my controller. "From what I've seen, people are always all over her. I don't want to be like that."

The way fans pose with her is too friendly, fingers grazing her hair, over her back, faces touching. It's like the stranger barrier falls because she's famous.

I don't know how she deals with it. I'm still sick to my stomach about having my photo taken by paparazzi as we left the restaurant. What are they going to do with it? Will it show up in an article, where people will speculate about who I am and what I'm doing at a restaurant with Cate?

It's violating, like an unwanted touch or getting pickpocketed—or having a video of me posted online without my consent.

My heart jumps into my throat and I grip my controller tighter.

I will not panic about this. I will not.

"Anyway, she told me she finds it hard to trust people," I say, hoping Abby doesn't catch the tremor in my voice.

"That explains why she's hard to read. She's cautious."

"True."

"Damn, girl," Abby says, leaning back on the couch. "You're going to have to test your hypothesis and gather some more data. Casual flirting, you know?"

My scientist brain begins to write a mental lab report.

Problem statement: I have a massive crush on Cate Whitney, and I can't tell if she likes me back.

Hypothesis: Cate Whitney is into me.

"That's what I plan to do," I say. "Gather more evidence."

"*Then* you can ask awkward questions and make things weird."

I smile. "Thanks, Abby."

"For confusing you even more? No prob."

———— ❦ ————

Bzzz-bzzz. Bzzz-bzzz.

What's vibrating?

I roll over, groggy, and see my phone lighting up.

Someone is buzzing to get into the building.

If this is an idiot with the wrong buzzer number again, I'm going to lose my shit. It's eight o'clock in the morning.

I grab my phone.

"Yeah?" I say, a little snappy.

"Hi. Rachel?"

Holy crap. That's Cate Whitney's voice.

I jump out of bed and get a fierce head rush. "Yes. Hi. Cate?"

"Hi. I'm sorry to bother you so early. Can I come up for a second?"

"Yes. Definitely." I look down at the underwear I fell asleep in and then around at the explosion of clothes all over my floor. "Third floor. Number 338."

I push the button to let her in and hang up.

"Fuck," I whisper-shout. Abby is still asleep, and I'd like to keep it that way.

I have about a minute before the elevator brings her to me. I have time to fix myself or the apartment, but not both. With a cry of despair, I sprint to the bathroom to relieve my bladder, use mouthwash, and apply deodorant, then bolt to my closet to put on clothes.

Knock knock.

"Fuck," I whisper, hopping on the spot to get my leg into my jean shorts.

I turn on the diffuser, hoping there's enough sweet orange essential oil in there to make the apartment smell less stale within the next five seconds.

On the way to the door, I throw dishes in the sink, kick garbage into cupboards, and close everything that's open. I shove my moose floatie, which I never bothered to put away after camping, into the hall closet. It makes a fart noise against the shoe rack.

I pause, take a breath, and put on a smile before opening the door.

"Hi, Cate." I'm lucky her name is short because my tongue fails me as I say it. She's in that extremely flattering steampunk outfit, completely out of place in the dingy hallway.

Am I in heaven? Maybe I did get eaten by a bear during my drunken walk around the lake last week.

"Rachel," she says, a smile lighting up her contoured, professionally made-up face. "Listen, I won't stay. I'm sure Sean is already panicking. I just wanted to come up for a minute while I have a chance."

"Okay," I say, disappointed but equally relieved that she doesn't want to come inside our disastrous place.

"Um—" She drops her gaze to her boots and tucks a lock of hair behind her ear, like she's nervous. "There's a red-carpet event this weekend. I have to fly out for one night and then be back in Vancouver the next day. Do you want to come to the gala as my guest?"

I gape at her. Do I want to attend a gala as Cate Whitney's guest? Is that even a question?

Arguments bubble up in my brain—the need to research for my thesis at the top, followed by the fact that I don't belong at a celebrity gala, followed by the unwelcome memory of paparazzi, and, worst of all, the idea of having my picture taken on the red carpet—but the cool, confident presence of the woman in front of me suppresses all of my concerns.

The silence must go on a beat too long, because she adds hastily, "Maybe I'm being selfish, but it would be good press for *Clockwork Curie* to have a medical physicist with me. People will be interested in who you are, and I can tell them I'm consulting with you about the scientific—"

"Yes," I say. "Abso-freaking-lutely I would like to come with you to a gala."

Behind me, a door clicks open. Abby must have woken up.

I angle my body and casually pull the door closer to me, doing my best to create a wall so she and Cate won't be able to see each other. There's a large chance that Abby is in her underwear right now. Once, she slept in nothing but a sock.

"Great," Cate says, breathing into a wider smile. "I'll pick you up at eight on Saturday morning. I'll arrange for your hair, makeup, and formal wear for the evening, so don't worry about packing much. Do you prefer a dress or a suit?"

It takes me a moment to process everything she said. "Either is fine," I stammer. "I'm more comfortable in pants, I guess."

"Would you prefer a masculine or feminine fit?"

I consider the suits I've worn in the past. "Feminine."

"I know just the tux to get you," Cate says. "Black and gold. You'll look gorgeous in it. Can I send a stylist to take your measurements tomorrow?"

"Sure. Thank you." My lips are numb.

She tugs her corset. "I'd better get back down there. The sooner we're done, the sooner I can get out of this thing. See you on Saturday, Rachel."

"Saturday. Okay. See you then."

She walks down the hall back to the elevator, and it takes me a long minute to realize I'm staring after her. I back up and close the door gently.

"Was that Cate fucking Whitney?" Abby says loudly.

"Shh!" I say, palms out. In this old building, sound carries through closed doors and into the hallway—and if Cate isn't in the elevator yet, she definitely heard that.

Abby, of course, isn't wearing pants. Her tank top is twisted so her boob is in danger of popping out, and her wild bedhead has given her hair an extra dimension. She has the squinty, unfocused look she gets when she hasn't put on her glasses yet.

"Yes, it was Cate Whitney," I whisper. "She invited me to go to a gala with her next weekend."

Abby must have forgotten that I shushed her, because she screams. You'd think we would have gotten out all of our screams by now, but clearly not. I skip and punch the air.

"You'll be there overnight with her," Abby says. "God, Rachel, imagine if she is interested in you. You're her plus-one."

My heart jumps, but I stay sensible. "She made it clear that it's for professional reasons. I'm her medical physicist consultant."

"A ruse," Abby says stubbornly.

"Don't be ridiculous. She's way out of my league and way older than me."

"Hey, Siri, how old is Cate Whitney?" Abby shouts.

"Cate Whitney is forty-one years old," her phone helpfully replies.

God, I hope Cate is in the elevator.

"Only eighteen years." Abby cocks an eyebrow. "Pah! I didn't know you were so shallow, Rachel Janssen."

"I'm not—how dare—"

"Stop making excuses. You're both hot and smart and good at what you do, and you're over here closing a door before you've even found out what's beyond it."

I bite my lip. I've always admired Cate, but that was the extent of it—a fangirl crush. I never thought dating her would be anywhere near the realm of possibility.

That begs the question: do I *want* to get involved with her?

I hesitate for so long that Abby raises an eyebrow.

"What about my…picture problem?" I ask, blinking at the ceiling. Attending a gala is one thing, but I'm not sure how I'll react to the red carpet and all of the photos of me that will inevitably show up online afterward. Whether I'm there in a professional capacity or a romantic one, I don't want to make an idiot of myself by breaking down and crying.

How embarrassing, how utterly shameful, that I've never been able to get over what happened five years ago.

Abby lets out a breath, then comes over and gives my arms a reassuring squeeze. "You should tell her about that so she understands why you won't want to be in the limelight. But Rachel, it's going to be impossible to stay out of pictures and videos if you're on Cate Whitney's arm. You know that, right?"

"Yeah," I say, drawing the word out for several syllables.

"So you need to make a decision. If you want to, you know, *test your hypothesis* with Cate, then you need to accept that it's going to involve cameras. But if you'd rather avoid all of that, then you should say no to the gala."

I open my mouth and no sound comes out.

Can I get over my aversion to the limelight?

"Also, what if I flirt and find out she's uninterested?" I ask, dumping my every concern onto Abby. "It'll be Julia all over again. My *heart*."

"That's why you have to test your hypothesis before you get invested. Turn up your charm and see what she does."

I don't tell her I might already be invested. In the short time I've known Cate, she's pulled me in so I'm a swooning mess. I'm hurtling down a one-way street and there's no stopping.

But I don't want to stop. She's worth the risk of another heartbreak— and worth standing in front of cameras for.

For Cate, I'll get over it. Even if this turns out to be a professional invitation, I can't say no to spending another evening with her.

The answer to my question is *yes*. If Cate Whitney is interested in me, then of course I want to get involved with her.

"I have to start cleaning," I say, dashing to my room in a rush of excitement. "Someone's coming over to take my measurements tomorrow."

Abby squeals. "This is so cool. I'll get the Windex."

"Thank you," I shout from my room, upending my travel backpack. My wrinkled, damp camping clothes tumble out, smelling terrible.

Time to get this stuff in the wash, plug in the vacuum, and make this place fit for a celebrity stylist.

Out of all of the people in the world, I'm the one Cate Whitney chose as her guest. No matter what way I spin this, it's good news. Whether she likes my field of study or is gauging whether there's a spark between us remains to be seen—but by the time the gala is over, I intend to find out.

Chapter 9
Mile High Club

After an awkward session with a stylist that lasts nine minutes, followed by several days of waiting that feels like nine years, I'm on a plane with Cate.

Flying first class is everything I hoped for and more. There's a champagne flute beside me, a TV screen in front of me, and I'm on a plush reclining seat with ample leg room. Beyond the window, the beautiful high-rises of Vancouver and Richmond get smaller while the sparkling Pacific Ocean seems to stretch out to infinity.

It's badass that Cate is successful enough to travel in luxury, and she does it with such confidence. She's earned these seats through years of hard work and has no shame about it. Sitting next to me, she's dressed casually in loose-fitting jeans, Vans, and a faded yellow tee with the *We Can Do It* woman on it. I'm in jeans and a tee too, but Cate makes even airplane-wear look fashionable.

She's the ultimate empowered woman, and it's both sexy and inspiring. She even has a team—Ken, Sean, her agent, her manager, her publicist, and whoever else works for her back home.

"This'll be my life once I start my career," I say with a wistful sigh, running my palms over the leather elbow rests.

"I imagine medical physics pays well," Cate says, leaning across me to peer out the window through her chic sunglasses.

Yes, *leaning across me*. Close. Her sweet scent meets my nose, and her soft hair tickles my face. Whether she cares about the view of British Columbia or is making an excuse to lean into me, I don't know. But normally when people look out windows, they don't lean quite so close to the other person and touch their thigh like this.

Also, I seem to recall her telling me that she was afraid of heights. And we're about 20,000 feet up, according to the TV screen.

"If I manage to become a diagnostic radiologist? Definitely," I say, ignoring the flutter in my belly. "I should be earning two or three hundred thousand."

Normally, I'd feel like an ass for talking about my future income, but seeing as Cate earns millions of dollars per movie, I'm less guarded.

"With a brain like yours and a passion for lifesaving work, I should hope you'd get a salary like that," Cate says. "Good for you."

There's a scuffle behind us.

"Miss, you need to go back to your seat," the flight attendant says.

"I just wanted to… Is there a bathroom up here?" a young, feminine voice says.

"First class only. Please go back to your seat."

A teenage girl is trying to push through the curtain, clutching her phone, craning her neck to look at everyone in first class.

Ken gets up, and that's all he needs to do. Under his stony glare, the girl shrinks back and murmurs apologies.

When she's gone and Ken sits, Cate looks at me as if none of this happened. "Where's the first place you'll fly to?"

"Um—the Netherlands," I say, bringing my attention back.

"Why there?"

"My grandparents live there. I've been a few times, and it's my home away from home."

"This would explain your affinity for crêpes—or should I say *pannenkoeken*."

I laugh. "Bang on."

She moves her sunglasses to the top of her head, and my abdomen tingles as I meet her gaze.

Her body is angled toward me, her legs closer to my seat than the aisle.

It's time to test my hypothesis.

"Ever join the mile high club?" I ask, my voice low enough that Ken and Sean won't hear.

Cate, who was sipping her champagne, covers her mouth to stifle a laugh.

She swallows and puts down the flute. "You'd think after flying private a few times it would have happened, but no. There are always people around who know exactly what you're doing."

"The risk of being caught doesn't do anything for you?"

She tilts her head in a gesture of indifference. "I think I prefer the opposite—knowing that it's just the two of us, alone, with nobody around to interrupt. You?"

It takes me a moment to get my brain back on track after that image.

"I did it in economy once, under a blanket," I say, "if that counts."

She looks sharply at me, her eyes glinting. "Do tell."

"I was headed to Mexico with a woman I was dating and a bunch of her friends. All-inclusive resort. Just a get-drunk sort of weekend." I haven't thought about that trip in a long time. She and I only dated for two months, and it was a fast and furious fling that ended as quickly as it started. Going on a trip together is a good way to figure out if you're into someone or not.

"It was an overnight flight, the lights were off, everyone was asleep. We had the row to ourselves. So, sharing a blanket…" I face her and touch her thigh, letting her draw the conclusion.

Her breath catches and her lips part. As I take my hand away, she clears her throat. "Was it hard to keep quiet?"

Her voice is husky and there's color in her cheeks.

"It's easy enough to avoid the obvious sounds," I say, "but it's hard to stop the quieter ones. Tiny hitches in the breath or too much movement could have given us away."

My heart beats faster. She hasn't angled away from me or changed the subject. In fact, she leans a bit closer.

The flight attendant stops by to ask us if we need anything, and we both give little starts, like we're guilty of something.

When she leaves, Cate and I look at each other and laugh.

Abby's warning lingers in the back of my mind, telling me to share my camera fears with Cate. But now that we're on our way, that fear seems far behind me and unimportant. The cameras on the red carpet won't even be focused on me with so many celebrities around, which means this could be a great opportunity to get over my anxiety. If I let myself enjoy the night, it might actually be fun and exciting.

Besides, if I tell Cate I'm afraid of cameras, she'll think I'm totally weird and damaged.

I'll be fine.

We land in Los Angeles and get into a limousine, where Sean jumps into assistant mode.

"To the spa!" he says, clapping. "Hair, makeup, manicures. I'll send your luggage to the hotel."

"I haven't had a manicure since I was thirteen at a birthday party," I say, a little anxious about the state of my nails. "I mean, I keep them pretty short. For reasons."

Cate casts me a knowing look and bites her lip.

I grin. I love that she caught the meaning, and I love even more that she acknowledged it.

The limousine takes us to a gorgeous spa that looks like it belongs in ancient Greece.

"We won't have time to get to our hotel suite until after the event," Cate says as we pull up out front. "We're on a tight schedule for the red carpet. But we're staying in the same hotel as the gala, and wait until you see it. It's a six-star. The room is like a full apartment."

"Wow." I've never been to a five-star, never mind a six-star.

Truthfully, I would be thrilled if we were in a dingy motel that could only offer us a tiny room with one bed, but this is amazing for different reasons.

I also love how she said *our* hotel suite.

The moment we get out of the limo, a woman in yoga shorts and a tie-dye shirt rockets toward us in the parking lot. Shit, another rabid fan? I wince, ready for Ken to football tackle her.

"Surprise!" she shouts.

Cate lets out an excited squeal. "Josie!"

I let out a breath of relief as they hug and scream.

Cate breaks away and motions to me. "This is Rachel. She's my plus-one tonight. Rachel, this is my little sister, Josie."

"Nice to meet you," Josie says, stepping in for a hug.

"Hi," I stammer, nervous and excited to be meeting a member of Cate's family.

She's a head shorter than Cate, brunette, and built like an athlete. They share the same ice-blue eyes.

"She forced me not to tell you, Cate," Sean says, typing on his phone.

"It's true," Josie says. "I threatened to roundhouse him."

"Josie's a kickboxing instructor," Cate says to me. "Among other fitness classes."

"Nice!" I say.

Sean gives Josie a side-hug. "You're lucky I told Ken, or else he'd be roundhousing you right now for ambushing us. Come on, let's head inside. I booked all three of you."

Josie rushes ahead, a ball of energy. "I've got the afternoon off, so I thought I'd surprise you. How's Canada? Have you seen a beaver yet?"

"Beautiful as ever," Cate says. "And no."

Sean checks us in and the staff whisk us into the lounge, offering iced tea and snacks. I can't help but grin at the prospect of spending the afternoon like this. Josie's energy takes the pressure off and is making me more at ease around Cate, which I desperately need.

"How's Waffles doing?" I ask Josie.

She lights up. "You told her!" she says to Cate, and then to me, "He's the best. I taught him to ring a bell when he's hungry and how to use the toilet so I never have to clean a litter box."

Cate laughs. "He's weirdly smart. He used to wait around the corner of the kitchen where Phil would trip over him. I lost count of the number of times it happened. I swear he did it on purpose to please me." She sighs wistfully. "Such a good cat."

She's relaxed with her sister here.

As we settle into cushy chairs for our manicures, I say, "Do you always get ready for events this way? Limos and a spa day and all that?"

Cate smiles, removing a couple of rings from her fingers. "Not quite so extravagantly. Today is different."

I want to ask why, but I'm afraid of the answer. I'm afraid she'll say that this gala is a big deal and merits the extravagance, when I want her to say it's because I'm with her.

A warm, tingling sensation fills my chest at the prospect that she's making today special for me—that she wants to impress me.

The technician sets to work on my hands and Cate laughs.

"What?" I ask, my lips pulling into a grin.

"You're supposed to enjoy a manicure. Your shoulders are up by your ears."

I shake out the tension. "It tickles!"

As our hands get massaged with tropical-scented moisturizer, I steal glances beside me. The technician moves slowly over Cate's delicate fingers and palms, and suddenly I wish I was the one giving her a manicure.

This surprise visit from Josie has switched something over inside me, making me see Cate as more than an actor. She's a sister, a friend, a cat mom, a woman who's lived a full life. I'm getting a glimpse into who she is when she's away from the set, and I like this side of her.

When we get to hair, the stylist asks what I want. I tell him to basically keep it the same, though I agree to subtle highlights.

"Go blue and a wolf cut, Cate," Josie says. "Get wild."

Cate laughs.

"I mean, you could probably pull it off," I say, trying to picture it on her.

"See? You're outvoted," Josie says. "Do it."

"I'll think about it for next time," Cate says. "But you'll have to do a better job of convincing me. I want a PowerPoint presentation."

"Done," Josie says, casting me a grin.

I think I'm in her good books—not that it should matter. But I want Cate's sister to like me.

"I had pink hair once," I say. "My roommate and I agreed to try fun colors a few years ago. It looked terrible."

"Everyone has to do something like that at some point in their lives," Cate says.

I raise an eyebrow at this loaded statement. "What did you do?"

Josie cackles.

Cate smirks. "Belly button piercing."

"No way," I say.

"When I was a teen. Big mistake. I fainted getting it done, and my dad was furious when he found out. It's long gone now."

Josie dissolves into laughter. "Dad was so mad."

"Until you got your shoulder blade tattoo," Cate retorts. "Forgot all about my little piercing, didn't he?"

"Yeah, well, I like to think I helped him become a little more liberal."

"Didn't do a very good job of it. He prays for me whenever I do a movie with a sex scene in it."

"He does not!" Josie exclaims.

"He does," Cate says. "He sprayed holy water on me last time I visited."

Josie lets out a laugh that fills the spa. Cate joins in, rubbing a hand over her eyes in exasperation.

I grin.

While Cate heads to the sink to have her hair washed, Josie says to me, "It's nice to see Cate like this. How long have you two known each other?"

"Just a couple of weeks," I say. "She's filming on my block in Vancouver."

Josie nods. "You wouldn't know it because of the brave face she puts on, but she's been a little shaken since the Phil ordeal. It's why I came today, actually. I thought she needed some family time. But she seems to be doing okay." She studies me up and down, opens her mouth, then closes it again.

My heart skips. What was she about to say?

After a moment, she says, "Be loyal to her, okay?"

"Okay," I say, though I'm not exactly sure what she means by this. "Or else you'll roundhouse me?"

Josie laughs. "Right."

Loyal. I shouldn't be surprised. Having a mega-public divorce and your secrets sold for money would hurt, even if she seems strong on the outside.

"You don't have to worry," I say, and Josie smiles.

"How do you want the sides?" my hair stylist says, pulling away my attention. "Do you want razor lines?"

"Sure," I say. "Surprise me."

It's a good call. He shaves in a gorgeous triangular design that I wish I had the talent to keep up once I return home. Between the cut and highlights, my hair looks better than ever.

By the time we finish getting our makeup done, I can't deny it: I look hot. So does Cate, but she always looks hot.

Josie grabs her purse, freshly beautified with rich brunette color, long bangs, and soft pink nails. "That's it for me. I've got to teach aerobics tonight."

"Okay," Cate says. "I'm so glad you came. That was such a nice surprise."

"It was nice meeting you," I say.

Josie hugs me and then Cate. "You too! Love you, sis. Have fun tonight."

She leaves the spa, and Cate says to me, "I hope that was okay."

"Are you kidding? That was so fun. I love her."

Cate's face breaks into a huge smile.

I can't get enough of the way she's looking at me today.

Before we can say more, the staff whisks us to separate changerooms. I enter mine to find a trickling fountain, a full-length mirror with an ornate brass frame, and a table with grapes and cheese on it. Good lord.

Sean tells me I'm stunning and hands me a black garment bag. "Your evening wear, m'lady. Alexander McQueen."

"Thank you," I say, breathless. I accept it like I'm cradling a newborn.

Alexander McQueen? Holy *crap*.

I've never paid much attention to fashion, but the prospect of wearing a designer outfit at a celebrity gala has me inwardly screaming.

Minutes later, I'm standing in front of the mirror with my jaw unhinged. The tuxedo is black and gold as promised, but that description hardly teases the surface of this piece of art I'm wearing. The single-breasted jacket has an hourglass shape, the waist embroidered with gold flowers. There was no shirt on the hanger, which means the jacket is meant to be on its own—and the plunging neckline comes down between my boobs to reveal the sexiest cleavage I've ever had. The trousers hug my thighs and flare out at the bottom, caressing me in all the right places. Whatever the material is, it's light and soft against my skin.

Paired with my professionally done hair and makeup, I look like I actually belong on a red carpet.

What is this jumping feeling inside me? Is that excitement? Impending cameras aside, I'm stepping further into a dream with each passing minute.

I'm slipping into a pair of modest black stilettos when there's a soft knock at the door.

"Come in," I say.

It opens and Cate enters.

My breath catches.

I've seen red-carpet photos of her many times, but it's different in person. She's in a gold floor-length gown that shimmers in the dim light of the spa. As she strides toward me, her bare leg peeks through a high slit, tipped with a gold stiletto that's perfectly matched to the dress. Her softly curled, shoulder-length hair is tucked behind one ear to expose a diamond pendant swinging from her earlobe. A matching pendant dips into the V-neck of the gown, settling between her breasts.

We stare at each other, unmoving. I could drink her in for hours. I don't think there's a more beautiful person on this entire planet.

She must notice my expression because she makes jazz hands and spins around to show off the full dress. "Imported from Italy."

My knees weaken as she spins. Her back is bare, the dress dipping low and coming to a point above her tailbone.

"Y-you look gorgeous," I say, tongue tripping over the words. It's hard to breathe in here. Isn't there a window I can open to let in some air?

"I was thinking the same about you," Cate murmurs, walking closer. "Absolutely stunning, Rachel. Lucky me, having you at my side tonight."

She stops in front of me, a head taller in her heels, and her presence wraps around me like an embrace.

Her words put a flutter in my chest.

Is it safe to fall for Cate? Does she like me for me, or would she shatter my heart?

"We match nicely," Cate says, eyeing the gold embroidery on my jacket. "We're going to look amazing together in photos."

I nod stiffly. This might be the right moment to tell her that I'm anxious about being on camera, before we get to the red carpet and are slammed with them.

I open my mouth, but I can't get the words out. How do I even begin?

The door flies open, and a woman in a black suit and tie strides in, stilettos clicking.

Cate and I step apart, breaking whatever thread had been pulling between us.

"Cate," the woman says. "You look perfect. How's the fit?"

"Feels okay," Cate says. "Rachel, this is Mandy Chung, my publicist. Mandy, this is my date, Rachel Janssen."

Mandy shakes my hand firmly. "Rachel. The tux fits okay?"

I nod. "Yes, ma'am."

Mandy walks a figure-eight around Cate and me, poking and tugging at our outfits before declaring us satisfactory. She checks her oversized watch and walks back out the door. "Ride's waiting out front."

Cate and I meet each other's eye before following Mandy. I can't tell what she's thinking.

We step outside into the blazing California heat to find our limo waiting. Sean tells us we look like queens and opens the door.

"The problem with tight dresses, crystals, and sequins," Cate says to me in an undertone, tugging the gown, "is that they're uncomfortable and scratchy. I'd rather be in a loose-fitting pajama shirt and no pants, wouldn't you?"

"Always," I say.

"Anyway, it won't be long until I can get into something more comfortable when we're back in our room later. You might have to help me take this off." She winks at me, and her hand trails over my waist as she steps past me.

My head spins as she accepts Ken's help to get into the limo. There's a tingling between my legs.

Okay, there is no misinterpreting that. "Slipping into something more comfortable" is *classic*. And that touch across my waist? Come *on*.

My pulse races as I climb in after her. I'm silently screaming, struggling to stay calm.

I've gathered enough evidence in support of my hypothesis.

It's time to write up my lab results.

Conclusion: Cate Whitney is totally flirting with me.

CHAPTER 10
Red Carpet Stresses

As our limousine approaches the red carpet, a gridlock of arriving vehicles forces us to slow down. Outside, noisy crowds line the street like they're watching a parade, craning for glimpses of the arriving stars.

Cars honk, the crowd screams, someone is using an air horn, and the reality of what I'm about to do settles in. My heart races and I'm light-headed. Beside me, Cate is taking deep breaths like we're about to cross the Capilano Suspension Bridge.

Is she nervous too?

My mouth is too dry to ask.

"You'll do two interviews on the red carpet, no more," Mandy says. She hasn't stopped talking since we left the spa. "I've arranged them with the networks already, so listen to my direction. Rachel, don't talk unless someone asks you a direct question. Tell them who you're wearing, and look to Cate if they ask about your involvement in *Clockwork Curie* or how you know each other."

"Okay." So the only words from my mouth will be "Alexander McQueen." I can do that. I think.

I swallow hard, my tongue feeling too fat for my mouth.

We pass through a security checkpoint, and for a long minute, the limo crawls closer to the place where we'll be let out. My heart is beating so fast that I'm trembling.

Why was I excited? This event is way out of my league. I thought it would be cool and fun to go to a gala with Cate Whitney, but the Rachel who agreed to this was an idiot. I can't go down a red carpet.

I turn to Cate, about to voice my anxiety, but her eyes are closed. Is she meditating? Praying to the angels of Lucille and Marilyn for strength?

Actually, that's not a bad idea.

I close my eyes and am immediately jabbed in the face with a makeup brush.

"Hey!"

"Just a touch-up," Mandy says, now doing the same to Cate.

My face is like a seven-layer dip.

She touches up our lipstick and hands Cate her clutch. "Ready?"

Cate nods.

Sean smiles, his face alight with excitement. "Have fun, ladies!"

Fun? Who said this was fun?

The limo door opens, and an explosion of shouting and clicking cameras slams my eardrums.

Oh, the *cameras*. I've never seen so many lenses in one place and never heard so many people vying for one person's attention.

Mandy gets out first and beckons to Cate.

I can't do this. My airway constricts, and I can't get enough oxygen to my brain. Black and white spots erupt in my eyes. I'm going to pass out.

Somewhere at the edge of my vision, a man helps Cate get out of the limo.

The screams get louder as people see her. The noise is weirdly hollow, like I'm underwater.

"Cate! Cate! Cate!" Shouts rise from fans, reporters, and photographers. They swirl in my senses, dizzying.

"Go ahead, hun," Sean says, touching my back. "Ken and I are staying here."

I can't move. My breaths are shallow, fast. Sweat prickles beneath my layers of makeup and runs down the back of my neck.

"Rachel?" he says, mouth turning downward as he leans over to search my face.

"I can't," I say, the words strangled. "The cameras. I shouldn't have—I'm not ready—"

"Don't worry, the cameras are all on Cate," Sean says. "You're secondary. And I mean that in the most loving, encouraging way."

I close my eyes as the camera flashes attack Cate outside, but the lights pass through my eyelids. I can't hide from them.

Breathe. Inhale slowly.

I cover my eyes and coach myself through breathing for a moment. When I force air into my lungs, I'm less dizzy.

Sean's hand comes to rest on my shoulder. Fuck, I have to hurry up and leave this limo. Cate will be waiting for me.

He has a point that I'm not the focus. It's like when I played a minor character in my elementary school production of *The Sound of Music*. When I compared my role to the leads, it seemed ridiculous to get nervous, and so I wasn't.

But am I really trying to compare today to being in a school play? I'm at a gala with Cate Whitney. I'm guaranteed to be in photos and videos that will show up online afterward.

I shake my head to get rid of that thought, my eyes stinging like I'm going to cry. "I'm a *student*, Sean. Those are celebrities out there."

Ken squints out the window, as vigilant as ever.

Sean grabs my shoulders and looks me dead in the eye. "Rachel, you are rocking an *amazing* tuxedo and are beyond gorgeous. Cate Whitney asked you here because she wants you with her tonight. Are you going to stay in this car and abandon her, or are you going to stand by her side?"

Outside the door, Cate turns away from the cameras and holds out her hand, inviting me to join her. Her brow furrows as she sees my expression.

"Rachel, come on," Mandy says sharply.

Sean is right. Cate set me up for success with this designer tux and professional makeover. Now I have to do my part and find confidence.

When I meet her eyes, I want to do this for her. I want to get through the evening with composure, like I belong at her side. I want to make a good impression on her, her friends, and the public. The alternative is to shake my head, shut the door, and leave—but I don't want that. I want to be here, even if I'm afraid. Because God, when am I ever going to get a chance like this again?

"Scrape me off the red carpet if I pass out," I say to Sean, giving him a quick hug before getting out.

"You got this!" he shouts.

I take Cate's hand and nod, pretending to be calmer than I am.

"Overwhelmed?" she asks.

"A little."

She squeezes, seeming to know it's an understatement. "You're doing great."

My consciousness seems to float outside my body as I follow Cate down the red carpet. She smiles and poses while Mandy fusses over her dress and the photographers order her around.

"Cate!" they shout, her name echoing down the line.

"Cate, look at me!"

"Turn!"

"Over the shoulder!"

"Move down, move down," Mandy keeps saying, shuffling us down the carpet to the next set of cameras.

I smile with Cate, hoping I look less panicked than I feel, and then stand back while she poses for more. She looks like a goddess as she works her angles for the cameras, and it hits me how much goes into looking nice in photos.

I have no idea if I have a good angle or if I should be posing a certain way, and I'm in no state to figure this out right now.

"Cate! Cate! Cate!"

My ears ring with her name until I want to plug my ears. How would it feel to have all of these strangers fighting for my attention, shouting my name until I'm numb to it?

The shouts begin to morph, like a DJ fading between songs. Someone else must have arrived behind us.

"Kristen! Kristen! Kristen!"

Their shifting attention brings an infinitesimal relief, like a cool breeze.

"Here, Cate," Mandy says, motioning her toward a woman with a microphone.

Cate walks forward while I stay behind with Mandy. But my moment of peace lasts only a few seconds before Cate looks back at me and Mandy shoves me forward.

"This is Rachel Janssen, my consultant on *Clockwork Curie*," Cate says to the interviewer, wrapping her arm around my waist and pulling me against her. "She's been helping me learn about Marie Curie's work."

"Lovely to meet you, Rachel," the woman with the microphone says. "Who are you wearing tonight?"

"Alexander McQueen," I say, my tongue too fat for my mouth.

"I thought so," the woman says excitedly. "Absolutely gorgeous, you two. Thanks so much and good luck tonight, Cate."

The woman turns back to the camera, and Cate pulls me along the red carpet.

Okay, that was fine. Nothing embarrassing happened. I said what I was supposed to say.

I grasp Cate's hand like it's a buoy and I'm lost at sea. I focus on her, trying as hard as I can to block out everything else.

And then, finally, we've made it. We're at the hotel doors.

"Good job, both of you," Mandy says as we go through. "Get into the ballroom and mingle. I'll get you registered and text you the seating chart. Call me if you need anything."

She waits until we both nod, then disappears through the crowd in the lobby.

I suck in a huge breath, like I was trapped underwater that whole time.

Cate takes my hand again, gripping tightly. She's cold, clammy, and wearing a blank smile, like she's checked out.

Maybe I'm not the only one having a hard time with this.

I squeeze her hand in reassurance.

"Ready for cocktails?" she asks, gaze unfocused.

"Do you want to hide in the bathroom for ten minutes first?" I ask. "It's my favorite party trick."

I get a brief glimpse of a real smile before another camera flashes and it's snuffed.

"I'm fine. Come on, let's find some drinks."

She lets go of my hand and I take in my surroundings, awestruck. This has to be the most gorgeous hotel I've ever seen. Crystals are everywhere, even the floor, and we follow an actual trickling stream to the ballroom.

Hundreds of the most elite, beautiful people in the world mingle beneath the vaulted ceiling, where a crystal chandelier the size of an elephant shimmers—almost, but not quite, as eye-catching as the woman beside me.

"Cate!" a woman shouts.

She must be tired of hearing her name by now. It brings to mind a dog owner I once saw at the park who called her Labrador's name so many times that he stopped responding to it. It made for an entertaining scene as she tried to get him to stop chasing a squirrel.

Sure enough, Cate doesn't seem to notice, and the woman has to call twice more before she looks over.

"Oh, it's Meredith," she says with a breath of relief.

The person calling her is a tall woman surrounded by a cluster of admirers—and holy shit, it's Meredith Cheema, multi-award-winning actor, director, writer, and more. She's looking curvy and dazzling in a floor-length red gown.

"I can grab us drinks and meet you over there," I say.

Cate meets my gaze, less guarded than a minute ago. "You're so sweet. That would be lovely."

I'm still jittery as we part ways, and there's sweat rolling down my back. I head toward the nearest person carrying a champagne tray, breathing deeply. That red carpet was a near-disaster. I was so close to slamming the limo door and telling the driver to keep going.

I hope Cate doesn't know what a coward I was. It's hard to tell whether she noticed my panic with everything going on.

At least I have the whole evening to make up for it. I'm going to be so damn charming that people will be asking what movie I'm starring in.

Weaving through the crowd, I pass so many A-list celebrities that I feel smaller by the second. This is surreal—and awesome. I make mental notes of every detail in the room and every person I pass, determined not to forget this night.

I can do this. I can make a good impression and act like I belong here. My confidence might be forced, but that's fine, right? I've faked confidence on exams countless times, and that always worked out.

I grab two champagne flutes from a server's tray, spin around, and nearly bump into someone.

"Sorry!" I say, gasping. "I'm so sorry."

A tall, middle-aged man stares down at me, the kind people tend to call a silver fox. He's so far into my personal space that I can smell his mouthwash.

"Nice date you two are having," he says, barely audible over the hum of the crowd.

"Excuse me?"

He raises an eyebrow like he's joking, but the way his jaw is set tells me he absolutely isn't.

It hits me who the man is. Phil Niles. Cate's ex-husband.

CHAPTER 11
THE WOLF AND THE KITTY

CRAP.

I spent so long dreading the cameras that I forgot to dread the other big thing—the fact that Cate's ex-husband might be here.

"I'm Cate's consultant for her role as Marie—"

"I've gotta say, it's a cute photo of you two." Phil holds up his phone. On it is a paparazzi shot of Cate and me leaving the Oceanfront patio in Vancouver last weekend. Cate's hand is on my lower back, and I'm watching my feet as we step down onto the sidewalk—and what I never knew until now was the way Cate looked at me at that moment. There's something tender and curious in her expression, and it sends a flutter through my chest.

"We were meeting to talk about science," I say.

"Ah. A business meeting." His eyebrows are still raised as he studies the picture.

My heart beats faster. He hasn't said anything threatening, so why do I feel threatened?

The fact that he's acting defensive after seeing Cate and me together is interesting. Did he read Cate's body language as flirting? Did he know before their divorce that she was into women?

"She told me about your divorce," I say, meeting his non-threats with a non-threat of my own. "Sorry to hear that."

His expression hardens, and I'm reminded of his latest role as a short-tempered werewolf. "She needed space. We've gone through this before. Kitty always comes back to her wolf."

"Kitty?" I say, judgment dripping in my tone.

He reaches past me for a champagne flute, his broad chest bumping my shoulder. "Pet name. You know, when you've been in someone's life for a long time and come up with nicknames—"

"I know what a pet name is."

A sick feeling churns in my gut. I fight the urge to punch his perfectly proportioned face.

He tilts his head. "Consider this a friendly warning not to get too attached, sweetheart. Soon, she'll get bored of entertaining an average girl and want someone more on her level."

"And you think you're on her level?" I say, stopping before I say something about tantrums and a delicate ego.

He raises a hand and I flinch, like he's going to punch me. "I've got more value in this cufflink than your entire net worth, sweetheart."

My airway constricts, and I focus on what's outside of us—the noise and laughter of the party. The world is bigger than whatever this idiot is projecting onto me, and I don't need to put up with him. I just need to get back to Cate and everything will be fine.

"Such a pleasure running into you," I say. Leaving him glowering at me with a raised eyebrow, I slip through the dense crowd before he can stop me.

A few strides later, I risk a glance over my shoulder. He's with a group of people, clapping a guy on the back and laughing heartily. They smile and hug like friends who haven't seen each other in a long time—like he didn't just act like an asshole five seconds ago. Do they know? Is he Jekyll and Hyde, or are those people perfectly aware of his unpleasant side and have decided not to care because he's famous?

Fuck him, anyway. What's his problem? Can't he deal with a breakup? Even if he's not over her, that doesn't give him the right to stalk anyone who hangs out with her.

I summon every drop of strength so I can return to Cate with a smile. I don't need to tell her I ran into Phil. It would upset her on a night that's already stressing her out.

Cate sees me coming, and though Meredith is talking to her, her eyes are on me, a smile on her face that melts me.

Yes, everything is fine.

"Rachel, this is Meredith," she says, accepting her champagne and putting an arm around my shoulders. "Meredith, this is who I was telling you about."

"The physics consultant! Lovely to meet a brilliant woman like yourself." Meredith shakes my hand and I'm starstruck all over again.

"Nice to meet you," I say.

"Cate was just doing a terrible job of explaining your program."

Cate laughs.

"I'm in medical physics," I say.

"I got that far," Cate says defensively.

"Yeah, but what that entails is another matter," Meredith says.

"It's about diagnosing and treating illnesses using X-rays, ultrasounds, MRIs, radioactive substances, that sort of thing."

"Amazing," Meredith says, drawing out the word, like I'm the first person in the world to study this. "We'll be seeing you on the cover of *Time* magazine one day. You'll be celebrated for a breakthrough in radiation therapy. Mark my words."

I smile, flattered. "That's the dream."

Maybe she's just being nice, but what she probably doesn't realize is that this sort of ambition has crossed my mind. When I chose this career path, I hoped to be part of a team that makes a medical breakthrough. It's a bold dream to have but not an impossible one.

Cate's gaze burns the side of my face. Maybe she's thinking about Meredith's words, wondering if I'm the sort of person who has that kind of potential.

"You know, Rachel, I never would have stayed in this business if it weren't for Cate," Meredith says.

"Oh, stop it," Cate says, turning her head in an adorable gesture of modesty.

"It's true! I got dropped by a TV series and was ready to give up when I met Cate on the set of *Rainfall*. I've never met a kinder person in this business. Never."

It's cute how Cate is blushing at the compliment, and even sweeter to hear someone confirm my theory that she's legitimately one of the nicest people ever.

"What was it like working on a Paulsen film?" I ask Meredith. "Is she as good a director as everyone says?"

Meredith looks delighted that I asked—and a bubble of hope rises in me. Tonight might turn out okay. Besides the red carpet and the Phil Niles incident, which I'd like to wipe from my memory, I'm holding onto my self-esteem in this crowd of incredibly successful people. Cate and Meredith are obviously friends, and if Meredith likes me, I'd say that's a win.

While Meredith regales me with stories, Cate takes several chances to smile at me. Her arm is around my waist, and when I lean into her, she moves her fingers gently—a secret shared between us.

The way her hand brushes over me is intimate, like what I'd expect from a girlfriend, and it sends my mind spinning.

As we mingle through cocktail hour, she caresses my lower back, my waist, even the back of my neck, driving me wild. I lean into her touches, squeeze when she takes my hand, and smile at her to let her know I like it.

Fuck, I want her. Badly.

I'm dying to return the touches—but this is her fame, not mine, and her gala, not mine. I don't want to do anything unwelcome.

But why would she be doing this when we're in the most public place imaginable, with cameras documenting everything?

Maybe it's as Abby and I suspected: celebrities are just outgoing and flirty. From the outside, our interactions might be unassuming. Everyone around us is touching and hugging and giving cheek-kisses.

Or maybe she wants the world to know. Maybe she wants rumors about her sexuality to get out, and she's showing it rather than telling.

Cate might have introduced me as a consultant tonight, but I can tell by her closeness and the way her attention lingers that my hypothesis holds strong. My heart beats faster as I wonder what might happen in our hotel room tonight.

Should I lean into her and say something about helping her get out of her dress later? Is that too forward?

Heat spreads through my middle as I imagine sliding that gold dress off her shoulders, kissing her all over, licking her in places that make her gasp and moan.

God, her hands feel good on me. I'm hopelessly attracted to them—like I am to every other part of her. I try to steal glances without lingering too long, but by the way Meredith catches my eye while Cate is talking, it's clear that I'm making my infatuation embarrassingly obvious.

I return Meredith's little smile and drop my gaze to the fancy ballroom carpet.

Then Phil's subtle threats swim forward in my memory. *Kitty… When you've been in someone's life for a long time… I have more value in this cufflink than your entire net worth.*

I let out a shaky breath. He was way over the line and not worth thinking about.

While Cate is wrapped up talking to a screenwriter she hasn't seen in years, Meredith leans in and says in an undertone, "I saw Phil talking to you over there. Everything okay?"

"Fine," I say too quickly.

Her mouth twists in displeasure, like she knows I'm lying. "He's been wheedling since they split, trying to pry for information about her from everyone they're connected to. I told him to shove it when he called, and we haven't spoken since."

"I knew I liked you," I say, and she smiles. I try to sound casual as I ask, "So what's his deal?"

Meredith sighs. "He and Cate were together for seven years. From the outside, it looked like they were crazy about each other. Luxury vacations, fancy dinners, parties—God, they had good parties. They were a power couple. No kids, and no plans for any. It was just the two of them and their adventurous life. But underneath… Well, I think he was delusional enough to see the same perfect image the public did. When Cate wanted a divorce, he was truly crushed. He's had a lot of failed relationships, a lot of heartbreak, and I think that gets to a person after a while."

"That doesn't give him the right to be a dick," I say, a little more sharply than I intended. The part about what an amazing life the two of them had isn't easy to digest.

"No, it doesn't." Meredith drains her champagne. "I don't know if I have the right to share it with you, but—well—his jealousy was a bit toxic. He kept close tabs on her and hated her having close friends, no matter the gender."

My insides twist uncomfortably. Is Phil afraid of what he sees between Cate and me? Is he jealous? I don't know how to feel about this. I don't want him to be thinking about Cate and me at all.

A deep voice booms over the speakers, telling everyone to please take their seats.

"Thank God," Cate says, putting a hand on my back. "There'll be bread on the tables. I barely ate lunch at the spa."

I jump a little, then try to cover it by straightening my jacket. "Great. It was nice talking to you, Meredith."

"You too, love," she says with a wink. "Stay confident."

It's like she knows what talking about Phil and Cate's marriage did to me. Confidence is hard to summon as my head swims with images of them, a Hollywood power couple who lived a wild and free life in the years before I met her.

"Doing okay?" Cate says as she guides me to our places.

"Yes," I say automatically. "This venue is incredible."

"Wait until you try the food."

Murmurs make me look around. People are parting, their attention on something behind me—and a firm hand claps my shoulder.

"Miss, please come with me."

It's a security guard, and not the chill kind from the movie set at home. This looks like someone from a SWAT team, complete with a helmet and vest.

"Me?" I say, voice high. "I think you have the wrong—"

"This way," he says, interrupting me.

For an absurd second, I wonder if they've realized I don't belong here— an average woman living in a separate dimension from Hollywood.

"Excuse us?" Cate says sharply. "Who are you?"

"Miss, step back," he says to Cate, pulling me away from her.

My ears ring.

Cate shouts something I can't process.

Another security guard closes in, the two of them flanking me. They force me to move my feet and drag me toward the lobby.

"What's going on?" Meredith says, her voice carrying.

People gasp. All eyes in the vicinity lock onto me, expressions shocked, perplexed, and, worst of all, pitying.

The security guards escort me from the ballroom while every A-list actor in America stares and whispers.

Chapter 12
The First Moose Back to Canada

Two security guards pull me across the opulent hotel lobby, down a quiet hallway, and into an empty, dim meeting room. Chairs and tables are stacked in a corner, and it smells like carpet cleaner and a depressing business conference.

"Do you have identification?" the one who grabbed me says. There's a pink tinge to his pasty, clean-shaven face, and his beady blue eyes glint with excitement. This asshat is getting a rush from playing a hero who's just captured a bad guy.

I pat my pockets before remembering that Sean sent our luggage upstairs. The only thing I have on me is my phone.

"It's up in our room. My name is Rachel Janssen, and I've literally never stolen anything or done anything illegal in my life."

Mr. Hero frisks me like a suspicious TSA agent, his hands painful as he checks my waist and legs.

"What are you doing?" I shout. "Get off me!"

Footsteps race down the hallway and Cate hurtles through the doorway. "Rachel!"

The second guy, a baby-faced kid, meets her in the doorway and physically stops her from coming any closer.

She tries and fails to shove him aside. "Someone tell me what's going on."

More footsteps race closer, and Mandy bursts into the room, panting. "What the hell is happening? Let go of her right now."

Mr. Hero narrows his eyes. "Is this woman Miss Whitney's date? We received a tip that she's carrying a weapon and is planning an attack—"

"For fuck's sake," Cate shouts, stepping closer so Baby-Face has his arms awkwardly around her. "Who told you that?"

"Ma'am, stay back!" Mr. Hero shouts with such volume that Cate is startled into stepping backward.

"Cate, stay calm," Mandy says.

Wait, did he just use the word *weapon*?

Mandy turns to Cate, her back to us, and says in a low voice, "I just found out Phil is here, so this might have something to do—"

Cate growls and steps around Mandy, pointing at the security guards. "Did Phil Niles tip you off? Or his assistant, maybe? Someone on his team?"

The security guards exchange a glance.

My head spins. *Phil Niles? What the actual hell?*

"Our divorce was all over the tabloids, and Rachel is my date tonight. Can you fit the pieces together?" Her cheeks are flushed, her curled hair becoming unruly, her earrings swinging.

The only time I've seen Cate in a rage like this was in a movie where she played a spy whose country betrays her. Seeing her this angry in real life is frightening.

The room goes silent. My pulse pounds in my ears.

"I suggest you boys look into this *tip* you received before you do anything you regret," Mandy says with an authority that makes them deflate a little.

"Miss Whitney, can you please come with me?" Baby-Face says with a cautious glance to Mandy. "I need to ask you a few questions."

Cate's gaze locks onto me. I nod, doing my best to convey that I'm okay—even though I'm not sure if I am.

He takes Cate out of the room.

Mandy backs through the door after them, pointing her phone at the aggressive asshole beside me. "Don't touch Rachel, don't speak to her, don't even look at her until I tell you otherwise."

"With respect, ma'am, I need to ask her some questions," he says, a lot less confident than a moment ago.

She curses under her breath. "Rachel, I'll be back for you as fast as I can."

I'm too stunned to respond or even nod.

With one more threatening look at the guy beside me, she storms after Cate, stilettos clacking.

I cover my eyes, struggling to slow my breathing. What the hell kind of toxic breakup have I stepped into?

Mr. Hero asks me an endless list of questions. Where am I from? How long have I been here? How do I know Cate? Which airline did I take? I answer all of them and throw back a few of my own—do you honestly think I'm concealing a weapon? Did Phil Niles tell you I'm a threat? Can I just leave and go home? He refuses to say anything about who tipped him off and what sort of weapon they think I'm carrying, leaving me to wonder whether Phil paid them to do this or they truly believe I'm a danger.

Humiliation rises, icy, smothering, like waves about to drown me. I can't believe all of those celebrities saw me get escorted out of the gala. I wanted to make a good impression on Cate's friends. I wanted to get through the night like I belong at her side.

I can never show my face to any of them again.

Then Mr. Hero looks into space and says, "Yep. Yep. Okay. Copy."

He must have gotten a message in his earpiece.

Without smiling, without a change in tone or posture, he steps aside and motions to the door. "You're free to go. Have fun tonight."

I stare at him for a long moment, struggling to form words, before blurting, "Are you fucking kidding?"

This asshole expects me to go back into the ballroom and act like I wasn't just publicly humiliated?

He offers no reply and instead shrugs and leaves the room.

Resisting the urge to shout at him, I walk shakily into the lobby, chest heaving, eyes stinging.

Breathe.

The ballroom doors are closed, and behind them a pair of muffled, lively voices are delivering a speech. The audience laughs.

The lobby is empty. Cate is nowhere to be seen. Is she still with the other security guard, or did she go back into the ballroom? What about Mandy?

I consider walking to the nearest beach to get outside and clear my head, but I have no idea where we are and I'm not up to walking around an unfamiliar city at night. So I run into the bathroom and lock myself in a stall.

With shaking hands, I call Abby before I hyperventilate.

"Oh my God, are you calling me from the gala?" she asks by way of greeting.

"Yes," I say, voice thick.

A pause.

"Fuck," she says seriously. "Are you okay?"

"I m-met Cate's ex-husband." I tell Abby about our meeting by the champagne and how he told security I was carrying a weapon, and by the time I get to the part where I'm currently hiding in a bathroom stall, tears are cascading down my face. And I haven't even told her about my earlier red-carpet panic.

"Shit," she says, breath hitting the phone. "We've got to get you out of there."

I draw a steadying breath. "I know. This whole night is a disaster. If this event was in Vancouver, I'd be sprinting home in my heels right now. I guess I could wait until morning—"

"You listen to me, Rachel Janssen. I'm getting you back to Vancouver if I have to charter a moose to pick you up."

I smile, wiping tears from my cheeks, chin, and neck.

Mouse clicks and keyboard taps carry through the phone. "There's a flight home in two hours," Abby says. "Can you catch a cab and make it to LAX?"

How long did it take us to get here? Can I make it?

"I think so."

More mouse clicks. "Okay. It looks like it's too late for me to buy you a ticket online, but you might be able to make the flight on standby. I'll pick you up when you land—it looks like it'll be midnight."

"You're the best, Abby," I say, rubbing my forehead. My makeup is so thick that there's a layer between my fingers and the skin of my face, like icing.

"Hey, there's someone on my dodgeball team who's totally gay and totally single," Abby says. "She's really cool and I think you'd like her. I can set you up, and you can forget all about this Hollywood side-quest you've been on."

I know she's trying to help me put this ordeal behind me, but my heart aches at the thought of being set up with someone—the thought of being with anyone besides Cate. Because despite all of this, I'm still into her. She's the most incredible person I've ever met, and I don't want Phil fucking Niles to derail what we had going.

Beyond the stall, the door opens and heels click into the bathroom.

"Rachel?" Cate says.

My heart skips at the sound of her voice.

Abby sucks in a breath. Cate's voice must have carried through the phone.

"I have to go," I whisper to Abby. "I'll keep you posted."

I hang up.

"Rachel, are you in here?" Cate says, closer.

I inhale through my nose, exhale through my mouth, and open the door.

She's right there, eyes red, like she's been crying too.

"I'm so sorry," she whispers.

"It's fine," I lie.

It's hard to meet those gorgeous eyes right now. A lot of emotions are raging through me, and shame is one of them. Cate wouldn't be going through this right now if I hadn't come here.

"Mandy is on the phone with my lawyer," she says. "I'm going to deal with Phil through legal channels. He's—um—he's been verbally abusive to me since long before the divorce." Her words are staccato, like she's having trouble getting them out. "His jealousy was intolerable at best. I've dealt with the situation privately, but tonight crossed the line. I never thought he would get that nasty. Rachel, I'm so sorry you had to be caught in the middle."

I nod, not sure what to say. The thought that Cate was verbally abused hurts worse than anything else.

"How does someone like you end up with someone like him?" I whisper.

"It didn't start out that way. It started out like…like we thought we were soulmates. He changed over the years, getting more jealous, making backhanded comments, expecting me to play the housewife and take care of everything—or maybe I was just noticing it more. He told me who I wasn't allowed to see a few too many times, and the last straw was when he insulted Josie. It was something mild, like he called her annoying—but that was the day I snapped."

It makes sense that she wouldn't notice a gradual shift in the man she fell in love with. I hate him, though. I cross my arms, shoulders rolling in.

"Why is he like that? What could possibly make someone so…" I wave a hand, not sure what word fits. *Vengeful? Awful? Dickish?* Meredith's explanation of him being jealous after a string of failed relationships isn't good enough. This is beyond feeling sad about being dumped a few times.

Cate lifts a shoulder. "He hated talking about his childhood, and I only met his parents a few times in all the years we were together. I gathered that he was never good enough for them. Even as he was winning theater awards as a teenager, they refused to support him or come to his shows. They wanted him to get good grades, and instead he dropped out and got into acting. I think he got overly attached to me as a result of his mommy issues and…couldn't deal with being dumped."

"That doesn't make me hate him less," I say, finding it hard to summon sympathy.

Cate steps closer, features pulled down, eyes brimming. "Rachel, you asked me earlier why I went all out today with the limo and spa day. It was for you. I wanted today to be perfect for you. I'm so sorry—" Her voice cracks. She swallows and shakes her head.

Those words might have sparked something in me earlier, but right now, I'm empty.

"It's okay," I say because even though it isn't, I can't stand to see her looking this sad because of me.

"I know this whole evening has been stressful. The red carpet was overwhelming for me too. I should have prepared you better."

"It's not your fault. How were you supposed to know I would be afraid of a red carpet?"

She searches my face, like she's trying to understand the meaning beneath those words. We never talked about my moment of panic earlier.

I have to tell her. She needs to understand why I seized up and why I might continue to seize up when we're bombarded by cameras. If she doesn't want anything to do with me, now is her chance to say so. I can go home, and that will be the end of us.

"Look, a few years ago, near the end of high school, I had a…bullying situation," I say. I speak to the sink behind her, because if I meet her eye, I might not be able to keep talking. "There was this girl, Lauren, who was nasty to me all through school. She threatened to kick my ass all the time. She never did, but God, the things she said to me were—" I shake my head. "She got nastier as the years went on. One day, everyone in my grade went to this backyard party, and I got pretty drunk and made out with my girlfriend, Sarah, behind a shed. And Lauren—um—she and her friends filmed it. They put it online, and everyone at school saw it."

I'm nauseous as the words come out, but it's like throwing up after eating something bad—it has to come out. I'll feel better when it does.

Cate isn't moving, giving me her full attention.

"The thing is, Sarah was in the closet," I say. "Her parents were super conservative and stuff. After that, she hated my guts and we never talked again. Her parents made her switch schools, and I ended up getting bullied a lot. People would, um—" I mime taking a picture. "—mock me, I guess. Try to get a rise. They pretended to take pictures of me in class, in the halls… Once, a couple of boys came to my house and took a picture of me through my bedroom window. My dad called the cops. Anyway, I was embarrassed, ashamed…and I regretted, like, everything to do with that whole incident. Even being gay. I started skipping classes, and I would've failed if it weren't for one of my teachers. She made sure I got the grades I deserved and that I didn't screw up my university admission."

My voice cracks and I clear my throat.

Cate steps closer. "Oh, Rachel…"

"It's why I get anxious in front of cameras. It kind of…triggered something. After it happened, if I ever turned around and someone was pointing a camera at me—like, even just my mom taking a video at family gatherings—I'd get this awful, panicked feeling in my chest. So I stopped agreeing to pictures altogether. I still break down sometimes. I'm working on it but…it's hard."

"And yet you still said yes to spending time with me, the queen of being in unwanted photos."

I lift one shoulder. "You're worth it."

Her cheeks flush. She opens and closes her mouth before getting her next words out. "Rachel, you should have told me. I wouldn't have asked you to come here with me."

I shake my head firmly. "That's just it. I need to get over it. I want to. I can't let that ruin my life—or ruin what could be a great evening for us."

"But we could have dealt with your anxiety slowly, not by hurling you straight into the fire," she says with a breathy almost-laugh. "We could have started with a selfie."

My mouth twists into a little smile.

It feels better to have confessed this to her. I'm not sure if she thinks less of me for it or if she pities me or something equally mortifying, but I feel lighter, freer, now that the words are out. Her response is as good as it could be, and now I'm not keeping any secrets.

"Do you want to bail on this party and go up to our suite?" Cate says.

I blink. "Bail?"

She nods, her loose blond curls bouncing.

"But...the gala," I say.

"We did our part on the red carpet, and I've already told Mandy and Sean that I'm done for the night. I'm heading up to our suite, so you're welcome to come with me."

Her expression is pleading, and it makes me want to step into her arms.

Though my heart has bottomed out, her invitation helps me stand a little taller. Even if I've been humiliated in front of everyone at the gala, Cate still wants to spend time with me, and she's the only person who matters.

"Okay," I say.

Her lips curve into what is almost, but not quite, a smile.

The flirty energy we had going earlier is long gone, and it's clear that the night is ending differently than I'd hoped.

As we leave the bathroom and cross the lobby, a round of laughter and applause breaks out beyond the ballroom doors.

We head up the elevator to our suite, not touching, not speaking, and I'm inwardly screaming at Phil fucking Niles.

Chapter 13
The Pros and Cons of Six-Star Hotels

The biggest gift basket I've ever seen is on the coffee table in our suite. Premium alcohol brands and truffles peek through the clear wrapping. Why is it that rich people get all the free stuff?

The suite has multiple rooms, as promised—full kitchen, living room, conference table, massive bathroom, two bedrooms.

A two-person tub is by the far wall, which is entirely a window overlooking a gorgeous California beach. My face burns as I take in the romantic setup around the tub—bubbles, champagne, glasses, mood lighting. They've even provided a basket of rose petals. The ceiling above it twinkles with crystals.

"I can't believe you get to stay in places like this," I say, ogling the suite. "When I was growing up, we stayed in budget hotels."

"Oh, I stayed in budget hotels as a kid too. Then, somewhere along the way, I got lucky and Hollywood wanted me. I mean, I say *lucky,* but there are drawbacks to this life. Things were a lot simpler back in the budget hotel days."

I wait for her to go on, wanting a glimpse into her childhood, but she saunters to the tub and tosses a handful of rose petals into the air like confetti. "Can't complain about swanky accommodations and gift baskets, though. Should we open this?" She examines the champagne.

"I feel like I've had enough champagne for today. Think the minibar has ingredients for Moscow Mules?"

She grins. "Let's find out. I'm in the mood to get drunk."

"You and me both."

Both of us are forcing casual tones. I don't mind it. At some point, maybe it'll stop feeling forced and we can forget about that godawful security incident.

I scan the minibar and menu, debating whether to order food. My stomach is in a knot, but I'm also starving.

"I'll have room service bring up a feast," Cate says, making the decision for me.

While I scan the minibar, she picks up the phone and asks for sushi, spaghetti, grilled cheese and fries, tacos, and brownies.

When she hangs up, I point to the gift basket, "This is more exciting than the bar."

Cate peers through the clear wrapping. "That's a lot of samples. Is that absinthe?"

I wrinkle my nose. "Yes, and it's triggering memories of bad decisions."

"Should we dissect the basket and try everything?"

"Dissections," I say with interest. "You know how to talk dirty to a medical student."

She cocks an eyebrow and makes a sultry face, which was probably meant as a joke, but it makes me bite my lip.

"First, I need to get out of this gown," she says, squirming. "God, I feel like I'm wearing sandpaper." She frees her arms on the way to her bedroom. Apparently, the open back makes it easy to remove.

I avert my gaze, having heart palpitations at the sight of her naked back. I recall her suggestive words from earlier that day—a lifetime ago—telling me I'd need to help her take it off.

Phil fucking Niles.

Cate comes out in an extra-large T-shirt and flannel pants with penguins on them. "Much better."

"I see the oversized shirt you promised," I say. "What about the *no pants* part?"

It was bold, but Cate smiles, and the look she gives me through her lashes would melt ice cream.

Still, the situation with Phil lingers. Beneath Cate's shell, it's clear she's hurting.

I'm not so sure where I'm at either. A few minutes ago, I was ready to hop on a plane and get out of here and pretend tonight never happened.

Cautiously, I say, "Are you okay?"

"Of course," Cate says at once. "I'm always okay."

It's a lie, and she doesn't meet my gaze, but I don't press.

"I'm here if you want to talk about anything."

This makes her meet my eye. Her shoulders drop, like the tension is leaving her body. "Thanks. But it's you I'm worried about, Rachel."

"I'm fine," I say, and with each passing moment spent with her, it's becoming the truth. "I'm here with you, and we have room service and this ridiculous gift basket, and that's all I need."

She offers a small smile. "You sure?"

I nod. Maybe if she thinks I'm over it, we can forget about the gala. Maybe tonight is salvageable.

She inhales deeply and rolls her shoulders. "Events like this are draining, even on the best of days. They look fun and exciting, like a party with the coolest people in the world—and I guess they are—but God, it's a lot of big personalities crammed into one room. Everyone here has made a career out of being outgoing and dramatic, and when you put them together and add cameras and press into the mix, it's like the room turns into a…" She makes a swirling motion with her arms.

"Energy vortex?" I offer.

She nods. "Witches have performed dark magic with the energy contained in a celebrity banquet."

I laugh.

She steps closer. "Anyway, I'm happier being right here tonight."

My heart leaps. "Same."

She opens her arms, and I step in, and she envelops me in a hug I didn't know I needed. It's warm and long, and her hand comes up to brush the back of my neck.

Tears burn in my eyes again because after what we just went through, it's amazing how good a simple hug feels.

As we hold each other tightly, I can feel her heartbeat against my chest. The shape of her body is perfect, melting into me like we fit together. Can we just stay like this for a while?

When we break apart, we avoid each other's gaze and Cate clears her throat.

"I'll get out of this tux, and we can start our dissection," I say shakily, making for my bedroom.

Oh boy. Maybe it would be smarter of me to run far and fast after getting a glimpse of what her ex is capable of, but there was a lot of chemistry in that hug.

In the couple of minutes of privacy while I get changed and Cate washes her face, I grab my phone and text Abby.

Things seem okay between me and Cate. I'll stay the night. Thank you for being so awesome, Abby. xo

Good to hear. Call if you need me. xo

I quickly open a browser and look up Phil Niles. I won't let him affect how I feel about Cate, but I need to know what I'm up against.

A few news stories are at the top of the search results, and Cate's name is in all of them. They all feature paparazzi shots of the two of them shouting at each other or walking away, looking miserable. *Divorce, court case, heartbreak,* and *nightmare* are scattered through the headlines and preview text.

My insides clench. Getting involved with someone who's recently had a messy breakup can be problematic, but this is another level. Not only is it mega-public, but it's with one of the most popular actors in North America. When I scroll down, Phil Niles's impressive filmography and social media accounts smack me in the face, a reminder of how accomplished he is. His headshots are smolderingly handsome—a far cry from the expression on his face earlier.

What made Phil decide to humiliate me after we spoke? Did he realize I wasn't about to step back from Cate and that he needed to take drastic action?

Maybe something about me threatened him, or something about the way Cate was behaving around me. Whatever it was, it made him want to physically remove me from Cate's presence.

It would be satisfying and exciting if he wasn't so scary.

The end of the evening flashes through my mind's eye—the security guards grabbing me, the embarrassment of being hauled away while all those famous people watched in pity, and then them telling me to go back in the ballroom like I hadn't just been violated.

Well, the asshole succeeded. I'm no longer at the party.

Neither is Cate, though. He probably didn't see that coming.

The bathroom door opens, and I click my phone off. I'll read more about Phil later. Right now, I just want to be here with Cate, the woman who ditched a celebrity gala to be with me.

She looks more adorable without makeup and in pajamas than she did all dressed up. My belly swoops at the realization that I'm seeing the real her tonight.

There's a knock on the door, which is thankfully just room service. While a man wheels in our feast, I take my turn laboriously washing off my makeup.

We sit on the plush carpet with our gourmet meals and the gift basket between us. Cate pulls the ribbon on top, letting it unravel so the plastic falls open. The movement is slow and deliberate, like undoing the laces on the back of a gown.

Jesus, Rachel. Keep it together.

But we're on the floor, sitting across from each other over a basket of alcohol, and something thick hovers in the air between us.

Discounting the mood-kill-and-a-half that just happened downstairs, if anyone else was sitting across from me after giving off flirty vibes all night, I would definitely be making a move right now. But this is *Cate Whitney*. Phil had a point when he said I'm too ordinary for her.

She upends the basket and sends bottles, chocolates, gift cards, and snacks tumbling across the carpet.

"Pick your poison," she says. "Literally. I bet half of this tastes like gasoline."

I mean, I could make a tentative move. Her reaction will tell me whether she's changed her mind tonight. It's better than awkwardly asking if she's interested in me and having the rest of the evening be totally weird if she says no.

"Oh, is that maple whisky?" I ask.

The rye bottle has rolled behind her. As I reach for it, I pretend to need her thigh for support and lean close so that our cheeks brush. Her summery perfume is gentle and calming.

She stays still.

When I sit back with the rye in hand, I hold her gaze longer than I otherwise would, grinning playfully. "Must be to make Canadians feel at home. Have you had this before?"

She shakes her head, lips parted, expression unreadable. A flush rises in her cheeks.

Okay, she didn't recoil or get weird about the closeness.

I open the bottle and take a gulp, letting out a satisfied sigh. "Tastes like home. Here."

I pass it to her, and she takes a tentative sip. "Oh, that's not bad! It's like liquified pancakes."

I laugh.

We sift through the items on the ground.

"I have an important point to raise," I say.

Cate cocks an eyebrow.

I pick up a snack pack. "Who came up with this shit? Crispy asiago bites with cilantro baked in? Are you kidding me?" I mime puking.

Cate laughs and takes the package from my hands. "This has to be a joke."

As we talk and laugh our way through everything on the floor, filling our stomachs with food that doesn't exactly go well together but is delicious anyway, pressure releases from my head. Cate's smile returns to the genuine one I haven't seen since we were in the spa hours ago.

We finish our feast, sample everything in the basket, and then move on to the minibar and champagne. The fanciness of the brand is lost on me, both because I have no palate for champagne and because I'm too drunk to taste it.

After a couple of hours, Cate presses the heel of her hand to her forehead. "Oh, gosh. I think I've had too many."

The way she says *gosh* instead of *fuck* or some other swear word is adorable.

Our gazes meet, and hers is as unfocused as I feel. We've definitely drunk way too much, and that international fusion we had for dinner doesn't help settle my stomach.

Her phone beeps on the coffee table and she gets up to check it.

"Just a flight reminder," she says with a sigh. "I guess we should go to bed. We have to be up at six."

I groan at the prospect of flying with a hangover and on very little sleep. I heave to my feet, drunk enough that the floor shifts beneath me.

We linger, the alcohol fumes turning the room into a haze.

"Um, good night," I say.

"Good night," she murmurs.

Am I imagining the intensity in the way she's holding my gaze?

If her thoughts were on getting ready for bed and going to sleep, she would be doing that right now. But she's not. She's looking at me, lips parted, something burning behind her eyes.

Heat licks through me.

If we were standing a foot apart, I could lean in, test the waters, see if she leans in closer in response.

But this damn hotel suite is huge, and there are so many steps between us. I would need to take three strides to get to her, and then what? What if this evening is unsalvageable?

The pause has gone on for too long. She breaks eye contact to look out the window, where lights on sailboats sway on the water, twinkling like fairies.

"Nice view," I say. "Everything about this hotel is so beautiful. Thanks for bringing me here."

"My pleasure," she says, gaze turning back to me.

"Good night," I say again, heart slamming into my ribs.

"Good night," she says, and there's a drop in her voice, like resignation.

I shut my door extra slowly, like I'm hoping she'll run after me.

What the hell is she thinking about right now? Why am I so chicken to ask?

Because she is an A-list celebrity who could have anyone in the entire world. She dated Phil Niles, world's sexiest werewolf. And as he kindly pointed out, I'm nobody. I'm Rachel from Vancouver, and I have a massive student debt and absolutely nothing going for me.

Ordinary. Average.

And with that humbling thought, I let the door click shut and get ready for bed.

When I take off my pants and slip between the cold sheets, I'm wide awake.

My pulse won't stop racing. I cycle between agonizing over Cate's flirting, being furious with myself for not making a move yet grateful I didn't because she should be the one to move first, and then back to analyzing her flirting.

The absurdly bright hotel clock passes two a.m.

I'm officially going to be a wreck on the flight home tomorrow.

Tap tap.

I sit up.

Did I dream that?

The noise comes again. *Tap tap tap.*

"Hello?" I say.

"Rachel?" Cate says softly from the other side of my door.

My pulse races all over again. I leap out of bed and run to my door as if I'm hearing a fire alarm.

I open it, and she's standing there in her T-shirt, legs bare, face dimly lit by the ambient lighting beyond the curtained windows.

"Is everything okay?" I say, lips numb.

"Yes," she says, breath tickling my face. "I—I couldn't sleep." Her breath catches as she locks my gaze.

She is absolute perfection. Her skin is smooth in the dim light, her eyelids heavy, her gaze smoldering beneath thick lashes. Her full lips are parted.

My body moves before my brain makes a conscious decision. In a blink, her body is against mine and she's kissing me back, our lips moving desperately against each other.

I wrap my fingers in her soft hair, pulling her closer, pressing my hips into hers. A moan escapes me as her lips move against mine. She bites and sucks my lip, teases me with her tongue, pulls my hips closer with confident hands.

"Cate," I whisper into her mouth, gasping, "I wasn't sure if you were into women."

She pushes me backward so that we stumble into my room. We're frantic, devouring each other, and every thread of tension that was taut between us snaps.

Her hands slide beneath my shirt, and the sensation of her palms against my bare waist sends a tremor through me.

"I've suspected it," she murmurs. "Just never acted on it. Never met the right woman to act on it, maybe."

The memory of being in the lake with Julia thrusts forward in my mind—drunk, curious, her first time with a woman. That rejection carved a hole in my chest that has yet to heal, and I don't want to put myself in that situation again. Should I stop this?

Then the back of my legs hit the bed and we fall onto it, Cate on top of me, and my doubts melt into a blissful haze. We shimmy up and I wrap my legs around her, agonizingly aware that neither of us is wearing pants.

Her skin is so soft against my inner thighs. I'm already wet.

"What changed?" I ask between kisses.

She pins my hands by my head and kisses my neck, taking her time to answer. "I think, sometimes, the universe brings you the right person at the right time. You were...exactly who I needed. You're smart, interesting, fun, sexy..."

I moan, the feel of her lips all over me making my head spin even more. "Wasn't—*fuck*—wasn't I on the ground covered in mustard and cobwebs when we first met?"

She lets out a breathy laugh that tickles my neck. "And after that, you were thoughtful and kind. You were an emotional connection I didn't know I was craving. I felt like you genuinely cared about me and wanted to help me. You were interested in what I had to say, not just going through the motions."

"Well, yeah," I say, confused. "Isn't that, like, a basic life skill?"

She smiles, and it makes her all the more beautiful as she claims my mouth again.

We rock against each other, grinding, all hitched breaths and soft moans. Her weight on me, hands pinning me to the mattress, is more intoxicating than the alcohol.

Victory erupts inside me. This is what I deserve—a woman who knows what she wants and is confident about her attraction to me. She *was* flirting. She knew what she wanted and she went after it, and God, that's hot. That self-assurance is how she got where she is—and it's why I'm so hopelessly attracted to her. She's done with the floundering, uncertain phase of life that everyone my age seems to be struggling through.

I flip us over and pin her, pausing to take in the sight of her spread beneath me, her blond hair fanned out, her cheeks flushed.

I run my hands down her front, the thin material of her T-shirt between us. I trace my palms over her breasts, down her stomach, and to her underwear. I slide a hand between her legs, where her heat radiates through the material and to my hand.

She gasps, rocking her hips into me. "I want you, Rachel."

I close my eyes, unbearably turned on. I'm dizzy, aching for her.

Everything that happened earlier tonight doesn't matter—my panic on the red carpet, Phil telling me I'm not good enough and then embarrassing me in front of everyone. Despite all of that, Cate is into me, and this moment with her makes everything else worth it. I would go through all of it again if I knew what waited for me on the other side.

I lean down to tease her lips with my tongue—and her expression changes abruptly. Her smile turns to open-mouthed surprise. Her eyes widen.

"Shit," she says.

I slide off her quickly, heart plummeting. Did I do something wrong?

"I'm going to—" She flies off the bed and into the bathroom, clapping a hand over her mouth.

I groan and go to hold her hair back, libido leaving me instantly at the distinct sound of vomit hitting a toilet bowl.

Chapter 14
Nothing to Hide

"Abby, remember when I got out of the apartment for a few hours while you had your interview?"

"Yes…" she says, eyeing me suspiciously. She's at the table, working on the web interface for Triple-X POV, and from a few strides away, I can see a header image of a woman really enjoying herself from the perspective of a man with a massive dick.

Interesting how well wish fulfillment sells. I wonder if technology will get to a place where people can put 3D renderings of their own bodies into the point-of-view video.

"Um, do you think you can stay out of the apartment for a few hours tonight?" I ask, my face burning as the words come out.

Abby gapes at me. I picture the gears grinding in her head, and then… *Click.*

"Holy fucknuts!" she screams, so loud that I'm pretty sure they'll have to reshoot the scene they're filming in the street below.

I cover my smoldering face. "Don't—"

"Are you fucking Cate Whitney?" Abby says, running over and forcing my hands down.

"That's the plan," I say weakly.

Abby backs up a step. "Oh my God. I—I need to lie down."

And she does, right in the middle of the living room, palms up, like she's in Savasana.

"I can't believe you're going to get naked with Cate Whitney," she says to the ceiling. "So she's really into you, then?"

"Apparently." The question, though innocent, stings—because the more I consider it, the more I'm not sure *why* she's into me. Is this all an experiment? Am I her "just for fun" while she's in Vancouver?

My heart does a double-skip. I guess I'll find out.

It's been a week since we had our rough, hungover flight home from LA. We've texted throughout the week to make plans for tonight, and based on the number of winking emojis Cate used, I'm pretty sure I know what's going to happen later.

It takes Abby twenty minutes to get off the floor. "I guess I can go out to a bar and get some dick tonight," she says with a glance to the header image on her screen. "For your sake."

I spend the afternoon giving the apartment a better clean than ever. I stack my textbooks on a shelf, water the plants, throw away the bits of plastic and twist ties that Abby tends to leave lying around the kitchen, and attempt to rearrange our travel souvenirs and photos of friends and family. We have so much stuff that there is no possible way to make our apartment look organized, but after dusting every surface and mopping the floor, it doesn't look half bad. Finally, I refill the diffuser on the kitchen island with essential oil.

With the apartment finally clean and smelling nice, I get ready in my sexiest backless shirt and smoky-eye makeup.

"Have fun tonight," Abby says in a saucy tone, emerging from her bedroom. She's in full makeup and a tiny white dress that flatters her curves and warm brown skin.

I whistle. "You too."

Alone in our apartment, I take a deep breath.

Cate told me she won't be able to get here until nine, so I probably have a couple of hours. I could use it to catch up on thesis research, or…

I grab my laptop and move to the couch, where I look up Phil Niles. I've been brushing off this urge all week, but I want to know what's going on with him. I want headlines to reassure me that he was spotted with another woman or that he's moving to Australia for several years to film a TV series or that he's had an epiphany and has gone to live in a monastery, or all of the above.

I scan the headlines at the top of his search results and stop on one that takes the breath out of my lungs.

"I'll never stop loving her"— Phil Niles opens up about Cate Whitney heartbreak

Torn between closing my laptop and plowing onward, I clench my jaw. I have to know. If he's going to be hostile, I can tell Cate that Phil is freaking me out, and she can...what? What do I expect from her? She already said she's getting her lawyer involved.

If I'm honest, I hope Cate can use her infinite power and money to make him go away.

But he also has infinite power and money, which is probably why the divorce is so nasty.

Grimacing, I click the article.

I scan quickly and start reading halfway down, like if I spend too long on this page, it'll detonate.

> *It's been months since the world watched the perfect couple split up. Now, Phil opens up and admits his mistakes, making our hearts ache for him as he shares his feelings about the woman he calls his soulmate.*
>
> *"I messed up," he tells us. "The same traits that make me a star leading man also make me a little selfish and stubborn. What can I say? I'm an alpha. That ended up pushing her away."*

Oh, God. Excuse me while I puke.

> *Fans have been keen to pick sides. In the wake of the couple's messy divorce, those on Team Phil feel that Cate is behaving unfairly.*
>
> *"I don't want anyone to say my Kitty should take me back," he says, wagging a finger. "She can make that decision when she's ready. I'll be right here—a prince waiting for the return of his strong, feisty princess."*
>
> *When asked if he hopes to win her back, those famously expressive brown eyes fill with tears. "I can't imagine life without her."*

I curse and close my laptop, chest tight.

Okay, that was not what I wanted to read.

If I have any sense of self-preservation, I'll bail out of this before Phil makes me the internet's current Most Hated Person. He already showed me what he's capable of. He can do that again, or worse.

But do I really want to let Phil get to me? No. What I want is to ignore his existence—and the existence of paparazzi.

I don't know if it's even possible to ignore such a prominent force in a celebrity's life, but I don't really have a choice. I have to fight this if I want to be with Cate.

My phone beeps. Speak of the devil.

Wrapping up soon. Sorry for the wait. We had to shoot a scene with a raven and he was being a little prick. See you in an hour :)

I let out a breath of laughter.

At the promise of having her alone in my apartment, my dread dissipates. Who cares about Phil Niles when I'm the one Cate wants to spend the night with? He's not here. He doesn't have to take up space in my head.

I might just have to spend forever avoiding celebrity events.

An hour later, when I let Cate in, my insides do a little dance. She's wearing a stunning buttercup-yellow suit that brightens the whole apartment. The blazer is open to reveal a white blouse. Her hair is still styled from the shoot, framing her delicate features and sharp cheekbones.

And I'm in ordinary clothes and makeup.

As Cate takes in my apartment, I've never been more self-conscious. What does my cheap furniture look like to someone who makes millions of dollars? Why is she even here?

This was a mistake. Phil Niles hit such a painful nerve when he called me average.

"What's wrong?" Cate says, stepping closer.

"Nothing," I say, forcing a smile.

She runs her fingers through my hair, sending a pleasant tingle down my back, and waits.

I consider insisting that nothing is wrong, but I won't accomplish anything by lying. "I don't know why you're interested in me. I'm so… normal. Average."

"Rachel." She guides my chin so she can lock gazes with me. "You are not average."

How is she so impossibly beautiful? Everything about Cate is ethereal, from the carbon that made her to the aura of confidence she takes wherever she goes.

"I sort of am," I say, not because I'm fishing for a compliment but because it's true.

"You're the most captivating, exciting, intoxicating thing in my life, Rachel." She kisses me, her lips soft and full, moving with a nimble expertise that makes me lose my balance.

If the heat of her kiss is any indication, I might be able to believe her. As fireworks go off in my midsection, I slide my hand beneath her yellow blazer, tracing my fingers over her back.

She sucks in a breath and pulls me closer. Her eyes have a blazing, hungry look.

"Nobody as smart as you should ever call herself *average*," Cate murmurs into my lips. "Nobody as sweet, as funny, as bold, as beautiful, as good a kisser…"

Her hand wanders low and she cups between my legs.

I gasp. "Okay. I believe you. Now, come here."

We kiss hard, our tongues exploring each other's mouths, biting and sucking. I make a small, involuntary moan, and she responds with a hiss, nails digging into me.

I press my body into her, grinding our hips together.

"Fuck," she whispers, wrapping a fist in my hair and pulling me in, devouring me.

I gasp, remembering to breathe, to be fully conscious of this moment, because it has to be a dream. I'm going to wake up soon and this will all fade, leaving me wet and panting, alone under my covers.

We stumble into the darkness of my bedroom and fall onto my bed. I roll on top of her, straddling her hips and grinding. I pin her hands by her head, locking our fingers, kissing and nipping her jawline and neck.

My shorts are tight, leaving me unsatisfied as I grind her. I can't get close enough.

"Cate," I whisper, panting, desperate to fuck her.

She moans, circling her hips with me, and it takes effort to string my thoughts together.

"One more thing." I need to get this out before we keep going. I can accept that she finds me interesting, by some stroke of luck, but I want to know more about what has been going through her mind since we met and what she expects from me.

Because last time I opened my heart to someone, the relationship came with terms.

"Hm?" She takes my hands and guides them beneath her shirt. I graze my palms over her stomach, up toward her breasts, and stop when her tight, white blouse prevents me from going further.

Struggling with the power of speech, I say, "I want to clarify where you're at with, um, how private to keep this. Because I've been at both ends of that spectrum. The ex I told you about, Sarah, was firm about keeping our relationship a secret. When we were out, we never touched and barely looked at each other affectionately. But with you…things have been different."

Cate is still holding my hands beneath her blouse, chest rising and falling. She says nothing, listening.

"With you," I say, "you touch me, look at me, hold me close in public." At a *celebrity gala*. "Like you want everyone to know."

"Yes," she says.

"Yes what?"

"If it's okay with you, then I do want people to know." She relaxes her hold on my hands, eyes softening. "When I was with Phil, all I did was hide the truth. I hid how unhappy I was, how he treated me, how I felt. I pretended we had a happy marriage for years. So when I met you…I decided I didn't want to hide and pretend anymore. I wanted to show you—and the world—how I feel. And it's going to be on my terms, not the work of paparazzi and gossip."

I nod, a flutter in my chest. I was always fine with keeping my relationship with Sarah a secret because she was afraid of how her ultraconservative parents would react. Her reason was valid, and her safety and happiness were important, so I was okay with hiding the truth until she was ready.

Of course, all of that blew up when Lauren posted that video of us online. That breakup never stopped stinging. I always felt like I failed Sarah by kissing her when other people were around. I could never apologize because I never saw her again.

Hiding our relationship was never easy, and maybe it was always doomed to blow open—so the relief of not having to hide my feelings for Cate washes over me like a warm bath, relaxing, freeing. If she's going to be transparent about her feelings, then so will I.

"I want people to know too." I bend and kiss her, slow and deep. I cup her face, then wander lower and tug the top button of her blouse. "Can I?"

"Do whatever you want with me, Rachel," she whispers. Her cheeks are rosy, her lips full from our kissing, her eyelids heavy.

I bite my lip, her hungry expression making me ache.

Slowly, I unbutton her blouse and let it fall open, revealing a beige bra and perfect breasts. I've seen her in a bra before in movies, but this is so different. This is so much better.

She sits up, and we kiss while I slide the blouse and blazer off her shoulders and remove her bra.

I pause, awestruck, and then she grabs my shirt and pulls it upward. I oblige, lifting my arms to let it come over my head.

I didn't wear a bra because the shirt wouldn't allow for it, so now we're both half-naked.

Holy crap.

She rolls us over, kissing me hard. Our breasts graze and her nipples trace over my stomach and chest, and oh, *God,* I think I'm going to come already.

I take her face in my hands, holding her so I can drink her in. "Cate, you are the most beautiful woman in the whole world. I—well, you know that already."

Complimenting her falls short because everyone tells her how incredible she is every day.

But she says, "Words from a magazine don't mean as much as words from the person you're getting naked with."

Maybe she has a point.

She slides lower, kissing my stomach, and I'm so wet, I'm afraid of the state of my underwear.

She unbuttons my shorts, and I gasp for breath as she pulls them and my underwear down to my ankles and tosses them to the floor. I reach up and help her take off her pants, and then we're both totally naked.

"Gorgeous," she whispers, running her soft hands up my thighs.

"Oh, fuck," I say, the words coming out as a squeak. "Cate, I want to taste you so bad—"

"Me first," she says, stopping me from sitting up.

Her head dips lower, her soft hair brushing my stomach, and I'm going to explode in about two seconds if I don't put a lid on this.

She presses her lips to my stomach, hips, and thighs.

Her warm breath passes over my swollen clit and I gasp.

She pushes my legs wider. Then she licks me, her tongue cool and gentle.

I let out a noise between a gasp and a scream, grabbing the pillow for support. Oh, *fuck,* this is going to be good.

"You taste sweet," she murmurs.

Her tongue makes slow circles, driving me wild. My lips tingle and my face heats up.

She moves faster, flicking my clit with her tongue. God, her tongue is fast. *Holy shit.* I'm at her mercy, and she licks me until I can't take it. I writhe, my legs bending, hands gripping the bed and pillows.

Her hands slide under my thighs and she pushes my legs up, getting a deeper angle. Her lips and tongue are agonizingly gentle.

A burning sensation starts in my core and grows hotter.

She quickens her tempo, sending a tremor through me, and I whimper. "Cate, I'm going to—I'm going to—"

"Mmhmm," she says, keeping her mouth on me, and the sound of her between my legs tips me over the edge.

I succumb to her, calling out, and waves of pleasure overtake me.

My hips buck and she locks her mouth onto me, not letting go, riding me until the waves stop and I dissolve into the bed.

She lingers another moment before leaving me panting, dizzy, totally limp.

"So you—you've never been with a woman before?" I ask weakly.

She crawls up to lay beside me.

"This is a first," she says, entwining a leg in mine. "Was it okay?"

I let out a breathy laugh. "It was mind-blowing."

She looks relieved. "Good. I was afraid of being disappointing, to be honest. Pretending to have sex with a woman in a movie is a far cry from having actual sex with a woman."

"Cate Whitney, it is literally impossible for you to disappoint me." I cast her a mischievous smile. "Also, those scenes you're talking about were critical to my coming out."

"Really?" she asks.

I avert my gaze to the ceiling, willing myself not to blush so hard. "I started to realize I was into girls in junior high, but it wasn't until I saw you kiss a woman that I admitted it to myself. I realized that was what I wanted—the happiness you showed in that role."

She holds my gaze, lips parted, like she can't believe the words I'm saying. "I had no idea that could be so impactful."

"It was. I know I'm not the only one. If you look online, you'll see a lot more queer people with the same experience. So, um, thanks for representing. Even if you didn't know you were into women at the time."

Cate smiles. "I'm glad to have played a part in helping teenage Rachel discover herself."

I kiss her, rolling us over so I'm on top of her. "Now, lie back and relax. I've been waiting to do this for a long time."

Chapter 15
Walking in a Breeze

I GRAZE MY LIPS OVER Cate's clavicle and down her chest, ready to give her as good an orgasm as she gave me.

"Can I ask you something?" Cate murmurs.

My heart skips. I love that question. Nine times out of ten, it means the conversation is about to get personal—and with Cate, I want that more than anything. I want her to know that she's safe to be open with me.

"Of course."

"What does your tattoo say?" She runs a soft palm over my ribs, where the black letters are written in cursive.

My lips pull into a little grin as I move lower to kiss her stomach. I should have seen that question coming. "*Uitwaaien*. It's Dutch. There's no English equivalent, but it basically means going for a refreshing walk outside. Like, walking in a breeze to clear your head. My parents do it; my grandparents do it. It's sort of a family tradition. It makes me think of them."

She's quiet for a moment. "Is that why you live near the ocean?"

I pause, lifting my head to meet her gaze. "Yes."

She runs her fingers through my hair. "That's beautiful."

Her hand moves softly over my ribs, and she's wearing an expression I've never seen on her before—not in any of the close-up shots in all of her movies. It's calm, unguarded, fully present.

Maybe one day I'll understand why this perfect woman is interested in me.

"Now, can I go down on you?" I ask. "You're being a tease and it's killing me."

Her mouth twists into what might be a smile, but there's something serious underneath.

"What is it?" I murmur. "We don't have to, if you're uncomfortable."

"No, it's not that," she says. "Actually, it's the opposite. I am comfortable with you. It's hard to protect my privacy, and it's hard to trust people. But I'm okay being with you—being vulnerable. Naked. Does that make sense?"

"It does." As elated as I am to hear these words, my heart aches that she has to be careful about something as pure as having sex with someone she cares about.

There's a familiar expanding feeling in my chest, like I'm catching serious feelings.

Not now. Cate is an out-of-my-league actor who's visiting Vancouver temporarily. Whatever happens between us can't last. She's probably only after a short fling anyway.

"Just so you know," she says with a tremor in her voice, like she's nervous, "I might not come. I get a bit of, um, performance anxiety."

"You? Performance anxiety?" I ask with surprise.

She shrugs and casts a guilty smile.

My heart swells for her. It's hard to cope with how stunning she is in the ambient lighting from the living room, her eyes glinting, her cheekbones sharp, an adorable curve on her lips. This confession makes her more real, more human, with insecurities like anyone else.

"Then I want you to enjoy the process," I say, making sure she's lying comfortably on my pillows. "Relax. Close your eyes. Know that I'm going to fully, completely enjoy being between your legs."

She closes her eyes, letting out a slow breath. When I run my hands over her body, I can feel her heart pounding hard.

I start at her lips and kiss her, working my way down her neck and to her breasts, where I pause to flick each nipple with my tongue. I circle and suck and she gasps.

I kiss her stomach and work lower, down to her thighs. She tastes as lovely as that summery perfume let on. I kiss her inner thighs and lick her soft skin. Goosebumps ripple up her legs.

"God, Rachel," she moans.

I push her legs wider, and a tremor runs through her.

Gently, slowly, I lick, circling her clit with my tongue.

The gasp she makes is the sweetest sound I've ever heard. It's a noise of absolute pleasure, a door opening for me alone.

I work my tongue through her, savoring how wet she is for me.

She wraps a hand in my hair. "Oh, God, that's good."

"Do you want me inside you?" I say, teasing her with my finger.

"Yes," she says, gasping.

Heat surges through my middle. I push two fingers into her and she moans, tightening her grip on my hair.

I slide my fingers in and out and suck her clit. With the other hand, I reach up and circle her nipple. I suck, work my tongue, and glide my fingers in and out of her all at once, putting everything I have into giving her the best orgasm of her life.

"Fuck," she says in a high voice, like she's struggling not to scream. "Rachel, oh my g—" She gasps when I push my fingers deeper.

I run them over her walls until she shudders, tilting her head back.

"Oh, you're amazing," she says, eyes closed, arching her back. "Rachel— how are you doing that?"

Satisfaction ripples through me.

"Yes, yes," she whispers, both hands in my hair.

I lick and suck, sliding my fingers in and out, moving faster. With the other hand, I brush my palm over her inner thigh, around her ass, up her stomach, to her breasts. I trace a finger around her nipple, teasing it.

I hook my fingers inside her, and I must have hit her G-spot because she screams, arching her back.

"Rachel!"

I tongue her clit and move my fingers faster, harder. With the other hand, I stop teasing her nipple to push her thigh up, opening her wider.

I change the pressure and tempo a few times, take little pauses that make her whimper, and play with different angles to see what makes her react. I'm lost in the taste and feel of her, enjoying every second.

Then Cate's thighs tremble and goosebumps travel up her legs. I glance up to see her eyes closed, her breath speeding up.

"Yes," she whispers. "Rachel—I'm going to—"

A spark of victory ignites in my middle. Despite her confession, of course I wanted to give her the pleasure of climaxing, and I secretly hoped I could. Maybe no partner has told her before that she's allowed to relax. Maybe it helped to know that I'm happy to spend as long as it takes down here.

She lets go, screaming as her orgasm ripples through her body. I wrap my arms around her thighs, keeping my mouth on her until it subsides.

She goes limp, panting. "Oh—my—God."

"I gotta admit, I'm feeling a little smug for making you come," I say.

She lets out a shaky laugh. "Rachel, that was the best orgasm I've ever had."

I stare at her. "Are you serious?"

She nods, flushed.

I can't stop my lips from pulling into a grin.

"Smug," she says, tugging my earlobe.

I laugh, snatching her fingers to kiss them.

We cuddle for a long time, wrapped in each other's arms, our foreheads resting together. Our breaths slow while the world darkens beyond my curtains.

I guess I'll have to let Abby come home soon.

Just a little longer.

"When did you know you were interested in me?" I say, sleepiness slurring my words. "Like, when you asked me to meet you on set, was it really because you wanted to talk about science?"

She stretches and makes a soft moan, like she was drifting off. "I wasn't lying when I said I needed to study for the role, and you helped me tremendously—but it was an excuse. Especially when I asked you for drinks afterward. I felt something between us, and I wanted to know you better. Is that weird?"

"No," I say, her words bringing a smile to my lips. "I mean, I never snuck into the craft services tent to try and get a job as a science consultant. I snuck in to try and meet you."

She bursts into laughter. "I suspected as much."

When we stop laughing, she runs her fingers through my hair and kisses me. The kiss is so tender that my heart swells.

"Can you see the set from here?" she asks with a glance toward the window.

"Yep."

She gets up and goes to my curtains.

"Don't!" I say quickly, pulling the blankets up to my chin.

She turns, mouth open in surprise.

My face burns. "Um, I like to keep them closed."

"Privacy?"

I nod. "The building across the street might be able to see in. Can't say for sure there isn't a creep with a camera over there."

"That's okay. I was just curious about what the set looks like from up here. It's probably too dark anyway."

I sit up and let out a breath, embarrassed for being so weird. "Sorry. I mean, I don't think anyone can see into my bedroom, but I can't say for sure, so I never open them because... Well, I know I'm being paranoid. Abby keeps hers open all the time and stands in her window naked. We're like two ends of a spectrum when it comes to privacy and..."

She comes back to bed and kisses my forehead, stopping my rambling. "I get it. You don't need to explain yourself. I'll look at the set from the living room when we're both clothed."

I try to smile but can't manage it. I wish I wasn't like this.

"Do you want to come on set again this week?" Cate asks, tracing a finger along my bottom lip.

I sit taller. "Hell yes, I would."

She rests a hand on my cheek and kisses me, our noses brushing. "And by come on set, I mean literally come on set. We can slip away between takes."

I let out a moan of longing.

So this wasn't a one-time thing?

My heart skips. I might still be a "just for fun" fling, and she might soon realize she lives on a whole other plane than me—but her invitation opens a door to something new and thrilling. It's something that could last, at least as long as it takes to film this movie.

And so far, I'm up for it.

CHAPTER 16
QUIET ON SET

WHEN I ARRIVE ON SET mid-afternoon and Cate comes to greet me, we step in for an awkward hug. Despite our promises that we're comfortable going public, neither of us is sure how friendly to act with her colleagues watching.

And they are watching. As she leads me across the set, gazes from the cast and crew linger. They must be curious about why I, a random local girl, am visiting Cate on set for the second time. Or else they heard about the gala.

"The smoke machine isn't working, so we're stalled," Cate says with a sigh. "I was hoping to break for lunch so I could spend a bit of time with you."

I catch the meaning beneath her words and bite my lip.

It's drizzling out, so we step under a tent for cover. Sean hands Cate the script and both of us green smoothies.

"Thanks!" I say, delighted by this VIP treatment.

"I'm glad you're here, Rachel," Cate says in an undertone, looking blankly at the script. "Everyone is driving me nuts. As much as I love the people I work with, these long days get to be a lot."

"Don't get me started," Sean says, typing on his phone. "I swear Veronica thinks I'm community property. But hey, no set will ever be as bad as New Zealand."

Cate laughs bitterly. "There's always that."

"What happened in New Zealand?" I ask.

Through the crowd, there's an outburst of swearing and a mechanical groan.

"So many things," Cate says. "Filming was rushed and chaotic. We had a lot of days where we couldn't break for lunch, which meant everyone was hangry on top of all of the other stress."

"Everyone hated each other so much that the crew went on strike," Sean says. "Plus, one of the actors set his trailer on fire, and there was some...other tension..."

His gaze shifts to Cate and back to his phone.

What was that about?

"And yet, all of that unhappiness wasn't the worst thing to come out of filming *The Woven Throne*," Cate says flatly.

The Woven Throne? Wasn't that the first movie she and Phil Niles costarred in? My stomach twists with the realization that they're talking about the set that she and Phil met on.

"But it was where you met me," Sean says with a winning smile.

"And for that, I'm grateful."

"I hope getting to visit New Zealand made it worthwhile," I say. "It looks beautiful."

"It is. We—I—stayed after shooting was done to travel around for three weeks."

She shifts, dropping her gaze. "We" clearly meant her and Phil. This must have been one of those adventurous trips they went on together.

Even when he's not here, he looms over me, a reminder that Cate's ex is infinitely wealthier and more successful than I am.

Sean's phone rings and he steps away to answer.

"You must have traveled to a lot of cool places," I say to Cate.

"A few." Her brow furrows like she's trying to decipher my meaning.

"Did you travel around New Zealand with Phil?" I ask hesitantly.

Cate sighs, fidgeting with her corset. "Yes. We started dating while filming that movie. I'm not proud of it, and I regret everything about it now. His ex was in the cast, fully aware of what was going on between us, and it made for some rough weeks during filming. Not to mention that it was the beginning of an awful seven years."

Her tone is clipped, like she is also regretting this conversation.

Heat rushes into my cheeks. "Sorry."

Ugh, why did I have to ask questions about him? I sound like a creep obsessing over someone's ex.

Except isn't he the one being the creep?

I don't know what I'm supposed to do here. I want to know what I'm up against with Phil, but I don't want to dwell on that asshole.

"It's okay," Cate says with a little smile.

A guy my age runs over to tell us the smoke machine is fixed.

"Great," Cate says, handing her half-drunk smoothie to Sean. She touches my waist as she leaves the tent. "See you soon."

Learning about Cate's work gives me a new appreciation for how hard actors have it. Between the long days, skipped meals, and being at the mercy of so many outside factors, Cate must really love her job.

"How long does she spend in hair and makeup in the morning?" I ask Sean.

"About an hour. Another half-hour for wardrobe. They're total pros and she doesn't need prosthetics, so it's not so bad. She's on set and in rehearsal by eight."

"Eight? What time does she get up?"

"Five-thirty," he says like this isn't a completely ungodly hour.

Doing the math on all the hours she has to spend working, it's a wonder she's had time to see me at all—and that she can function when we do see each other.

As Cate shoots her scene, I attract more stares. Crew members whisper and glance my way, and while Cate is getting her makeup touched up, the two lab assistants in the scene with her lean close. They stop talking when they notice me watching.

Are they speculating about what kind of relationship Cate and I have? Did rumors spread after the gala?

One of the lab assistants looks over her shoulder at Cate, and they both angle away from me to keep whispering. I recognize that gossipy look on their faces, and it brings forward unwelcome memories of high school.

"Cool cool cool," I say under my breath, trying to ease the tightness in my chest. Just what I wanted—to be the subject of gossip.

Finally, the director shouts, "Print, moving on!" and everyone shuffles around.

When the director's attention turns to a burly, bearded man with a massive raven on his arm, Cate rushes over.

"I'm sorry this is taking so long."

"Don't be! I love watching you do your thing."

"You're too kind. But I was getting impatient for a couple of reasons."

Sean appears out of nowhere and hands Cate water and the script.

"Protein," he says, offering her a granola bar.

"In a bit," Cate says. "Thanks."

Sean looks affronted, like she's never denied his snack offering before.

"Is that the raven you mentioned?" I say, pointing. The bird looks around with a mischievous expression in his beady eyes, like he's debating what to steal.

"Little prick," Cate says. "He told me to fuck off yesterday. The trainer was embarrassed, but I couldn't stop laughing."

I look at her sharply. "The raven told you to fuck off?"

"They mimic human sounds. Smart animals. I guess the swearing comes from spending so much time on film sets."

I laugh.

The raven flies from the trainer's hand on cue and goes to land on a sign that says *Freta St.* After a pause, he flies back, and the trainer feeds him a treat.

"He's fantastic when we get something out of him," Cate says, "but that only happens when he's in the right mood. They'll be a while getting this shot. Want to come with me to my trailer?"

She says it casually, but a glint in her eyes tells me her intent—and my heart leaps.

She passes the water and script back to Sean, who either didn't catch the meaning of her words or is pretending to be oblivious.

"Anything in particular you want to do in your trailer?" I murmur as we cross the set.

"I could use you to warm up my tongue for the next scene."

She opens the door, motioning for me to go in ahead of her.

While my pulse speeds up, Cate closes and locks the door, then checks all the blinds.

She's over to me in two steps and we kiss, wrapping our arms around each other, teasing each other with our tongues.

"Hang on and let me look at you properly," I say, holding her at arm's length.

I take in the steampunk outfit with the help of my hands. The top hat and goggles rest tilted on her loose, blond curls, which are silky between my fingers. Her bare shoulders and arms are smooth, the brown corset softer than it looks as it hugs the curve of her waist.

Her breath quickens as I run my palms further down, savoring her bare thighs between the short, black skirt and fishnets.

"How long do we have?" I say, my voice coming out husky.

She takes my hand and brings it up to the apex between her legs. She's warm and soft. "Long enough, I think."

I press my hips against hers and kiss her, our mouths moving tenderly against each other.

"This outfit really works on you," I murmur, gripping her waist.

"It doesn't fit great, to be honest."

"Oh? Let me test this." I tug the corset, and to my satisfaction, it slides down enough to expose her nipples.

She lets out a noise between a gasp and a laugh.

"Hm, I see what you mean," I say, giving it one more tug so her breasts come free.

I lean down and flick my tongue over each of her nipples, making her moan. Her chest heaves as her fingers wrap in my hair.

"Rachel…" She reaches for my waistband, but I stop her.

"Can I eat you out?" I whisper into her skin, kissing her softly.

"Okay," she says, the word a gasp.

Heat burns through my middle. I must have been a saint in a past life if today I get to go down on Cate Whitney while she's dressed like this.

The skirt is so short in front that there's not a lot to navigate. I tug her underwear down and push her so she's sitting on the white couch. I spread her legs apart, kneeling on the floor.

Holding her blazing-hot gaze, I slide her underwear all the way off and toss it aside. I push the skirt higher, kissing her inner thighs above the garters of her fishnets.

She moans, bracing her gloved hands on the couch.

I spread her apart with my hands and lick her with the tip of my tongue, working up and down on either side of her clit.

"Oh, God," she says, her voice high. Her legs are trembling.

I suppress a grin and work my tongue faster, then close my mouth over her and suck, enjoying her sweet taste. I reach up and swirl my fingers around her nipples, pulling and teasing.

Fucking a woman in a sexy steampunk outfit is something I never knew I needed. God, this is hot.

She's breathing fast, thighs tense, and when I slide two fingers into her, she wraps a gloved hand into my hair.

"Was—that okay—standing around for so long?" she asks between gasps.

I pause for long enough to say, "I love watching you work."

"Good. Sometimes film people can be…blunt."

"Everyone was nice," I say, discounting the gossip that was going on around me.

I shimmy closer, working my tongue while sliding my fingers in and out, and she moans.

"Maybe—I can watch you work one day," she says, her grip tightening in my hair.

I let out a note of laughter. "That's sweet, but at this point in my career, you'd be watching me stare at a laptop for hours."

I run my other hand up and down her fishnets, over her leather boots, up to that tantalizing skirt, and over the corset. I pull my fingers out to grip her waist, holding her in place while I close my mouth over her and flick her clit with my tongue.

She lets out a loud gasp and angles her hips into me. "Yes…"

The way she's losing control, head tilted back, she must be close to finishing.

There's a knock at the door. "Cate? The raven behaved. You're up in five," Sean shouts.

She claps a gloved hand over her mouth. I pause.

"O-okay," she calls back, stammering. "I'll be out in just a minute."

She gives me a blazing look that says, *Keep going.*

I work my tongue and grip her waist, savoring the sight of her losing control as she rocks on the couch. Her face is flushed, her nipples erect over the top of that excruciatingly sexy corset.

"Rachel," she whispers, gasping, hips bucking. "Yes. Yes."

I move my grip to her thighs and lock my mouth onto her, holding her to me.

She suppresses a scream as her orgasm shudders through her body.

Her hands grasp either side of my face, like she's not sure whether to pull me closer or push me back. I keep licking until she falls back, panting.

"God, you're good." She moans. "I wish I had time to return the favor."

"Next time," I say, grinning uncontrollably. That was easily the hottest sex of my life.

Cate rushes into the trailer's tiny bathroom, a little uncoordinated. "Sean totally knows what we were doing."

Unable to wipe the grin from my face, I wait for her to finish cleaning up, then help her fix her corset so she can get back outside.

She's panting, her cheeks flushed, and I run my fingers through her softly curled hair to set it back to what it was. The hat miraculously stayed in place. Good costume design.

"I was wondering," she says, stealing a glance at my face before returning her attention to her twisted skirt, "if I could take you to dinner. I'll be busy filming all week, but are you free on the weekend?"

A real date with Cate Whitney? Like, she wants to do more than just bang?

My heart lifts. "You want to date me? This isn't just…um…"

She tilts her head, smiling. "Yes. I want to buy you dinner and share a bottle of wine and stumble back to your place afterward to do this again."

I throw my arms around her and plant a firm kiss onto her lips. "I would love to go on a date with you."

We finish fixing her costume and head back outside, both of us flushed and giddy.

The crew is setting the scene and fussing over Cate's stunt double, who looks alarmingly like her from behind and not at all like her from the front.

"Sorry, I had to get started on the others while we waited, Cate," a woman with a makeup brush says, dabbing powder onto one of the lab assistants. "I'll be just a minute."

"No rush," Cate says.

We catch each other's eye. She's blushing, and it's obvious what we were doing.

"A real date," I whisper, still absorbing this new reality. "My God. Pinch me."

Cate pulls me back a few steps, out of everyone's earshot.

"Remember how I told you I've always suspected I was into women?" she murmurs.

"Despite being ridiculously drunk when you told me? Yes, I remember it vividly."

"Well, my first crush on a girl was in eighth grade, though I didn't know it was a crush at the time."

I face her, grinning widely. "Oh? Do tell."

Her lips curve upward. "In drama, I overheard a classmate, Sandra, telling someone that she was bi. I became so curious about her, and painfully awkward. I would catch her eye a lot, think about her, want to talk to her but be too shy to say a word… I remember fantasizing that she would kiss me."

"And you didn't realize you might be into girls?" I ask teasingly.

"I told myself I just thought she was cool. I guess I was repressing how I really felt. Anyway, we ended up being partnered for two weeks for a drama assignment—a dialogue scene—and I remember blushing so much that she must have thought there was something wrong with my face. We were going through a stack of papers to pick which scene we wanted to act out, and I suggested this one that was supposed to be an argument between two lovers. A man and a woman. I played it off as some sort of boundary-pushing thing."

I raise an eyebrow. I love that she's telling me this. I can just imagine teenage Cate in drama class, already singled out by teachers as having extraordinary talent.

"Sandra was into it?" I say.

"Oh, yes. We got together to practice more often than we needed to, and we kept playing with ways to touch and hold each other during the scene. I suggested—well—we kissed. Just once, under the guise of trying different things for the scene."

"And?" I ask eagerly.

"And nothing came of it, but we sure had fun working on that assignment."

I absently watch the crew work, imagining Cate's journey to figuring out her sexuality. "Wow. So your first kiss with a girl was at…thirteen?"

Cate nods, lips quirked in a little smile. "And it took me fifteen more years to realize that was a crush."

"Still. You were younger than me when I had my first kiss with a girl."

She fidgets with her gloves. "All of this is a long way of saying that I'm certain about my feelings for you, Rachel. I've known for a while that if I met the right woman, I could be in a happy relationship with her. So I mean it when I say I want to take you on a proper date."

She looks around and bites her lip, but the only person near us is a tattooed guy with a boom mic—the same one she was talking to the first time I laid eyes on her. He looks too busy with his setup to have overheard us.

My insides dance at her words.

"Teenage Cate, smooching a girl," I say, nudging her.

"I've never told anyone that before," she says, an adorable pink hue in her cheeks. "I had a boyfriend at the time, so I kind of felt like I was cheating on him."

"It was for a drama assignment, so it doesn't count," I say with a wink. "Plus, I think you get a pass since you were only thirteen."

She lets out a breath and puts a hand over her heart. "Thank goodness. That weight has been pressing down on me for decades."

I laugh.

The crew calls Cate over, and she touches my waist. "Help yourself to snacks if you're hungry. You know where the craft services table is."

Leaving me smirking, she goes to shoot the scene.

I'm flattered that she opened up to me, especially since she told me how hard it is for her to trust people. Her words also mean more than she knows. She called me *the right woman*, which means I'm more than an experiment or a fling.

I draw a breath and stand taller. Whatever people are gossiping about, Cate Whitney just told me that I'm someone she's interested in dating, and that feels pretty amazing.

Chapter 17
Foraged Mushrooms

When Cate told me she would take me to a fancy place, it flashed through my mind that she might be talking about Obsidian Grill, the most upscale restaurant in the area, but I immediately dismissed it out of guilt. I shouldn't expect her to take me to a place that extravagant.

Turns out my hunch was right.

I've set foot in this place once with Abby, and it was to order the cheapest thing on the menu—a martini glass full of chocolate mousse—just to say we've been here.

Now I'm about to have a three-course meal with the most incredible woman I've ever met. How is this my life?

Cate is rocking high-waisted brown pants, a tight yellow sleeveless shirt, and yellow stilettos like a runway model. Her hair is gelled back from her face, giving her a "just emerged from the ocean like a sea goddess" look.

I'm in all white—wide-leg pants and a top that shows a generous section of midriff—praying that I don't spill anything colorful onto my lap.

The ambience is dark and sultry, all woodsy tones with black accents. A white rose in a slender glass vase makes up our table's centerpiece.

As we read the menu, Cate notices my smirk.

"What?" she asks with a grin.

"I love pretentious menu descriptions." I point to the first item. "Heritage chicken tenders with a smooth honey Dijon foam? So, chicken nugs and honey mustard sauce?"

She laughs. "I was eyeing the handcrafted gnocchi with delicate foraged mushrooms and aged Parmesan flakes. I wonder which staff member foraged the mushrooms."

"I'm sure the chef goes foraging in the woods before his shift." I chew my lip, unsure what to order. Are the portion sizes going to be tiny? I rarely come to restaurants this nice. Living on sparse savings and student debt, it's hard to justify spending so much on food. But I don't feel like telling Cate about my mediocre lifestyle, so I'll just pick at random when the server returns.

Meredith's words about Cate and Phil's extravagant life drift back to me, and I stomp them down. I'm not letting him loom over me right now, not when Cate's gorgeous eyes are piercing me in a way that takes the breath from my lungs.

"You're in trouble later," she murmurs, barely audible, a wicked gleam in her eyes.

And I'm tingling between my legs.

Cate doesn't seem to be comparing me to Phil, so why do I keep dwelling on him? I need to stop this. I'm the total opposite of him, and that's the point. She wants me, not him.

"What are you thinking?" Cate says, searching my face.

"About your high school drama class," I say, grinning. "Was that around the time you decided to become an actor?"

She smirks. "Much earlier than that. As a kid, I used to put on plays for my parents."

"That's adorable."

"And a little desperate."

"Were you a ham?"

"Absolutely," she says, inclining her head and making a smoldering expression.

I laugh.

"I…was also trying to entertain them to distract them from each other," she says more seriously, her gaze lingering like she's gauging my reaction. "They argued a lot. Ended up getting divorced when I was twelve."

My shoulders slump, like I'm melting for her. "I'm so sorry. Please don't tell me you blamed yourself."

"Don't all kids think they had something to do with it? I thought I didn't do a good enough job keeping them happy. It made for a miserable first few years as an actor—it's not a career you want to jump into with the feeling that you've never been good enough—but I got over it with the help of an expensive therapist and time."

"How are your parents now?" I say, reaching across the table to take her hand.

"They're together again, but they bicker a lot. They're also more right-wing than I care to admit, and Josie likes to provoke them with hot topics when we go there for the holidays. It's a nightmare."

As she shares gasp-worthy stories of their family functions, I can't help feeling like something inside her is opening up to me. She's a different person than when we met. Her posture is relaxed, her smiles coming easily.

"Anyway, tell me about your family," she says, rubbing her thumb across the back of my hand, and her interest in my life makes my smile widen.

Without doubt, it's the best date I've ever had. I tell her about my parents, grandparents, and cousins. She tells me about growing up in the Midwest before moving to California. We talk about our favorite foods, songs, and places and have a passionate disagreement over the best movie franchises of all time. ("Marvel is the hill I will die on," I declare a little too loudly, and she argues that nothing can beat what *Jurassic Park* did for filmmaking.)

We're reading the dessert menu, leaning over the table toward each other, hands linked, when a light flashes beside us. I look over, startled.

A woman two tables over puts down her phone quickly, a flush in her cheeks. She turns back to her date, avoiding eye contact.

"Did she just take a picture of us?" I say, my face going numb as the blood rushes from my head.

"Yes," Cate says flatly. "Amazing how many people forget to turn off the flash when taking secret photos."

We've stopped holding hands across the table, both of us leaning back in our chairs.

My heart is racing, like I'm running up a hill.

I'm fine. I'm fine.

"I'm sorry, Rachel," Cate says, her voice seeming to come from the bottom of a pool. "If I'd let Ken come inside with us, that wouldn't have happened. People tend to think twice when he's lurking."

"No, it's okay," I say, my lips numb. "It's nice just the two of us."

I meet her concerned gaze and my breaths slow. I run my hands over the napkin in my lap, grounding myself.

Since meeting Cate, I keep getting thrown into entirely new situations—paparazzi chasing us, strangers whispering and gossiping, a ridiculously successful ex to compete with, unwanted photos while we're trying to have dinner. I'm doing my best to deal with all of this, but God, I hate it.

Cate must see something on my face because she raises a hand to summon the waiter. "Could we have the check, please?"

"Absolutely, Miss Whitney," the waiter says. "Would you like me to ask the patrons over there to leave?"

"No," I say quickly, "it's okay. No need to make a scene."

Cate searches my face, then nods and gives the waiter a warm smile. "Just the check."

"Right away."

He leaves and I sit back, forcing myself to relax. "Bill."

"Sorry?" Cate says.

"We call it the bill in Canada, not the check."

She pauses, then lets out a small laugh. "I'll remember that."

I try to smile but can't quite manage it.

"You okay?" she asks, leaning closer.

I nod, trying to convince myself. "It's not like we're a secret. You said you don't want to hide the truth, and neither do I."

"Yes, but we never consented to be in a photo. There's a difference, and you're allowed to feel upset."

I shift in my seat. I am upset, but I don't want to be. I'm not sure how to voice that without sounding pathetic.

She squeezes my hand across the table. She continues to amaze me with how confident she is and how much wisdom she's gained from being in the spotlight for so long.

"Talk to me if you're uncomfortable with any part of this, okay?" Cate says, holding my gaze. "There are things we can do to make people like that go away. We can also work harder to avoid them."

I nod. "Thanks."

Her eyes glint in the soft light, pulling me in. A flutter low inside me tells me I'm ready to take her home now.

"Abby is on a date tonight, if you want to come up to my place," I say.

Cate's lips twist into a mischievous smile. "I do. And have I got plans for you."

The way she says it sends a lick of heat through me. I crane my neck to check on the waiter, murmuring for him to hurry up, which makes Cate laugh.

Ken drives us the short distance back to my place. What a boring night this is for him, chaperoning us around and waiting in the car while we have a great time. But I guess that's the nature of his job.

In my apartment, which Abby thankfully left clean before she went on her date, I put on music and grab a bottle of wine.

I have yet to open it when Cate presses into me from behind, her fingers and lips on my neck, swaying with the music.

My breath hitches, and suddenly I forget how to open a bottle. I stand transfixed as she kisses and touches me.

"Wine can wait a few minutes," she whispers.

Heat spreads through me as she slides her fingers beneath my waistband.

I gasp as she makes a V and glides her fingers up and down on either side of my clit, slow and deliberate. She kisses my neck in time with her movements, teasing me with her tongue, until I'm dizzy. The wetter I get, the more the sensation of her hand intensifies.

"My legs are going to give out," I whisper, clutching the counter for support.

She guides me firmly to the couch and sits. "Pants off. Sit on my lap."

The curtains over the sliding glass door are open. I dash over and close them tightly before obliging.

"Is this the 'in trouble' you promised?" I say, taking my pants off in what I hope is a sexy way.

"Oh, you are definitely in for it. I've got a lifetime of pent-up sexual feelings for women to release."

"Lucky me."

She grabs my hips and turns me around, then pulls me down so I'm in her lap with my back to her. As she reaches around me and parts my legs, I close my eyes and sink into her.

Except my brain drifts back to the restaurant and the camera flash that interrupted our dinner.

Should I have confronted the woman who took the photo? It's not okay for people to take photos of others without their permission, even if they're famous. I was a coward for not doing anything about it, both for my sake and in defense of Cate.

Cate slides her hand down and draws a circle around my clit. "You're wetter by the second."

I gasp. She taps, rubs, and circles my clit gently, and all of my worries dissolve. I lean back against her, my head on her shoulder, and she kisses the side of my neck.

The sensation of her lips on my neck and her fingers on my clit brings a moan to my lips.

She spreads her thighs wider, forcing mine to open with hers, and I let out a little scream of pleasure. "Cate!"

I tremble as she explores me with gentle fingers.

"Do you want me inside you?" she whispers in my ear, sending a shiver through me.

"Yes," I whisper.

Slowly, teasingly, she slides a finger into me. At the same time, she licks and sucks my ear.

I whimper, trembling as she pushes deeper into me. "Oh…"

She glides her finger in and out, then circles my clit. I'm lost in the feel of her fingers, her lips and tongue on my neck, her breasts pressing into my back, her other hand running up and down my inner thigh.

My breaths quicken as she moves faster, in and out, palming my clit, biting and kissing my neck. Her lips on such a vulnerable part of me sends a wave of heat through my middle.

Her fingers move expertly, her breath warms my neck, and I unravel.

I cry out as waves of pleasure overtake me, lifting my hands to grab onto her. Her soft hair runs between my fingers, her body is pressed into my back, and she claims me with her hands and lips and arms wrapped tight around me.

I lay back against her, panting, and she kisses my neck and shoulders. Her lips and soft hair brush my skin, sending a shiver through me.

"Everything about you is incredible," she murmurs. "I'm so lucky I found you."

"Thanks," I say. "You're okay, I guess."

She laughs and nips my earlobe.

I spin around and kiss her. "Your turn."

An irresistible naughtiness gleams in her eyes.

Kissing her neck, I murmur, "Undress for me?"

She raises a playful eyebrow.

I pull her to her feet.

Where an average person might get shy, Cate thrives. I watch, intoxicated, while she sways her hips in time to the music and unbuttons her pants. She pulls them down, torturously slow. Her shirt is next, first revealing her stomach and bra, and then it's over her head and on the ground.

She turns a circle, rotating her hips, in the best striptease I've ever seen and probably will ever see.

Her bra comes off and then her underwear.

I grab her and lay her down on the couch, ready to devour her.

There's a rustle outside the apartment door and we both freeze.

The grinding of a key in a lock.

"Abby!" I whisper.

Cate springs to her feet, panicked. Her clothes are inside out and scattered across the floor. I'm pantsless, still in a tiny white shirt that barely comes past my ribcage.

I shove Cate toward my bedroom with one hand and grab my underwear with the other.

"Quick! Wear something from my closet. Anything."

Cate barely makes it into my bedroom when the front door opens and Abby walks in.

"Hey, fart-face," she says loudly. "You are not going to fucking believe what pics came out of the night that bitch-ass dickwad had you frisked—whose shoes are these?"

My bedroom door slams at the same moment as I get my underwear over my ass. My cropped shirt, which I was so proud of earlier, is suddenly infuriatingly short and in no way hides the fact that I was totally pantsless a second ago.

Abby stands there for what is probably the longest pause ever to exist. Her gaze darts from me to the closed curtains to my closed bedroom door.

Then she gasps and drops her purse and the magazine she's holding. She claps her hands over her mouth.

"Is Cate Whitney in our apartment?" she asks through her hands.

Cate definitely heard that.

I close my eyes and pinch the bridge of my nose. "Yes. She's in my bedroom. Can you please give us a minute to get our clothes back on?"

"Yes. Sorry. Oh my God." Abby stumbles to her bedroom, seeming to forget how to walk, an excited gleam in her eyes. "Can I come out and say hi when you're both dressed?"

"Yes."

"Sorry. My date sucked. I would have been home later."

She shuts her bedroom door, and I grab Cate's clothes, heart pounding.

I'm more exasperated than embarrassed. Abby and I are nothing if not open with each other. We share graphic details of our sex lives and see each other pantsless regularly.

Cate, however, doesn't have that rapport with Abby, and when I open my bedroom door, her face is the color of a tomato. She's wrapped in my unicorn bathrobe, the hood up so the ears and rainbow horn are over her forehead.

I smile and kiss her, passing over her clothes. "It's fine. Abby and I are tight. She's excited to meet you."

"Good," she says with a shaky laugh. "She didn't see my ass as I was running to your bedroom?"

"Nope. Just mine."

When we emerge, Abby is in the kitchen, still in her tiny white dress, pouring a glass of the wine I was about to open before Cate and I got distracted.

She spins, red wine slopping out of her glass and onto the floor. "Cate Whitney! Hi! Wow, you're even prettier in person. I'm Abby Yousefi."

"Lovely to meet you," Cate says, pushing past the awkwardness like a pro. I guess she has years of experience navigating cringey situations.

"I've never met a celebrity," Abby says, sipping her wine and staring at Cate without blinking. "I mean, I've seen them from afar. I used to work downtown."

"Oh? What do you do?"

And it's time to divert this conversation before Abby says the words "point-of-view porn" to the woman I'm trying to impress.

Recalling Abby's greeting when she came through the door, I look over at the dropped purse and magazine in the entryway. "Abby, what were you saying about a dickwad who had me frisked? Were you talking about Phil Niles?"

Her eyes widen. "Um. I can show you later."

Cate follows my gaze. She strides over and picks up the magazine.

She stares at the cover for a long time, expression blank.

Dread floods through me, icy cold. I race over. "What is it?"

It's a tabloid magazine, and the cover is a photo of the security team hauling me away at the gala. Inset is a picture of Cate shouting from the same night, an ugly expression on her face. I think they've edited the photo to make her look twenty years older. They've definitely added some shadows into mine because I've never seen a picture of me that's quite so unflattering.

"Cate Whitney's lesbian affair blows up," Cate reads. "An affair? Really? Dimwits."

She looks at me, offering an exasperated smile, but I can't return it. I'm breathing fast, sweat prickling all over my body.

"Are you okay, Rachel?"

I nod reflexively, though I'm not sure.

Twice in one night, I've had my privacy violated. I want to scream or throw up or change my name and face and everything else about my identity.

The worst part isn't even what I thought it would be. My anxiety about having my picture taken is secondary to how this is going to affect my career. Will anyone take me seriously after this? Will I forever be seen as some celebrity's squeeze? Gracing the cover of a tabloid is not a good look on someone trying to go after a medical career.

Meredith Cheema's words from the gala trickle forward.

We'll be seeing you on the cover of Time *magazine one day.*

She wasn't far off from my ambitions. I got into my field to make an impact, to use my brain to do something world changing.

Instead, I'm on the cover of a tabloid, painted as a hot mess, being dragged out of an event I never belonged at in the first place.

Chapter 18
Mystery Mistress

Wow, so Cate decided to lower the bar, huh?

Imagine going from Phil Niles to this.

She looks like Conrad's most recent kill, the one with no lines whose only job was to die in the opening scene.

Conrad is Phil's werewolf character. And his most recent kill is about how I feel right now.

It's 3:42 a.m., and I'm lying wide awake, gaping at my phone after being pulled from sleep by endless notifications. It took me a groggy moment to process what the notifications are. The only reason I have social media apps are to follow dogstagram accounts, celebrities, and food bloggers. Any notifications are usually just Abby or my mom sending me memes.

Now my screen lights up my bedroom as strangers talk about me, comment on my appearance, and send me direct messages.

Apparently, my name and ancient profile picture are public enough that strangers can still find me.

"Shit," I whisper, sitting up.

It feels like a rock has dropped into my stomach. After the tabloid article, people must have taken it upon themselves to track me down. The problem is that my profile photo is from when I was sixteen and had braces. It's a ridiculous class photo that I never bothered to change.

Someone saved the picture and made a viral post that says, *Wait, so is Cate adopting her or dating her?*

As I frantically clear the notifications from my phone, face burning, another one comes in.

lol Phil must have really done a number on Cate if she's suddenly into women.

I grind my teeth. On top of it all, they're even speculating about how real Cate's feelings are. Awesome.

Though the damage is done, I go into my privacy settings to turn everything up to maximum. I change my profile picture to a random picture of an otter and block anyone who's requested to follow or friend me since last night.

What, exactly, has happened since that magazine was published?

I open a browser and type my name in the search bar.

Big mistake.

There are photos of Cate and I running from the paparazzi after our first date, having dinner last night, leaning into each other at the gala, and Cate touching my waist on set the other day. The headlines call me Cate's *mystery mistress* and *lesbian lover*.

The word choice infuriates me. Why can't they just say we're dating? Why do they have to make it sound scandalous? I'm over here, innocently falling for Cate, and they're trying to ruin our happiness by painting this as something secretive and shocking.

Between the tabloid magazine in our recycling bin and my name appearing all over the internet, it's hard to breathe. I pretended to shrug off the tabloid before Cate left last night, but inside, I'm icy cold. So many strangers know who I am.

Have my parents seen any of this?

No, they would've called if they had.

But God, how will this affect my career?

My chest is so tight. Am I panicking? I'm as mortified as I was when that video made the rounds in high school.

What if Cate dumps me over this?

"Stop it," I whisper.

I breathe deeply, counting as I inhale, hold, and exhale while scrolling through endless commentary on social media. Most people are supportive and full of well-wishes, but even those comments sit uneasy in my stomach. Who are these strangers, and why are they thinking about us at all? This is *our* relationship. We don't need or want their blessing.

Beneath the kind comments, layers of slurs and loyalty to Phil Niles roil like lava. A lot of people hate me for keeping Phil and Cate apart, as if I'm the only thing blocking the Hollywood Power Couple from making up.

As much as I try to skim past the comments about me, my eyes are too quick, and I catch words like "mousy" and "plain."

In other words, ordinary. Average.

I reflexively look at my closed curtains, half expecting some of these commenters to peek through or try to catch a glimpse of me with a long lens.

I type Cate's name into the search bar.

Sure enough, every headline is about me—not her movies, not *Clockwork Curie*, but *me*. The Rachel Janssen scandal.

By the time the sun rises, after I've spent a couple of hours spiraling into an abyss, Abby meets me in the kitchen and tells me I look like shit.

I shove my phone in her face, search page open with Cate's headlines at the top.

"I should break things off with her, shouldn't I?" I say, my throat tightening as the words come out. "I'm ruining her career. She's making headlines for her sex life rather than for the movies she's working on."

"Hold up," Abby says, squinting at my phone without her glasses on. "Let me process what's going on here."

Abby makes coffee and toast, wipes the smudges off her glasses before putting them on, and settles on the couch with her laptop. I follow her like a dog and stand over her, pulse racing, tears threatening to spill.

Abby must have been working the last time she used her laptop, because there's a Triple-X POV page open with a *Categories* header and a list of words—*Threesome*, *Squirt*, *Milf*, *Feet*. She opens a new tab and clicks the search bar.

"Cate Whitney and Rachel Janssen," she murmurs, typing. There's a pause while she looks at the headlines. "Huh. I see. Interesting."

I appreciate how calm she's being because I'm dying inside.

After a long moment, Abby closes her laptop and clasps her hands over it. "No."

"No?"

"You shouldn't break up with her. This is Hollywood. All of this—" She nods toward the laptop. "—is a symptom of fame. Cate knows this. She signed up for it."

"Okay," I say slowly. Maybe she's right that Cate can handle the media attention. The problem is, I can't. The paparazzi, nasty headlines, tabloids, Phil…all of it is adding up to something I don't want to deal with.

"As for you," Abby says, reading my expression, "you have to decide whether you want this."

"Of course I don't. If I wanted fame, I would have become an actor or whatever. I'm a freaking science student, Abby."

"If your dislike of fame outweighs your feelings for Cate, then okay, you should break up with her. But I've seen the way you look at her. I've seen you smiling into your phone in a way you haven't done since…well, since Sarah, to be honest."

Yeah, of course I have real feelings for Cate. I'm head over heels. But there's an uncomfortable twist in my gut because I'm also letting what happened with Sarah affect my relationship with Cate.

The thing is, Cate and Sarah couldn't be more different. If I can get over my fears, the potential for an incredible relationship is there.

I flop down next to Abby on the couch. "I don't *want* to break up with her. But am I supposed to suffer through all of this?"

"No. You're supposed to decide that you want to endure it. There's a difference."

I raise an eyebrow. "Is there?"

"Of course there is! You can keep fucking Cate and suffering through the side effects, or you can choose to embrace this as part of it. You don't have to enjoy being labeled a skank by the press, but you can accept it as part of the deal. What sounds better: suffering through something or accepting it?"

"Accepting it. But I *don't* accept being labeled—"

Abby grabs my face. "It's part of the deal, Rachel. Your other option is to fight the press and the haters and try to make everybody like you, but they're going to spin your image however it serves them. So either accept the shitshow as part of being with Cate, or don't accept it and break up with her. But if you keep resenting it and dating her, guess who you're going to end up resenting?"

I stare at her, my face in her hands.

She's right. If I stay with Cate and treat the negative press as something awful that I have to fight, I'm going to end up resenting Cate for putting me through it. If I accept that it's part of dating a celebrity and I can choose to live happily in spite of it, then it doesn't have to affect me.

I just don't know if I have the strength to accept it. My feelings are kind of delicate.

Part of the deal. Can I learn to accept Hollywood crap the same way an actor does when they get into the business?

"Everything comes with baggage, Rachel. This is Cate's baggage."

I sigh. "I guess I accepted stress and studying as part of being a student."

"Exactly."

"So I should learn to accept bad press and shitty internet comments as part of dating Cate."

My tone is not convincing.

Abby grimaces.

My phone beeps. I open it to find that Cate has sent a pornographic GIF of two women scissoring.

I'm curious...

I purse my lips, a smile tugging at my face. My insides tingle.

"How can you say no to that?" Abby says, leaning over my shoulder to peer at my phone.

I click the screen off and swat her away, laughing.

I rub an arm across my eyes, drawing a deep breath.

"Yeah, I can learn to accept the baggage."

Though my tone wavers, Abby gives me two thumbs up. "That's the spirit. Now get out there and live up to your reputation, Mystery Mistress."

⎯⎯⎯⎯✦⎯✦⎯✦⎯⎯⎯⎯

On Saturday, Cate invites me to the hotel where she's staying, and it's as nice as the one in LA. We eat dinner in the hotel restaurant and head for the elevators in a hurry. Her filming schedule and my schoolwork only leaves us with Saturday nights and Sunday mornings, and the dry days in between make us hornier than ever. We can't even have sex in her trailer between takes anymore, because after we set her costume askew and made her late, she may have gotten in a *teeny* bit of trouble for bringing me onto the set.

In the elevator, I push her against the wall and kiss her. She moans into my mouth, her hands wandering up and down my back.

I bite her neck and suck.

"Don't leave a mark," she says, laughing. "I'll have to spend longer in makeup."

"Right. Sorry," I murmur.

The doors open and she takes my hand, pulling me down the hall to her suite.

The room looks out on Vancouver and has everything from heated floors to a king bed with chocolates on the pillows. It's the perfect place to have sex—it's totally ours, it's romantic and gorgeous, and the suite is big enough that our neighbors should, hopefully, not have to listen to us.

We shove the chocolate-adorned pillows aside, clawing at each other to get our clothes off.

She pulls my shirt over my head and I do the same to her, taking extra care since the pastel blue material is obviously designer.

Our pants come off with fumbling fingers, and then we're both naked. She pushes me onto the mattress, and before I can sit up, she's on top of me, holding me to the bed with firm hands. She straddles my thigh, already wet, and the sensation on my leg sends my head spinning.

"God, I needed you today," she says, closing her eyes as she grinds on my leg.

I push up, giving her a resistance that makes her moan. "Rough day?"

"Long. And I keep thinking about you and getting horny while I'm working."

Laughing, I roll us over. She lets out a noise between a gasp and a laugh.

I've accepted that Cate is into me. I've accepted that something about me has snagged her attention and she's interested in dating me. But it still feels like a dream. I'm still holding my breath, hoping she won't realize that she's settling for someone far beneath her.

The public knows it. Phil Niles knows it. How long before Cate realizes it?

"Ready to try that GIF you sent me?" I whisper into her mouth.

There's an excited gleam in her eyes. "I'm all yours."

I lean back and position my legs over hers, closing the distance between us. We're heat to heat, wet with desire.

She moans, rocking her hips.

Below me, her head tilts back and her eyes close. Her blond locks cascade onto the pillow.

I move my hips in a slow circle. Her soft hands caress my thigh.

She moves with me, and the sight of her body making slow waves is enough to make me burn with longing. The sensation is unbearable, and knowing she's feeling the same thing makes me lose my mind in a haze. Soon, my hips move without conscious thought, up and down, left and right, faster and faster.

Cate's fingers dig into my thighs, no longer gentle.

We move faster, gasping, and I bend over her leg, aching to get closer. I'm losing myself in her, losing track of the world around us.

A burning starts deep inside me and gets stronger.

"Yes," Cate says, breathless, and I know her intimately enough now to catch her tone.

"You close?" I ask.

"Yeah."

The heat in my loins intensifies, building fast. "Me too."

Our hips move faster, our breaths come out shallow. Her face is flushed and her skin glints with sweat, making her all the more tantalizing.

She meets my gaze, and the look in her eyes tips me over the edge.

Ripples of pleasure overtake me, dizzying, breathtaking, and I'm holding Cate's gaze as she grips me hard. Her hips buck against me, making me gasp.

Sex with Cate is the best I've ever had. It's something about our body chemistry, the way we move together, react to each other, and know exactly what the other needs.

We lean in and kiss, bumping noses. We're both sweaty, too spent for words.

As we lay next to each other and cuddle, I run my hands over her cheek and shoulder and down her waist.

My phone lights up, and I grab it with a huff—an email from some TV channel asking for an interview.

That's a firm no.

How the hell did they find my student email address anyway?

Scowling, I unlock my phone to turn off all notifications. My browser is still open with Cate's name in the search bar.

I tap out of it quickly, but not before Cate sees.

"What was that?" she asks.

"What?" I ask reflexively.

"I saw my name. What were you reading?"

"Just…I've been keeping track of news about us," I say, face heating up. "I'm not used to making headlines. It's all a little weird for me."

"Oh." She's silent, gazing at the ceiling. "I'm sorry, Rachel. I should have been checking in with you more. Are you doing okay?"

I hesitate, debating my words. "It's hard seeing some of the headlines and comments, but I'll get used to it."

"It takes time to get used to. But it helps to know that the public's memory is fleeting, and there are always new scandals to focus on. We're hardly the most newsworthy people out there."

"That's true."

"And what about Phil?" she asks.

The mention of her ex-husband stabs through me like an electric shock. "What about him?"

"Are you okay after what happened at the gala? I haven't heard from him since I threatened him with legal action, so I hope that was the last of him."

I hesitate. Maybe it's time to tell her that he spoke to me.

"Tell me," she says, reading my face.

"Before that whole thing happened with security, Phil talked to me."

She sits up. "What?" Her voice turns sharp.

"He seemed bitter about seeing us together. It's fine. I told him to get over it."

She gets out of bed and grabs her phone from the TV stand, her mouth drawn in a tight line. "Rachel, you should have told me. Mandy will—"

"Don't." Heart beating fast, I sit up. "I don't want to be the cause of more drama between you two."

She gives me a stern look. "First of all, the *drama* of our divorce was no different from any average divorce. The media is making it out to be an ordeal. Second, if my ex-husband is threatening my girlfriend, you bet your ass I'm going to make him pay."

I gape at her while her thumbs tap aggressively on her screen. "Your girlfriend?"

She looks up, eyes wide, and bites her lip. "Sorry. Am I making assumptions?"

"No!" I jump out of bed and kiss her. "Cate, nothing would make me happier."

Her grin brightens the whole room. "Me too."

I pull her back to bed, but she's distracted.

"Can I arrange for you to have a bodyguard?" she offers.

I laugh, though I know she's not joking. "That won't be necessary."

"It might make you feel more at ease. I can lend you Ken. He's trained in judo *and* karate, you know."

"Has he ever needed to put those skills to use?" I say, unsure if I want the answer.

She tilts her head, considering, then says carefully, "Sometimes, people think they're entitled to me. Those are the times when I'm grateful to have Ken. Though thankfully, he's never had to injure anyone and I've never had to go so far as a restraining order."

I kiss her hand, filled with admiration over everything she has to deal with. "You're strong, Cate."

She smiles. "So, can I interest you in the same protection?"

I'm struggling to accept the attention I'm getting, and Abby has spent a lot of time being supportive and coming up with creative insults for online trolls—but I don't think a personal bodyguard would help me deal with all of this. It would draw attention to the fact that my life has changed since dating Cate. I want to feel normal at least some of the time, and adding a security detail would make that impossible.

"I promise I'm fine," I say. "But if I change my mind and decide I want a martial arts pro stationed outside my apartment, I'll let you know."

CHAPTER 19
CHOICES BEFITTING A WOMAN OF SCIENCE

"WHY ARE YOU HOME?" ABBY says in surprise. It's nine a.m. on a Sunday, and she's frying up something that smells potatoey.

"Good morning to you too," I say as I emerge from my bedroom. "Cate had to work late last night and be up early today."

"Oh. Want to share my breakfast scramble?"

"Sure, if you have enough."

"Coming right up."

"Thanks, bestie." I settle on the couch in my usual spot, put my laptop on a TV tray, and pull it close.

"I guess this was bound to happen at some point," Abby says. "What's it been, two months of seeing her every weekend?"

"Seven weeks."

That's seven Sundays of waking up with Cate, and every time has been as blissful as the last.

I guess I should be grateful we've had that many weekends together, given how filming schedules are. But I can't say gratitude is my primary emotion. I'm more feeling sad that I won't see her for two weeks and maybe a little horny.

While Abby makes breakfast, I open my laptop to work on my thesis.

I'm still unsure how dating Cate will affect my professional life. Have my supervisors seen any of the paparazzi photos? My stomach clenches as I imagine Dr. Wee in the checkout line at the grocery store, jaw unhinging as she recognizes me on the cover of the tabloid magazine beside her.

"Do you think I should tell my supervisors I'm dating Cate?" I ask Abby.

She pauses with an egg in one hand and a spatula in the other. "Um. Why?"

"With all of the gossip and stuff, I'm afraid that I won't be taken seriously. My public image is…scandalous." I wrinkle my nose. "I don't know if this is going to affect my career and what I'm supposed to do about it."

"Hm. I guess *celebrity* and *doctor* don't look good together."

"I think that's the literal definition of a quack." I cup my cheeks and let out a little moan. "Imagine my future patients or coworkers recognizing me from this."

"Yeah, okay, you could bring it up," Abby says with a grimace. "Supervisors are there to guide you and give advice, right?"

She cracks the egg and keeps cooking.

I purse my lips. The advice is supposed to be for school-related stuff, not my love life, but I desperately need some guidance here. The last thing I want to do is ruin my professional image.

I open a new email to my supervisory committee. I tell them I'm still reading papers and trying out software and will set up a meeting soon to go over my progress. Then I add,

I don't know if you pay attention to celebrity gossip, but you might have seen me in some entertainment programs or online recently because of who I am dating… and I just wanted to ask your opinion on what to do about this. I don't want my personal life to interfere with my career, but it's hard to stay out of the public eye when I'm in a relationship with Cate Whitney.

If they think this is a terrible idea for my professional image, they'll tell me.

The problem is, I don't know what I'll do if they say that this is the worst idea ever and that I'm doomed to struggle in my career because of it.

I send the email and immediately get an automated out-of-office reply from Dr. Wee.

I groan. I guess I'm going to be left hanging for a while.

Abby brings me a plate of an amazing-looking hash—potatoes, eggs, spinach, red peppers—and a side of multigrain toast.

"You're the absolute best," I say.

She beams and sits next to me.

"So, say I do get past fame and Phil and all that crap," I say. "What's next? Filming is going to wrap up soon. Could my relationship with Cate actually go somewhere?"

Abby takes a bite of toast and stares at me, clearly not sure how to answer.

"It would be a long-distance relationship," I say. "Which sucks."

Abby waves her toast through the air. "Cate has enough money to fly back and forth."

"But even if she flies here to see me once a week—or has me flown out to LA—it's not the same as living in the same city. I don't want our relationship to depend on whether she's able to fly here or not."

"So move to LA," she says, then seems to hear her own words, and a look of horror crosses her face. "Actually, don't. Please. You're the glue who holds my life together."

I smile. "I couldn't. I'd be so homesick. My whole life is here."

"Would Cate move here?"

There's an excited swoop in my gut at the prospect. She wouldn't have a problem applying to live here, if she wanted to. The prime minister himself would probably arrive at the border to welcome her across.

"It's a topic we'll have to broach as filming wraps up," I say carefully and stuff my face with savory, salty goodness. "Anyway, how was your date last night?"

"Meh. We went to the art gallery, and they're featuring one of those pretentious abstract exhibits that doesn't make any sense. But we went back to his place after and made up for it."

After breakfast and hearing about Abby's sex life in intimate detail, I open my laptop, and Abby retreats to her bedroom. I have to put Cate out of my mind and do at least a few hours of research today.

I've figured out how to use the defense and intelligence software, and I can input MRI scans, but I haven't been able to make an accurate machine learning model. It's no better at recognizing tumors than the human eye, which renders my idea useless. I think I need more sample data to train the algorithm.

The only reason I have access to this program is because Abby dated a software engineer last year who worked on it. Their relationship went nowhere, but Abby was able to wheedle some free career-advancing software for me, so there's that.

See? Some people have normal exes, I think bitterly.

My phone lights up with a new email from someone named Amber Scott. The preview text is short.

rachel… hope u sleep well at night knowing u broke up a happy relationship. homewrecker.

I swipe it away, rage bubbling inside me. I have the urge to reply with a middle-finger emoji. How did the public find my email?

I search the internet for my name, and it takes all of two minutes to find my name and email published on the university website, along with my field of study.

"For fuck's sake," I whisper.

Why is so much of my information out there without my consent? Why is the internet so violating?

None of these strangers have any idea what's going on between Cate and me, and it enrages me how many of them assume they know the story. I want to stand on a roof and scream at all of them to leave me alone. I don't want any of this.

But separating Cate from fame would be impossible. It was, after all, the reason we met.

Like Abby wisely said, I should accept and embrace it. I have to, if I want to be with her.

I just never knew it would be this hard.

My phone rings.

I snatch it up, my heart jumping, expecting to see Cate's name and the heart-eyes emoji I put next to it.

But it isn't Cate.

Instead of heart-eyes, there's the tulip emoji I associate with the person I care most about in the world.

"Hey, Mom!"

"Rachel? I saw you on the cover of a magazine."

Oof. I put a hand on my stomach.

I probably should have called them sooner. I guess I was hoping they would never see the paparazzi photos.

I get up and pace the living room. It'll be easier to talk about this if I'm in motion.

"Oh, you saw that?" I ask casually.

Clattering and hissing in the background tells me she's making brunch. Probably pannenkoeken. I can picture her in her white terry towel robe, bustling about the kitchen with a flipper in one hand and her earphones in, a fresh vase of tulips and a stack of mail on the counter next to her. It was the same scene every Saturday and Sunday morning growing up.

"I was at Carly's house," she says. "You know, from my ukulele classes? And she had some magazines on her coffee table. And I said to her, 'Look, that's my daughter,' and she didn't believe me. Well, it's you, isn't it? I have it right here."

Pages rustle as if she's picking it up to show me through the phone.

"Yes, it's me."

"I knew it," she says, then shouts into the distance. "Jack, it's her! Rachel, why were you with Cate Whitney?"

"I'm—I'm dating her, Mom." My lips are numb. It's like coming out to them all over again.

They reacted supportively then. But they've never been particularly smitten by celebrities, and somehow, I think this conversation will be a little bumpier.

"Dating her?" Mom says. "You're dating Cate Whitney?"

Dad shouts something inaudible in the background.

"That's what she just told me," Mom shouts back.

"She's yanking our chain," Dad shouts in the distance.

"I'm not," I say. God, why is talking to them always so chaotic? "Cate is filming a movie on my street, and we met. We went on a few dates and… she invited me to that gala."

"But what's going on in that picture?" Mom says.

I can feel Abby's eyes on me through her open bedroom door. I keep my gaze on my feet as I pace. "Security, um, mistook me for someone else.

It's fine. The pictures just make it look bad. You know how those magazines are—"

"Jack, come eat!" Mom shouts. "Rachel, I don't like you being so public like that. You should be careful. Tell Miss Whitney that you're a woman of science and you need to focus on your studies."

I open and close my mouth. Of course she'd make this about school. I love my parents, but it's always about grades and careers with them. A social life is secondary.

"Mom, I'm not going to break up with her!"

Abby sidles out of her bedroom and comes to sit on the couch, getting a front-row seat to this conversation.

"If this is what dating her looks like, I'm not sure I like it. Think of your career, honey. That was a terribly unflattering headline. Jack, the syrup is here."

"I am thinking of my career! It's fine!"

More clattering in the background. She's always multitasking when I talk to her.

"Just be careful. You seem to get into trouble when cameras are involved—"

"Don't," I say sharply. "Don't even go there, Mom. This isn't at all like that. I'm an adult who is dating another adult, and I'm dealing with the cameras just fine."

The last bit might not be true, but I can't believe she said that. She knows how much that wrecked me.

I'm breathing hard, my fists clenched.

"I'm sorry," she says, a little more softly. "You know this comes from a place of love. I care about you and don't want to see you mess up your schooling. You're such a smart cookie."

"I—yeah—thanks," I say, rubbing the back of my neck. "I'll be careful. I was doing research right before you called, so I'm not letting my schoolwork slide. Don't worry, Mom."

Her breath hits the phone. "All right. I—Jack, I've got another ready here. I'll leave you to your love life, Rachel. I trust you."

"Thanks," I say, hollow.

"And for the record, I am excited for you. So is your dad—he's giving a thumbs-up. Cate Whitney looks like a lovely person, and so talented."

"And beautiful!" Dad shouts. "Good catch, Rach!"

This makes me crack a smile.

But despite their change of tone, I'm agitated, this conversation putting me in a worse state than ever. I love my mom and I value her opinions, but when it comes to dating Cate, I don't know if I want to listen to her.

I can balance dating Cate with my schoolwork, right?

I wish I could take my own advice and not worry, but I'm more confused than ever about what I'm supposed to do. What if my supervisors tell me this is a bad idea too? What if every reasonable person in my life tells me dating her is a mistake?

"Hey, why don't the two of you come over for dinner?" Mom says, pulling me out of my thoughts.

My knees give out, and I sit down on the couch without looking, ending up half on Abby's lap. "What?"

"Dinner! Bring her over. It's been so long since you've had a partner, honey, and Dad and I would love to meet her."

CHAPTER 20
MEAT AND POTATOES

THROUGHOUT THE WEEK, I'M SUDDENLY more studious, like my brain can only manage to procrastinate on one thing at a time and asking Cate about meeting my parents has won as The Thing I Am Most Avoiding.

When we meet up on the weekend, no moment seems like the right one to ask. Not when we're enjoying each other's company at a sushi restaurant, nor when we're naked and sweaty, nor as we're drifting off to sleep, nor as I'm about to leave the next day.

But the texts and calls from Mom grow persistent, my phone burning a hole in my pocket as we have dinner the following weekend.

What if this is too much, too soon? Cate and I haven't talked about what'll happen to our relationship when filming wraps up. Are we serious enough to be meeting parents? Will she freak out if I ask?

I could tell Mom no. I could say Cate's too busy filming.

But deep down, I want to invite her. Bringing her to meet them will make us more real in each other's lives—and if she says no, then at least I'll know where we stand.

When we get to Cate's hotel room after dinner, my heart is in my throat. It's been two weeks since Mom brought it up, and I can't put this off any longer.

"My parents invited us for dinner," I blurt as we take our shoes off. "I'm sorry. We can say no if it's too uncomfortable. They found out about us because of the tabloid, so I told them about you, and then they asked to meet you, and—"

"I thought you seemed quiet tonight," Cate says, stopping my rambling. She walks to the desk across from the bed and takes off her earrings and necklace. When I continue watching her in silence, she says, "Were you worried how I would respond?"

"Do you want to?" I say, my mouth dry.

She hesitates for the tiniest space of time—one second, maybe two. "I'm up for meeting your family."

My heart jumps. What was that hesitation? Am I reading too much into it, or does she not want to go?

I plunk on the bed, watching her. "Really?"

She meets my eye through the mirror. "You met Josie. Now it's my turn."

"Yeah, but Josie's cool. My parents are…parents."

She shrugs. "They can't be worse than mine. We haven't had an argument-free family dinner since Josie and I were kids."

I flop back on the bed and stare at the ceiling. "Sorry. I shouldn't be acting like my parents are awful. They're not. They're great." I hesitate. I should be relieved that Cate said yes, but my insides are twisting worse than ever. "I guess I'm nervous about bringing home a girlfriend—and you, of all people. They're going to embarrass the hell out of me, I know it."

"I'm sure they won't."

She pulls her arms through her sleeves and begins to undress, and my brain starts to derail. Before it's too late, I say in a rush, "I've never brought a partner home to meet my parents." My tongue is numb. I swallow hard. "Not really, anyway. They only ever met Sarah as my friend. No one else I've dated has been serious enough."

Cate studies me and, after a pause, smiles. "Then I'm honored to be the first."

"If it's awkward, we can—"

"It'll be just fine, Rachel. I promise."

She crawls onto the bed, suspended over me.

Melting under her gaze, I believe her. If I'm going to bring someone home to meet my parents, I'm proud and excited that it's Cate.

So, the next Sunday afternoon, we get into my rusty old SUV, which I spent two hours cleaning. We're both wearing capris and blazers—Cate's a lavender set that's clearly designer and mine, black-and-white and pieced together from a sale rack. I look nice by normal standards. Cate has her celebrity aura shining as brightly as ever.

"Last chance to switch rides," I say apologetically. "We can get Ken to drive us in your fancy car instead of this old beater."

"It's not a beater," Cate says. "It's charming. Does she have a name?"

"Old Blue," I mumble, driving us out of the parkade. Maybe one day I won't feel like nothing in my life is good enough for Cate.

She reaches over to squeeze my thigh. "I argued with Ken for this freedom. Don't make me waste it."

"What do you mean?"

"He wanted to come with us today. I told him I could handle meeting my girlfriend's parents without security detail."

Ken thought he should come? Would it be smart to listen to him? He is, after all, a professional.

Cate must read my hesitation, because she says emphatically, "I'll be fine. I don't need security for something like this."

I'm not sure whether to be honored that she trusts me enough to leave her bodyguard behind or concerned that she's letting her desire to be normal cloud her judgment.

But it's not my place to decide this for her. She's been in this business for a long time and knows what she's doing.

So I smile. "Just the two of us."

I take her down the highway toward the suburbs, cruising at a leisurely pace to let her take in the mountain views I told her about when we first met.

"Oh, it's just gorgeous," she says, leaning across to take a picture out the window.

I smile and turn up the music, letting the radio dictate the soundtrack to our day.

But even Ed Sheeran can't keep my heart rate down for long, and by the time we arrive at the house I grew up in, my pulse is racing.

As we get out of the car, Cate's gaze sweeps over the gray siding, wood accents, stone walkway, freshly mown lawn, and roses out front. Her expression is unreadable.

I take her hand and draw a shaky breath. What if my parents tell some embarrassing story about me? What if we can't manage to make conversation? What if Cate gets uncomfortable with the questions they ask?

We walk up to the door and I knock, and the ensuing pause is the longest of my life. My pulse pounds in my ears.

The door flies open, and Mom and Dad stand there with wide eyes. I haven't seen them looking this excited since I told them I got accepted to my master's program.

Mom looks like she can't get her breath. "Hi. Hello. Wow."

"Hi—nice—meet you," Dad says.

Well, now Cate knows where I get my awkwardness from.

My parents haven't looked at me yet. Their eyes are fixed on Cate.

I guess they care about celebrities a little more than they claim.

"Please, come in," Dad says, stepping aside and making a sweeping gesture with his arm. I've never seen him like this. Last time I came home, he told me to "get the hell over here" and wrestled me into a one-armed hug.

My tongue feels too fat as I stammer the introductions. "Mom, Dad, this is Cate. Cate, this is my mom, Ann, and my dad, Jack."

"Beautiful house," Cate says.

"Built in 1976," Dad says. "They don't make 'em like this anymore!"

"It's humble compared to what you're used to, I'm sure," Mom says.

Yes, start off by pointing out how rich she is, I think, looking at the ceiling.

"I grew up in a house like this one," Cate says. "Same split-level layout. Those stairs will go down to the basement, right?"

"That's right!" Dad says. "How about that, Ann? Same house."

"Do you live in Hollywood now?" Mom says, clearly not letting the subject drop.

"Outside of it. But I do live in a big house, if that's what you're wondering. Infinity pool, home theater, personal gym."

"Wow." Mom's eyes get starry. She's always dreamed of living in a mansion, though I'm not sure why, because she constantly complains about this house being too big. I guess it's more about the idea of living luxuriously.

My parents finally turn their gazes to me and then take turns wrapping me in warm hugs.

"I'm so glad you could make it, honey," Mom says. "Rach has been so busy with university, Cate. I'm sure you know."

"Oh, yes," Cate says, though between the two of us, her work schedule puts her as the busier one.

"Come on. Give me a few minutes to make the cheese sauce, and dinner will be right up."

"Thanks for cooking, Mom."

"Thank you," Cate echoes. "It smells wonderful in here."

We shuffle to the kitchen—fresh tulips on the counter, a stack of mail in the same spot, most of the furniture and decor unchanged from my childhood. There's a cuckoo clock on the wall that they brought back from the Black Forest, which Dad and I rigged using a microcomputer so it makes velociraptor sounds instead of chirping. Mom doesn't know how to fix it, so it's been like that for a decade.

"Did you go to university, Cate?" Mom says.

Of course she asks that. My parents are so stuck on the old-fashioned idea that everybody should have a degree, even if your career path is clearly headed elsewhere. Heaven forbid if I'd told them I wanted to get into a trade.

"I went to UCLA until my acting career called me away from my studies," Cate says, expertly rewording the dropout version she told me when we first met.

Mom beams. "UCLA! Wow, you're smart *and* talented."

She gives me a raised-eyebrow look that she doesn't even bother trying to hide. Cate sees, I see, Dad sees. At least Mom's impressed.

"We were thrilled when Rachel got accepted into her program," Mom says, still beaming. "She's going to be the first doctor in the family."

"The first on both sides!" Dad says.

"She's certainly smart enough," Cate says. "Building her own computers and whatnot. She must have learned from the best. Rachel tells me you build houses, Jack."

Damn, she's smooth. Dad inflates at the praise, his chest literally expanding by a couple of inches.

"Oh, yeah. Houses, furniture, whatever else I come up with. Has Rach told you about the projects she and I have worked on?"

Cate shakes her head.

"Come look," Dad says, giving her no choice.

He walks out the back door and into the yard, and Cate follows. After a pause, I dash after them. They've manicured the lawn and garden, but there's still a large pile of stuff beside the house from Dad's various projects.

"Rach and I built this when she was in grade seven," Dad says.

I groan. He shows this to anyone who will listen—guests, the neighbors, the septic guys—which I guess is cute but also a little mortifying.

"Is that a solar panel?" Cate says.

"Charges these twelve-volt batteries!" Dad shows her four RV batteries wired together, the final and most expensive step of the project. "I've had to replace the batteries here and there, but the panel keeps on working. Flawless. Our electricity bill is next to nothing in the summer, and it's saved us in how many power outages, Ann?"

"Dozens," Mom calls from inside.

"Dozens!"

"He gets excited when there's a threat of a power outage," I say.

"I like to put our hard work to use!"

"What parts did you need to build it?" Cate asks.

Dad looks ecstatic that she asked. "A sheet of tempered glass, epoxy, soldering iron… The main thing is the solar cells. They're cheap. You give the glass a good clean, then lay them out in rows, see? Then you wire them up so you connect the positives and the negatives like a circuit…"

While Dad goes through the riveting process of building a solar panel, Cate looks around the yard, and I can see her picturing me growing up here. The tire swing still hangs from the maple tree, the tree house above it weathered and well-loved, the expansive lawn home to many games and water fights.

She catches my eye. I don't know what look I expected to get from her—maybe exasperation over Dad's rambling—but what I get instead is something tender. Maybe she's seeing me in a different light. Something about the way her gaze hits me sends a flutter through my chest.

The way Dad is talking, it's clear he likes Cate. Of course he does. Who wouldn't? She's the most charming woman on the planet, in my completely unbiased opinion.

Mom calls us inside, and I'm spared from him showing Cate our other DIY projects in the garage.

We have roast beef, mashed potatoes, gravy, boiled broccoli with cheese sauce, and buns. It's a meal I had hundreds of times growing up.

While we eat, the cuckoo clock chimes seven velociraptor barks, and Dad and I erupt in laughter while Mom rolls her eyes. I explain it to Cate, who laughs and offers a home for the clock if my mom ever wants to give it up.

We get through dinner with my parents asking Cate basic questions that thankfully don't make me cringe—her favorite films to work on, the celebrities she's met and which ones are interesting in person, her family, how she got into acting. Cate holds their attention, and I can see my parents growing smitten with her. Slowly, I let go of some of the tension in my shoulders.

Then Dad says, "They can sure get nasty to celebrities on TV and online."

I freeze, silently begging him not to veer any closer to mention of Phil or paparazzi.

"Sadly, it's true," Cate says. "It helps to have a security detail, but my privacy is always on a precipice. The nature of the job, I guess. Every career has its downsides."

"Does it ever," Mom says. "I've had a few jobs in my day—retail, insurance, an admin job at a software company…"

"Dog grooming," Dad adds.

"Nannying," Mom says.

"And good at every single one of those jobs," Dad says.

Mom smiles at him. "But no matter the skill, every job came with a catch."

Cate watches the conversation bounce between my parents, a smile playing on her lips. I remember what she told me about her parents divorcing as a kid, and it hits me how long it must have been since she's seen a marriage like this one. My parents might bicker sometimes, but they've never stopped being in love.

"That's an impressive resume. It sounds like you're a woman of many talents," Cate says, and Mom blushes.

I relax a little, grateful to Mom for guiding the topic away from how awful the media is to Cate. I wonder if she caught my tension when Dad brought it up.

"Rach wanted to be a vet," he says now. "Didn't you? Decided you couldn't handle the sad parts?"

Cate looks at me with interest. I haven't told her about my range of career ambitions.

"I did," I say. "But I also wanted to be a spy when I was a kid, so let's not get carried away."

Mom laughs and pats my arm.

"I wanted to be a war photographer," Cate says.

"Really?" I look at her in surprise.

She nods. "Traveling to far-off places and sharing untold stories appealed to me. Still does. But I'm glad I got into acting. I'm not sure I'm brave enough to run into a war zone with a camera."

I try to imagine Cate as a thrill-seeking photographer. How would that Cate be different from the version of her sitting across from me? Less strained from the pressure of Hollywood, maybe, but more strained from the hardships she would face while traveling.

Maybe some people are meant for careers that put them under pressure. Not everyone is resilient enough for it, but Cate is. Beneath her glamorous exterior, she's rock solid.

"It would suit you," I say. "You'd just be telling stories through pictures instead of through acting."

As Dad goes off about how he's always known he was meant to be a builder, Cate and I hold each other's gaze. Whatever passes between us makes my heart skip. She seems to be enjoying herself, I haven't collapsed from embarrassment, and my parents are acting decently normal.

I think this dinner is going well.

After dessert and tea, we say goodbye with a round of hugs, and Cate thanks my parents for inviting her over. They seem flustered and pleased, which is about how I've felt since the moment I met Cate. Something about her is so charming that it would make anyone blush.

On the way home, she reaches over and takes my hand. "Your parents are so sweet. It's clear they're proud of you."

"That wasn't too awkward?"

"No." She gives me the same look as when Dad was explaining the solar panel to her, the one that sends a deep flutter through me. I'm afraid to ask what she's thinking.

Beyond the windows, the sky turns pink as the sun sets over the pristine mountain range.

Cate lets out a breath and says, "It was perfect."

Chapter 21
Cursed Hotel TVs

"Come on, you can't tell me this isn't hilarious," I say passionately. We're in Cate's hotel, and I'm making her watch a French-Canadian prank show that I loved as a kid. It's eleven p.m., and we're sweaty after marathon sex.

"I just don't get the appeal of making someone think they've let a stranger's Pomeranian fall down a manhole."

I wave my arms at the TV. "Look at the woman's face! That's priceless!"

We dissolve into giggles.

I can't get over the way her face changes when she laughs—the crinkle in her eyes, the way her cheeks lift, the curve of her lips. It's the most beautiful look on her.

"I never watch TV except for when I'm staying in hotels," Cate says, lying back against the pillows.

I curl up next to her. "Same. We don't have cable, and I had to give myself a streaming ban when I started university."

"Dangerous business," she says gravely. "People have wasted away binge-watching."

Her fingers brush up and down my arm, growing slower, sleepier. As we finally settle down, the program ends and there's a commercial for a home renovation show.

"I want to move to Hawaii when I retire," Cate says sleepily. "Imagine being in the tropics year-round."

"You'd move away from LA?"

"In a heartbeat."

"Mm. In a perfect world, I'd live in the tropics for four months out of the year."

"Why four?"

"November to February, when winter sucks here. I'd miss home if it were longer than that."

I feel her gaze on me. The subject of what will happen when filming wraps up lingers on my tongue. Should I ask her? It's been three months since we met, and while I don't want to pressure her into getting serious, I do want to know how she feels. We'll either need to talk about a long-distance relationship, one of us moving, or…

I'd rather not think about the other option.

Afraid of the answer, I leave my question unasked and cuddle closer, letting my body drift into dreamland.

"Rachel Janssen…"

I jolt awake at the sound of my name coming from the TV.

What? Did I dream that?

Cate sits up, staring at the screen.

It's a late-night celebrity news program. Cate's picture is in the top corner.

"…exclusive interview where he broke his long silence about the divorce," says the host, a high-maintenance looking woman with silver-blond hair and absurdly thick eyelashes.

"His *silence?*" Cate says, aghast. "If they think he's being *silent*, I'd hate to see—"

She stops as the program cuts to an interview between the host and Phil Niles. He's wearing a baby blue dress shirt and is clean shaven, looking more approachable than his usual wolfy vibes.

"We were in each other's lives for seven years, you know?" Phil says, soft spoken, nothing like the man I met at the gala. "This is hard for both of us. And with our fans involved…"

"Do you feel support from them?" the woman says, her voice solemn and gentle.

"The public is divided, but it hurts to know that so many are taking my side against Cate. I want to say thank you to my fans, but please be nice to her. I still…I…"

The host leans in. "You still love her?"

Phil nods. "I think I always will. I wish she knew how sorry I am. I've been working on myself—going to therapy, journaling, meditating. It's been a process of growth."

"Wow," the woman says, a hand over her heart, like this is a bombshell. "How do you think she feels?"

"I think she's…" He shifts, sighs, and gives the audience a moment to absorb the pain on his face. "Look, I take responsibility for the role I played in the divorce. But, you know, it takes two, and I hope she takes responsibility for her part in it, too. We both have growing to do."

"What do you think her part is? If you could hear an apology from her—or an admission of some kind."

Phil takes a moment while the camera zooms in, and when he lifts his gaze, his brown eyes are glossy. "I want the truth. I want to know how long she's known she's a lesbian, and I want to know how long she's been involved with that girl."

"You think there could be overlap?"

"Did she cheat on me with this woman? Who am I to say? But the two got cozy pretty fast. I'll be honest, Vanessa—it was tough to see them together." He wipes a veined, muscular arm across his teary eyes.

The show cuts to a commercial for toilet paper, which befits the interview.

Phil's words roil in my stomach. *Fuck—this—guy.*

For him to talk about the divorce like it's Cate's fault, like she coldly shattered his heart, like she cheated on him with me…

Cate gets up and paces the room, scowling, silent.

It infuriates me that he's assuming her sexuality, calling her a lesbian when she might identify differently. Considering she's been in relationships with men, she might identify as bi or otherwise. For him to talk about her sexuality in an interview, to out her like that, is a dick move.

"Are you okay?" I say, the question barely coming out.

She shakes her head once.

I struggle to find words of comfort, fighting the urge to throw something at the TV.

"Nobody believes that you cheated on him," I say, wishing I sounded more confident. "The divorce happened months before we met."

"His fans believe anything he says. I've seen it before. Fuck, this is going to be a mess for me." Cate grabs her nightshirt and puts it on, continuing to pace.

I put on my shirt, too. I'm nauseous. I want to fix this but have no idea what to say. All of my efforts to accept the Hollywood bullshit dissipate, and Cate is growing more distant by the second.

What's going to happen once the world sees this interview? Will the nasty comments start coming in tenfold? What if Phil Niles fans start coming at me?

The program resumes, the silver-blond woman looking energized by the juicy interview clip she just showed.

"Phil's accusation is justified," she says to the camera. "That *exclusive* interview happened shortly before I found out that Cate Whitney allegedly admitted to *cheating* on her boyfriend in high school with a *bisexual* girl. Did she repeat old behavior and cheat on Phil Niles? Is Cate's hidden sexuality and adulterous behavior what split the—"

Cate snatches the remote and turns off the TV. The abrupt silence and darkness are jarring. Streetlights beyond the sheer, white privacy curtains turn the room a dull yellow.

I stand, horrified that the host would slander her like that. "Cate…"

"How did that get out?" Cate says.

"What?" I say, mind whirling.

"Sandra. She was talking about—about what I told you." She doesn't meet my eye.

The implication hangs.

"I didn't repeat that to anyone," I say, a little sharp.

Does she think I sold the story of her sexual orientation? Of course I wouldn't do that. The fact that her brain even went there is insulting.

When the silence stretches on, I say, "You don't trust me?"

"It's not that, it's… Things slip, sometimes. Or a friend or roommate overhears, or—"

"I didn't tell anyone, Cate, and I didn't let it slip," I say fiercely.

"Okay," she says, sounding no more reassured.

She's deep in her own head again, thinking hard, eyes darting over the floor.

"What, then?" I ask. "Talk to me."

When she meets my gaze, her expression has hardened. "What do you want me to say?"

My throat tightens with emotion. She's shutting down, and I don't know how to get her to come back to me. "Tell me what you're thinking!"

"I'm thinking," she says, voice rising, "about what a fucking mess this is, and how Phil came across as a puppy I decided to kick, and how I'm going to have to retaliate with a bombshell interview of my own, and how this is going to pit our fanbases against each other and make for some miserable public appearances, and how, if I don't do enough damage control, this could affect my entire public image and career. Most of all, I'm thinking that I need to be more careful with what I confide in people. I knew this already, and I was an idiot to let my guard down."

I open my mouth, all of her worries crashing over me. They're valid, and I want to be there to support her—but the last one stings. Does she honestly feel like she can't confide in me? "You can lower your guard with me, Cate!"

"Everyone likes to think they're a loyal friend, but money is the strongest motivator, no matter who you are. It's human nature to compromise our morals for money."

"I disagree," I say, and not just because I'm defending myself. "I think the strongest motivator is love." My voice catches. I swallow hard.

Cate sits on the edge of the bed and drops her face into her hands. "Sometimes I think it's better to be alone in this business," she says, voice muffled.

I shake my head, feet rooted. "It's not. Don't say that."

"It's too hard to be in a relationship, Rachel. I want to trust you, but my—my profession doesn't allow for it. I have to be careful. One wrong step and my image is ruined."

"That shallow TV gossip doesn't matter, Cate. Ignore the outside world." My throat is painfully tight, and my advice is so damn hypocritical. I haven't been great at ignoring public opinion, so why should I expect anyone else to be?

Cate says nothing, still not looking at me.

A long silence passes.

Then she says, barely audible, "I can't believe he still loves me."

Bile creeps up my throat. What does that matter? Why does it mean anything to her?

"You—you didn't know?" I say, the words barely coming out.

"I thought that was just the press spinning it that way."

"But there were interviews. Headlines. I saw one—"

"I don't have social media, Rachel, nor do I look up my name online," she says, snappy.

I shut my mouth, tears burning.

I want her to clarify but my throat is too tight to speak. Does learning that Phil still loves her change anything?

I could shout that those were fake tears coming out of that bastard's eyes, and he's probably not journaling and meditating, and he's a manipulative liar who's trying to win over the public. But that wouldn't help. It would only make Cate feel worse.

Cate's phone rings.

"I need to take this," she says, her tone cold. She doesn't meet my eye.

A knot forms in my stomach. I've been so absorbed in my struggle to come to terms with celebrity life that I never realized Cate has issues to come to terms with, too—and she doesn't trust me enough to confide what they are. What are her feelings about Phil, exactly? How does she usually deal with shitty press and slanderous interviews?

"Do you still care about—"

"I don't want to talk about this, Rachel. I don't want to talk about anything with anyone, okay?"

The ringing goes on, much too loud, filling the room.

I grind my teeth, eyes brimming. "I'm doing my best to adjust to all of this, Cate. I guess my best isn't enough."

"It's not about you—"

"I know it's not. It's about both of us. We're both being attacked here, so we could at least stick together."

She meets my eyes, and she's vacant. It's like I'm looking at her while she's sleepwalking.

The pressure has built for too long, and now, we're both cracking. I was never strong enough for this to begin with, but Cate? I guess her seemingly rock-solid interior is more brittle than I thought.

She answers the phone before it can go to voicemail. "Hi, Mandy. Can you hold on one minute?"

She looks at me expectantly—waiting for me to leave, I guess.

Anger bubbles inside me. I'm fighting for us, and she can only be cold and dismissive.

"Fine. You take some time and text me when you're ready to talk." I snatch up my clothes and get dressed.

I can't decide if I'm furious with Cate or sad for her—or both. If she needs to process this, okay. But I haven't done anything wrong, and she'd better come to that conclusion.

"We're on the same side, Cate," I say as I open the door.

Without looking back, I grab my bag and leave the hotel, wiping tears from my eyes.

CHAPTER 22
The End of Summer

PHIL'S ACCUSATIONS AND THE SURROUNDING gossip spread like a wildfire over the next few days, adding to the permanent tightness in my chest. I walk the beach for hours, getting sunburned, waves hissing in my ears, the bottoms of my feet sore from stepping on rocks and shells barefoot.

Cate and I were supposed to be in this together—us against bad press. So why am I alone in dealing with this?

Abby is here for me, of course, full of insults for Phil and his supporters. Mom called to ask whether that interview was true and offered words of comfort when I told her what happened, which made me break down in tears after we hung up. But Cate? Not even a text. It's an effort not to stand on the balcony and look down at the set, just to check if she's still real.

After four days, I grit my teeth and call her while I'm walking the beach, expecting her to have blocked my number.

But the phone stops ringing, and there's a beat of background noise, and a soft "hi."

"Hi," I say, mouth dry. I keep walking, treading slowly over the rocks.

Cate waits.

I didn't plan what I would say. I didn't think she would answer.

If she's been dealing with the same attention as I have over the last few days, she's probably not doing great.

"Are you okay?" I say, forcing my legs to keep walking.

"I can't talk about this, Rachel."

I grip my phone tighter. "I thought we'd made it to a place where you would talk to me when something upset you. That's what couples do."

"This is different. This isn't just something that's upsetting me. This is a harsh reality. Mandy is in a frenzy, and we've been on damage control all week."

My heart sinks. "That many people believe Phil?"

"You're underestimating his fanbase," she says, her tone as sharp as a knife. "We're going to be up to our necks in statements and interviews for the next while. As if I fucking have time for that."

I step on a jagged rock and curse, regaining my balance by stepping on several more jagged rocks. My eyes water. "If you're getting interviews, that's good, isn't it? You can tell everyone the truth about how he treated you."

She's quiet for a moment. Shouts and clanking fill the background. I'm close enough to the set that the same sounds echo in the distance and through the phone. It's a reminder of how close we are to each other, even though it feels like we're a world apart right now.

"I don't want to go there," Cate says. "I don't want my public image to have the word *victim* attached to it. I don't want to fight him in another legal battle after we finally got over the first one. And I sure as hell don't want to drag my fleeting high school crush into all of this."

I watch my step, walking slower, but the stones are getting hard to see behind my blurry vision.

"And this all came back to that fucking *story*," Cate says. "Me cheating in high school."

"You were thirteen and curious," I choke out. "They can't pretend—"

"The public doesn't care. Phil has been hurt by women before, and as far as they're concerned, I'm the bitch who's hurting him again. I've had to—" Her voice catches, and she clears her throat. "It makes me reconsider things. Letting someone into my life is self-destructive."

"Reconsider?" I say, the word barely coming out.

But it's not like this is coming out of nowhere. She told me she's been betrayed before. I've experienced the media and paparazzi. I've obviously underestimated how much pressure Cate is under and everything she's had to deal with over the years.

"If I hadn't told you that story about Sandra, he wouldn't have had so much kindling to work with."

A long silence passes. The implication that I'm the only link between that story and other ears swells between us. I don't know what else I can say to convince Cate that I didn't tell anyone about it.

"I thought I made it clear that I would never spill your secrets." I swallow hard, trying not to cry. "Are you having a crisis about life in the spotlight, or are you genuinely wondering whether you can trust me?"

Her breath hits the phone. "I want to trust you, but I really can't, Rachel. It's a fact that I need to accept about my career. I can't let my guard down for anyone. It's nothing personal—"

"It sure as hell is! Nothing has ever been more personal! After spending all summer together?"

She pauses. "I enjoyed the summer. But reality caught up with us, and my dwindling free time is going to be spent mending my public image for the next few weeks."

I can't hold back the tears anymore. They spill from my eyes, and my throat is unbearably tight. "That's it, then? We had a fun summer and it's over because of something I didn't even do?"

"It's over because my life has no room for it."

The breath leaves my lungs. I scrunch my face, trying not to break down. I wish I could unhear that sentence. But she said it, and there's no going back. *It's over.*

"Look, Rachel, filming is wrapping up soon, and they need me here on weekends. Between that and publicity, I'm out of free time." Her voice seems to come from a long way away, drifting at the edge of my hearing.

"Sure," I say. "Well, good luck."

I end the call without a goodbye, my throat too tight to say it.

I step on another sharp stone and curse, stopping for a moment to regain my balance. Everything Cate said loops in my mind, leaving me short of breath.

It's nothing personal.

My life has no room for it.

Reality caught up with us.

Was this whole summer a dream? She didn't think of our relationship as real life?

When I get back from my walk—sweaty, miserable, and dehydrated—I spend the whole evening continually picking up my phone to text her, then stopping with my thumbs over the keypad.

What is there to say?

It's over.

She made that clear.

The next day, I leave my phone behind. And the day after that. I spend my waking hours in the next week away from my phone, doing research in the library and walking the beach in the hours when I can't focus.

I fell too hard for Cate. I should have known I was in trouble when I brought her to meet my parents and saw the way she looked at my house, my family, my memories.

A word drifts at the edge of my consciousness and I block it, refusing to let it materialize.

I can't go there. She doesn't feel the same.

For the first time, uitwaaien is failing me. Over a week of walking the beach and my mood is no better.

Friday rolls in, rainy and cool, and I leave the beach shivering. My feet are numb from the water and there's seaweed between my toes.

I don't know how I'll ever get over her.

When I get home, Abby is in her room, watching something that involves a lot of epic music and battle cries.

I check my phone and open Instagram to try and cheer myself up with cute dog pictures.

A lot of notifications are waiting for me in the app. Friends and strangers still manage to tag me in stuff, even though I made everything private.

I curse under my breath. Maybe it's time to delete my social media profiles and say goodbye to following cute dogs and food blogs.

I flop down on the couch and tap the first tag. Apparently, all of these people are eager for me to look at a paparazzi shot of Cate and Phil kissing, bodies pressed together, his hands cupping her face, hers resting on his broad chest. They look so perfect that they could be posing for an engagement photo. Her blond hair gleams in the sun, skin tanned, back arched.

"Yeah, and?" I mumble with a spark of anger. Obviously they would have kissed before, given that they were married.

The caption on the post reads, *Are Phil and Cate an item again?*

I blink at the picture.

Cate is in her steampunk outfit.

What?

If she's filming *Clockwork Curie*, does that mean this picture was taken recently? Like, since we met?

The post is from today.

"No," I say, standing.

There's no way the two of them made up. Would Cate honestly forgive him after the way he treated me—after the accusations he made? Would she go back to him that quickly?

Pacing the living room, I call her. The phone rings and rings until her voicemail picks up.

Surely that kiss didn't happen and it's a photo manipulation.

Unless she was lying to me about lingering feelings for Phil. She's good at acting, after all.

I shake my head, dismissing the thought. There has to be an explanation. I haven't known Cate for long, but I've known her intimately, and she wouldn't do this.

I call her again, hand trembling over my phone, tears threatening to spill.

Voicemail.

Maybe she's in the middle of shooting a scene.

The other part of the photo I don't like is that it means Phil Niles was here, in Vancouver, on set with her.

Is he still here?

Most importantly, *why* is he here?

"Abby," I say, my voice coming out sharper than I expected.

The battle cries and epic music stop. Abby's feet hit the floor and she steps out of her bedroom, eyes wide.

"I think—I don't know what's going on." I show her my phone. "Phil Niles is in Vancouver, and there's a picture of him and Cate kissing. I think this was taken, like, yesterday. Maybe even today. I should go down there, right? To the movie set?"

She stares at the photo, brow furrowed. "This was just taken?"

"Look at her costume."

Someone knocks on the door.

Abby and I freeze.

"Did you order food?" she asks.

I shake my head.

Is it Cate? Did she miss my call because she was in the elevator?

No, she never buzzed in.

Whoever is on the other side of the door got in without my letting them into the building. It's happened before—usually someone letting a delivery person in behind them.

But I'm not expecting anyone.

"Maybe it's Jehovah's Witnesses," Abby says. "Or Girl Guides selling cookies."

I leave her and tiptoe to the door to peer through the peephole.

My heart jumps into my throat.

Phil Niles is standing on the other side.

CHAPTER 23
NO SOLICITING

AVIATOR SUNGLASSES HIDE PHIL'S EYES. His salt-and-pepper hair is perfectly styled and swept to one side. He's in a black polo shirt, his muscles straining out of the sleeves.

I step back from the peephole and clap a hand over my mouth to stop from swearing.

"Is it him?" Abby whispers, barely audible.

"Yeah."

What does he want?

He knocks again and I jump.

"Rachel? Can I talk to you?" His tone isn't aggressive. In fact, he sounds worried.

Worried about Cate?

I look at the ceiling, inwardly cursing. I don't want to open the door, but it would be super weird and confrontational not to, wouldn't it?

Abby is with me. She'll back me up.

I glance back at Abby, who nods, rooted on the other side of the kitchen. She doesn't seem to care that she's pantsless.

I draw a breath and open the door.

"How did you get into the building?" I say, standing in a way that does not invite him to come in.

He raises an eyebrow. "I'm Phil Niles, sweetheart."

Pompous ass.

"Where's Cate?" I ask.

"Busy."

Okay, so his tone of concern was acting.

I wish he would take off those sunglasses so I can see his eyes. Instead, I'm treated to my reflection in the lenses—and I look small, afraid.

He moves to walk past me and I block him, palms out. "I'd rather you didn't come in."

He hesitates for half a second before pushing past me anyway. His dark eyes rove over Abby and the apartment, and his mouth quirks like he finds my life amusing.

My pulse pounds in my eardrums. "Why are you here?"

Phil sighs. "Love triangles are so passé, Rachel."

This is rich, coming from a guy whose most famous role is one where the lead woman is trying to choose between him and another werewolf.

"Who says this is a love triangle? We were in a monogamous relationship, and you butted into it!"

He shakes his head and looks at his phone. After an infuriatingly long pause, he holds it up to show me the picture of him and Cate kissing.

"I saw that," I say flatly, trying not to betray the confusion and fear rampaging through me.

"Then you know how she feels about me."

"If she feels so strongly about you, then why are you here threatening me?"

He steps closer, right in my face, and says softly, "Do you honestly think you're good enough for her? Do you think she cares about a science student after being married to me?"

I bark out a note of laughter. "After being with me, I wonder why she ever cared about a self-centered ass in the first place."

A tremor runs through me as the words come out. I sound more confident than I feel. I want to believe it, but in truth, I'm a mess of a human. I'm swamped in student debt, I have no time for hobbies or friends, and I barely have my shit together. Before meeting Cate, I tried to hook up with a woman who has a boyfriend, for fuck's sake. How did this summer with Cate even happen?

"I thought I made myself clear at the gala, sweetheart—"

"Okay, that's enough from you," Abby says firmly. "Get out. Right now."

"Who are you, her other girlfriend?" Phil says.

"I'm Abigail Yousefi, and you're in my apartment." She grabs a kitchen chair on the way over and holds it like a wrestler ready to use it. With the other hand, she holds up her phone like a weapon. "You have three seconds or I'm calling the cops."

"Everyone, chill," I say, holding my palms out to each of them.

"Why?" Abby snaps. "You didn't invite him here."

I open and close my mouth. I'm not sure why I told her to chill. It's like some part of me is treading carefully because he's a celebrity. Like I'm afraid of who he is and how much power he has over me—afraid of upsetting a man in his position.

Which is bullshit.

"No," I say with an apologetic glance at Abby. "Phil, I don't know what's going on between you and Cate or why she kissed you after all of the shit you've pulled, but you got your wish. I won't see her again. Now get out of my apartment."

My heart aches, but Cate told me we're done, and I'm not going to fight for her if she still cares about Phil. She has the right to make her own decisions. I can't force her to love me.

Footsteps thunder down the hall, and Cate appears in the doorway, panting.

My heart leaps at the sight of her. She's wearing flowy blue pants, a white sleeveless blouse, and white flats, with her hair and makeup still professionally done from filming.

"You liar," she says, pointing at Phil, her teeth bared like she's ready to rip into him.

"Cate!" he says, like he's surprised to see her here.

"I knew as soon as you disappeared that it didn't feel right," she shouts, a wild look in her eye. "Sean showed me that nasty stunt you pulled. Fuck you."

Phil opens his arms apologetically. "Come on, Kitty. You know I have your best interests—"

"Don't—call—me—that," Cate says through gritted teeth.

My heart stutters. What's going on?

"Cate," I say, her name bittersweet. "The picture of you two—"

174

"It's my stunt double," she spits out. "He wanted to make it look like we're still in love. You'd better get the fuck away from here, Phil, because you can be sure I'm getting that restraining order."

I should be relieved that Cate didn't kiss Phil, but relief is the last thing I'm feeling. Anger bubbles inside me that he would do this to her—to *us*.

Phil puts on a puppy-eyed face I've seen on TV before. It's the face fangirls swoon over. "Don't overreact, Kitty."

"Overreact? You've been telling the world I cheated on you! I was loyal until the excruciating end."

"Kitty—"

"Don't!" Cate shouts.

"Oh, just admit that you've been lying, Phil," I say, beyond done with all of this. "You've been making shit up to try and come off as the heartbroken victim."

Phil opens and closes his mouth as he seems to debate what to say. Finally, the words burst from his lips. "It's not just about my image. I wanted you to see that you made a mistake. I love you, Kitty, and I miss everything we had."

Cate steps back, expression stunned.

"And you show that by getting the public to choose sides against her?" I ask with a note of laughter, though there's nothing funny about his fucked-up thought process.

I can't decide whether to feel sorry for him or hate him. Maybe he does love her and is heartbroken, but his way of dealing with it is completely unacceptable.

"I thought the public opinion would help sway you," Phil says, still addressing Cate. "If everyone thinks you're wrong, then sooner or later, you'd realize that you are. I deserve another chance. We were so good together. Please, don't throw that away."

Cate growls in frustration. "So you made up a story about me cheating on you to manipulate the media to take your side?"

"It didn't come out of nowhere," he says. "It's a possibility, isn't it?"

"Oh, come on," I say. "She and I met months after you got divorced and you know it."

"But you cheated on your high school boyfriend," he says to Cate, "and that means you could cheat again."

Cate throws her hands in the air. "For fuck's sake, Phil! That's completely irrelevant—"

I gasp. "It was you! You sold the story of her kissing a girl. How did you hear about it?"

He grits his teeth, like he wants to tear me to shreds. "I heard the story from Ricky. He overheard you and I sold the tip to the media. Happy? Is that what you want to hear?"

There's a brief, heavy silence. It doesn't matter who Ricky is—the knowledge of how that story got out is an infinitesimal relief. It wasn't me, and now Cate has confirmation that I never betrayed her.

"Fuck you, Phil!" Cate screams, and she takes off her shoe and throws it at him.

"Hey!" he roars, flinching as the shoe hits his chest.

"You lying bastard. You don't get to follow me to Vancouver and invade my privacy. You don't get to sell bits of my personal life in order to manipulate me into crawling back to you."

Cate throws the other shoe, and Phil catches it this time. A wolfy expression crosses his face, and a muscle in his jaw flexes.

The threatening look he gives Cate is my last straw. Any hint of pity I felt for him vanishes beneath a rush of anger. I step forward, pulse pounding in my ears. "Get out of my home. *Now.*"

He rounds on me. "Stay out of—"

"Leave!" I grab his arm, trying to direct him toward the door.

I'm done with him and I'm done with all of this. I want to go back to my life the way it was a few months ago—just me and Abby and school and my houseplants.

Phil jerks away from my grasp hard enough to make me stumble. I stagger sideways and grab the counter for balance.

Abby gasps.

"Phil!" Cate cries.

I raise my fists, ready for him to get in my face, yell, swear at me—but he stops. He's frozen with his jaw set and his fists clenched. For some reason, his gaze fixes on Abby. His eyes widen and he steps back.

"I know a lost cause when I see one," he says, his tone soft. "I'll leave you to your life, then."

Eyes brimming, he storms out of the apartment, leaving me with my heart pounding out of my chest.

Beyond the open door, several neighbors are looking in, their hands over their mouths, their phones up to either record the incident or call the police.

Cate is breathing hard, her hands up by her temples, her eyes full of tears.

Abby lowers her phone. "Got all of that on video," she says casually. "Cool that he admitted to being a lying dick on camera."

CHAPTER 24
HEAVY BAGGAGE

AFTER APOLOGIZING TO THE NEIGHBORS and assuring them that we're okay, Abby retreats to her room to give Cate and me a minute.

Cate's eyes are pink around the edges, with more tears brimming. "Rachel, I'm so sorry. I never thought he would come to your home like this."

I shake my head, scrunching my face against the tears threatening to spill down my own face. "I can't handle this anymore. I've heard so many apologies from you, and I know none of this is your fault, but…God, Cate, this is so far beyond anything I've ever dealt with. *Him*, the paparazzi, tabloids, all of the internet bullshit. I never wanted any of this."

"I know." She opens and closes her mouth like she's debating how to continue, then shakes her head and rubs a hand under her eyes. The way she does it is careful, like she's spent a lifetime figuring out how to wipe her tears without smudging her makeup.

"And then *you*," I say, voice cracking. "I told myself that being with you makes it all worth it. But I tried so hard, and you wouldn't even trust me. You were so quick to jump to the conclusion that I betrayed you and sold your secrets."

Cate steps closer, eyes pleading. "I'm so sorry. It happened to me before, and my brain just…went there."

"With me, though? You think I would betray you?"

She gives a feeble shrug, dropping her gaze.

"Phil said a guy named Ricky overheard us," I say. "Was he the one with the boom mic and all the tattoos? He was the only person nearby."

Cate nods. "I knew him when I was with Phil. I should have clued in that they were still friends."

"But you had to hear it from someone else before you decided I wasn't the one to spill your secret."

She slumps, eyes glossy. "I don't know what to say except that I'm sorry."

"Okay. Apology accepted. I guess I'll see you around, then."

I cross my arms, waiting for her to leave, but she doesn't.

"Rachel, I've missed you since we last spoke. If—if you give me a chance, I can work on myself."

I blink. "Give you a chance? You broke up with me."

She looks so sad and ashamed that my heart shatters all over again.

I look at the ceiling, blinking back tears, and draw a breath. I should be weak at the knees at her change of heart. She wants me back.

But even if I agree to another chance, our relationship would forever be on the edge of a precipice, ready to topple at the lightest touch. "How do you think I feel, knowing I'm untrustworthy unless proven otherwise?"

"I know."

"And even if you do figure out how to trust me, I—" I swallow hard. "I don't think I have the emotional strength for this. I tried to deal with the cameras, the media, online bullying, every nasty part of this whole fucking situation, but Phil coming to my house? I'm not cut out for the life you have."

Mom was right all those weeks ago. I shouldn't be involved with a celebrity. I'm in my early twenties and supposed to be two feet into building my career, not spiraling into an abyss of relationship troubles and public image catastrophes.

"That's fair," Cate whispers.

Our gazes lock. It's hard to breathe.

"It was a good summer," I say. "I'm glad it happened."

She nods.

"This is the last week of filming," she says, barely a whisper. "Just so you know."

The words wash over me because it's impossible to feel any worse right now.

"Okay."

She doesn't meet my gaze before turning and leaving, a hand over her mouth. I wish she had, just to give me one last look into her eyes.

But that might make it worse. Neither of us is strong enough to make this relationship work. Cate won't trust me because the world has been cruel to her, and I'm a coward who never learned to accept the tough parts of her life. I can't handle fame, and I've been foolish to think I can date a celebrity.

So I let her walk down the hallway and get into the elevator—and the best woman I've ever met in my life is gone.

———⟡———

The next morning, I'm eating oatmeal at the table when Abby sits across from me, her hands clasped, with the air of someone about to bring up a serious topic.

"What?" I ask flatly, spoon hovering.

"What would you like me to do with the video of Phil Niles losing his shit?"

I sit back, anger flaring inside me like a volcano about to destroy the nearest village. Any reservations I've had about appearing online are secondary to my absolute rage toward that genital wart of a human.

"Post it," I say venomously. "Share it all over the internet and show everyone what kind of person he is. Tag the media and make sure they see it."

Abby grins, jumping to her feet and giving me a salute. "You got it, boss. I was hoping you'd say something like that. You deserve better than what that asshole did to you, and the world needs to see it."

As hollow as I feel, her loyalty warms me a little.

Two hours later, I'm on the couch with my laptop when she emerges from her bedroom.

"I sold the video. I'll e-transfer you half."

I blink. "Sold? Like, the media paid you for it? With money?"

Abby nods and shows me her phone. "It's trending on Twitter."

I push the phone away before I can accidentally see the video. The prospect of reliving that moment churns my stomach.

She puts the kettle on. While the water boils, she rewatches the video, much to my dismay.

I try to focus on the wall of text on my laptop. *Image segmentation with deep learning algorithms.*

"I wanted you to see that you made a mistake," Phil says.

Multimodal medical imaging.

"…you made up a story about me cheating on you…" Cate says.

I play jazz music, turning up the volume to drown out the video.

Cate's voice rises over it. "Fuck you, Phil!"

The part where I thought I would need self-defense is coming. I scrunch my face, as if that'll close my ear canals.

I can't tell if I regret publicizing what he did. He deserved to be exposed, and people needed to know the truth, but I didn't like doing it.

I'm about to ask Abby to spare me and mute it when she says, "Wow, the comments are overwhelmingly good. People are screaming for you to get a public apology."

"An apology from who?" I ask.

"From everyone who said you weren't good enough for Cate. The media, trolls, Phil… You look like a hero who put up with unjust bad press."

I should feel relieved and victorious, but even if that video helps my case in the public eye, it doesn't change the fact that Cate and I broke up.

I stand by my decision not to take her back. Even though Cate apologized, I'm not convinced that this won't happen again. I should be with someone who is willing to trust me.

And Cate should be with someone who can handle the limelight.

I force a grin. "Thanks, Abby."

She must see through me because she gives me a sad smile.

I lean back in my chair and sigh. "It's for the best, right? Me and Cate splitting?"

"Hm…" Abby grabs her favorite hazelnut instant coffee from the cupboard, which to me tastes like it's been burnt to ash, rolled in high-fructose corn syrup, and dipped in some dirt where a hazelnut tree used to grow. "She made a big mistake, pushing you away for something you didn't do. I hope she knows it."

I picture the look on Cate's face before I asked her to leave yesterday. "I think she does."

"Do you feel better having broken up? Some sense of relief?"

"Yes?" I say, my tone completely unconvincing. When Abby raises an eyebrow, I add, "Well, I hated fame. Phil showing up here was one too many sour moments, and I'm over it."

"You hated *everything* about Hollywood life? Even the gala?"

"Especially the gala! Are you forgetting what happened?"

"Before the security incident, I mean. Did you hate the part where you got to fly to LA in first class, wear a designer tux, and talk to A-listers while on Cate's arm?"

I scowl at her. Because I didn't hate that part. And now I'm more confused.

Abby grabs her mug, which says in Comic Sans, *I like my coffee like I like my men.* I wonder if that means she likes them cheap and instant or burnt to ash.

"Babe, if dating Cate was seriously affecting your well-being, then, yeah, it was the right call," she says. "It's worth taking some time to think about things."

I nod, a little reassured.

She mixes her ash-syrup-dirt coffee and heads back to her room.

"Hey, can you set me up on a date with your gay teammate?" I ask, blurting the words before I can chicken out.

She raises an eyebrow. "That wasn't exactly *some time to think.*"

"I have a fast brain. I need to get over Cate, and going on a few dates is the best way to do it, right?"

Abby gives me a half smile. "It's your call. Yeah, going on a date might help you sort out your feelings."

I can't quite read her tone, but it doesn't matter. She agrees to set us up, and I'm ready to move on from this ache in my chest.

I turn back to my laptop with a scowl. Abby's teammate had better be so charming that I forget Cate Whitney even exists.

Her name is Jaz, short for Jazmine. We go to an improv show, and I've got to hand it to Abby for having good judgment. Jaz is funny, flirty, androgynous, and incredibly smooth. By the time we sit, she's got her arm around me.

"I'm pointing to you if they ask for volunteers," she says.

I laugh and nudge her. "Don't you dare."

The improv show starts, and she's got hilarious ideas every time they ask for audience suggestions. She's probably the coolest person I've ever met, and I should be making heart-eyes at her while silently congratulating myself for landing such a hot date.

Except watching the actors reminds me of watching Cate act out her scenes, and being on a date makes me wish she was the one with her arm around me. I almost ordered a Moscow Mule at the bar, and the mere thought of that drink put a lump in my throat. I can't stop thinking about how her body feels against mine, how she smells like coconut and summer, how her eyes crinkle when she smiles.

My chest hurts.

On stage, an improv team plays the one-word-story game, and everyone is laughing. To me, it's obnoxious. I don't want to laugh right now.

I run through my reasons, needing to reaffirm my decision. *Lack of trust, tabloids, paparazzi, strangers with cameras, celebrity galas, jealous ex-husbands... I should be with someone more average...*

Those reasons suddenly feel weak. Cate tried to apologize, and I could give her another chance if I wanted to. Can't I learn to get over having my photo on the cover of a trashy magazine? Can't I block and ignore everything that comes at me from the internet? Why is this so hard for me?

Jaz laughs at whatever is happening onstage. A props game. One of the actors is playing an upside-down vase like a bongo. I sip my beer, trying to look like I'm paying attention.

All of that aside, the local buzz is that *Clockwork Curie* will be done shooting tomorrow. That means Cate will return to California.

Our relationship was never meant to be a long-term thing. It had to end.

Except I was happier than ever this summer. Every moment I spent with her was a gift—even the weird moments like hiding in a changeroom to escape the paparazzi. Nobody has ever made me smile so much before.

Could I forgive her?

During intermission, we line up for the bar and Jaz says, "I used to do improv."

"Oh?" I say, suddenly aware that I'm not being very conversational. "Um, did you like it?"

"It was fun. Pretty amateur, but the fact that we sucked made it less stressful."

"I would've thought that constantly flopping would make it worse," I say teasingly.

Jaz buys our drinks and I thank her.

"I guess when you do any sort of performance, there's always the fear of making a bad joke." She tilts her head so that a dark curl falls across her eye. "Laughter is fuel when you're up there, and you care deeply about a good audience response."

"I can imagine."

"It sucks when you miss, but you do it anyway," she says with a shrug.

I nod and sip my drink. Everyone onstage tonight cares about a good reception, but they don't let the fear of a bad performance stop them. They learn to have a tough skin. They keep showing up because despite their fears coming true once in a while, it's worth it. Sometimes you flop, but that's part of the deal.

"Jaz, do you think some baggage is worth enduring?" I ask.

She looks at me with an eyebrow raised. "Baggage? Like, the shit people carry into a relationship?"

"Never mind," I say. God, why did I say that out loud on a first date?

After a pause, Jaz says, "My ex had two cats. I'm allergic to cats. I kept dating her because she was worth living on antihistamines for. Does that count?"

My lips pull into a smile. "Yes."

We head back to our seats and watch the second half of the show, where the actors and audience all have a good time—no matter how many jokes flop.

When the show ends and Jaz and I leave, she says, "I had a great time."

"Me too," I lie.

We're silent as we cross the street to get to our cars.

"I can tell you're heartbroken and not super into this," she says.

Shit.

I stop and face her, ashamed for being a bummer tonight. "Jaz, I'm sorry—"

"Don't. I've been there."

"It's not you. I have a lot to think about. I'm a bit of a mess right now. You're cool, and you deserve better than what I was dishing out tonight."

She nods, looking a little sad but also like nothing can take away her confidence. God, she's cool.

"I won't expect a text from you," Jaz says. "But if you decide you want to see me again, that would be great."

I nod. "Thanks. I really did enjoy your company tonight. I'm just…not ready for dating, apparently."

We part ways with a hug and go to our cars, which are parked adjacent to each other.

"Hey," she calls out as she opens her door. "Life's full of baggage, you know? Some of it is heavier than others, but it's always there. Nothing's perfect, and that's a good thing. Life would be pretty boring and easy if there were no challenges."

She winks, gets in her car, and drives away.

And she's got a point.

I've been calling fame baggage, but maybe it's just a challenge—and challenges are meant to be overcome. Other people learn how to deal with bad press and unwanted attention, so why can't I?

There are things I can do to make fame more tolerable. I can ignore headlines, purge social media from my life, and focus on living here and now. Strangers' opinions don't have to affect me. I can choose to focus on myself, on Cate, and on our life together. I can welcome all of the lovely people who support us and ignore the rest.

Above all, I need to take control of my fear. It's time to face the trauma that's haunted me through all of this.

Chapter 25
Bullies

When I get home and tell Abby that I ruined my date with Jaz, she isn't surprised.

"I knew you regretted pushing Cate away," she says, her eyes on the TV. She's playing some Viking video game I've never seen before. "Christ, I'll have to apologize to Jaz for setting her up with a disaster."

I grimace, flopping next to her on the couch.

"Do you think Cate would take you back?" Abby says.

"I...don't know," I say honestly. "I was pretty firm about our worlds being too different."

"And yet, opposites attract."

I rub my face. "I have to work on my issues."

"Your mental health is the priority," Abby says, mashing the controller buttons. "You don't deserve to be dragged on the internet, and if it bothers you that much, then you should stay broken up. But if you really care about her and want to get over your—I mean, your anxieties are totally valid. It's just...it's possible that you could learn to overcome them."

She gives me a sidelong glance, and if I'm not mistaken, she's uncomfortable. It's a rare look on her. I appreciate that she's trying to choose her words carefully.

"I know. You're right," I say. But from here, I'm not sure where to go. My aversion to attention is part of me and it has been for years. "How do you do it, Abby? You walk around the apartment in your underwear with the windows wide open." I nod to the glass patio door.

She shrugs. "I've never cared much about others' opinions. You can't control other people, and you especially can't control what they think. What's the point in worrying about that? The only thoughts that matter are your own. I like my ass, and if our neighbors across the street don't, they can close their blinds."

I chew my lip. Is fear of other people's opinions the reason I'm bothered by fame? If I cared less, it wouldn't matter what was posted online or talked about on entertainment programs. It wouldn't matter what anyone gossiped about. My opinion is the only one I should care about.

I've never felt good enough for Cate, but, really, the only people who told me I'm not good enough were Phil Niles and some trolls on the internet. If I ignore them and let myself believe that I am good enough, all the signs say that I am. Cate flat-out told me that she's into me, and here I am, insecure about it.

"I guess I've been caring too much about what other people gossip about," I say.

"You shouldn't, because you're awesome," Abby says. "Not that my opinion matters."

My lips curve into a smile. I *am* awesome. I'm smart and fun and pretty hot when I manage to get enough sleep. Why wouldn't Cate Whitney be into me?

"Thanks, buddy," I say.

I stand, stretch until my spine cracks, and head to my room to get ready for bed.

When Cate and I met for drinks the first time, her interpretation of radioactivity struck me. Right now, I feel like I'm the one self-destructing and harming everything around me. I'm struggling with my scary new reality and hurting the woman I care about in the process.

Across my bedroom, the closed curtains sway in the breeze, looking the same as always. In the four years that I've lived here, I've only touched them to dust the windowsill.

Now, I stride across the room and pull them open, letting in the city lights. The ambient glow turns my walls and floor orange. The street looks gorgeous from this angle. The ocean is visible, a strip of dark water with twinkling lights reflecting off the surface.

A sense of peace overcomes me.

While Abby swears at her game in the living room, I grab my laptop and sit on my bed.

Since meeting Cate, I've been forced to revisit what happened in high school. Before, I could avoid being in pictures by turning away and shielding my face. It became a habit, something people stopped questioning. Those who didn't know my story assumed I was shy.

Lately, I've had to think about that incident, talk about it, and try to move past it.

And I've failed.

Yes, Cate was wrong to mistrust me, and she has to work on herself in order for this relationship to work—but I have to work on myself too. Therapy will be part of it, but there's also something I can do right now.

I open Facebook, and for the first time ever, I type my high school bully's name into the search.

Lauren's profile picture takes me a long minute to process. Her face is older, rounder, and happier. She cut off her long brunette locks and is sporting a pixie cut. In school, it never occurred to me how rough she looked, but comparing my memory of her to this picture, she's taken care of herself since then.

I scroll her page. She's married to a handsome realtor. There are a few pictures of them with a dog—they have a rescued greyhound. She's shared some posts about volunteering, some pictures from charity organizations, and she's posted videos of herself speaking at some events.

After a moment, I stop, absorbing the trend in her posts. She volunteers at a child protection charity, and she shares a lot of posts supporting victims of childhood abuse. She's even done public speaking gigs to talk about it.

I don't want to jump to conclusions—it could be a cause she cares about for various reasons—but this might explain a lot about the way she behaved in school.

I rub a hand over my face. This doesn't change the fact that she bullied me and ruined my relationship with Sarah, but it helps to understand that she was fighting her own demons. I was the unfortunate target of her misery.

I hope she's found inner peace. Through loved ones and self-care, it looks like she has.

I should have done this a long time ago.

Fingers trembling, I type Sarah's name next.

It takes me a few minutes to find her because her last name has changed. But there she is, a close-up shot that looks like it was taken at a fancy dinner, her facial features achingly familiar. She's leaner, all of the baby fat I knew and loved gone.

Seeing her puts a flutter in my chest. I never got closure, and it's like all of my feelings for her have just been sitting in my heart, waiting to be addressed.

It's not that I feel anything romantic for her—far from it. I just never knew what happened to her. I never found out if she was okay and if she got over what happened between us.

I click her profile and scroll down.

She's married to a man.

They have two boys, a toddler and an infant.

I wipe an impatient hand across my eyes, clearing the tears, and draw a shaky breath.

She looks happy. I hope she is. I hope she wasn't forced to hide her feelings for women because of what happened between us.

There are endless pictures and videos of her and her family. She posts something every day, usually her and her boys smiling, laughing, playing.

One thing is certain: she isn't as damaged as me when it comes to having an online presence. She never let Lauren ruin her ability to be in someone else's pictures and videos. She's out there in the world, sharing what brings her joy.

I could add her as a friend. I could message her to tell her I'm glad she's happy.

But what would be the benefit of that? It would bring up the past, when she's probably eager to forget it. She's moved on, and so should I.

I close the browser tab and send her love from afar. I hope she can feel it. I hope she knows how relieved I am that she's found happiness when the world was so cruel to her.

She deserves it. We both do.

I open a new tab and search for therapists. It's time to work through this with someone who can help me.

Seeing Sarah and Lauren living full lives in spite of what happened gives me hope that I can learn how to move past it too. I want to, and I owe it to myself. Life is so much more than whatever embarrassment I dealt with as a teenager. Life is about partners, families, experiences, pets, passions, and everything else represented in what those women have posted online. They've been posting snippets of their lives since high school, and, meanwhile, I've been frozen in time, paralyzed by fear and embarrassment.

My life is so much more. I want to learn how to think of that incident as a distant memory, a part of my life that doesn't have to control me.

Tabloids, paparazzi, Phil Niles, and online trolls—they're all strangers. They're people I can choose not to care about. They can say what they want about me, and it doesn't affect how I feel about Cate.

And how do I feel about her?

That's easy. I'm completely head-over-heels in love with her.

Chapter 26
I Am Not a Stunt Person

Clockwork Curie is in its last day of shooting, so I'm pausing my thesis research for the day. The scene looks exciting, and Abby and I are going to watch from our balcony.

Also, I need to make sure I don't miss my chance to see Cate before she leaves.

I fling open my curtains, letting the morning sun bathe my room for the first time in years. It stings my eyes in the best way. The movie set buzzes below, traffic rolls down the streets beyond it, and the ocean sparkles in the distance. A sailboat drifts past, and I wonder what adventure those people are going on.

I get dressed in the pants I bought from Rainbow's witchy shop and a sports bra, then settle into a wooden patio chair between Abby and the hydrangeas we occasionally remember to water. She's set up a tray of snacks and tea between us.

For a couple of hours, we watch Cate's stunt double fly along the zip-line while explosions go off below. The zip-line starts on the crane about fifty feet off the ground, zooms past the steampunk storefronts, and ends in what is ordinarily my favorite pizza place. She holds onto a T-bar and is clipped in by a harness that will presumably be edited out during post-production. Soaring over the set in a steampunk outfit, skirt flapping, looks pretty badass.

Our neighbors all step onto their balconies to watch too—it's the most exciting thing to happen since a restaurant down the road caught fire five years ago.

"I had no idea Marie Curie was such a daredevil," Abby says, reaching for a chocolate chip cookie.

I blow on my tea. "Don't mess with a physicist. She's probably on her way to defend her thesis."

My stomach twists at the sight of Cate's stunt double, both due to her resemblance to Cate from behind and the barely healed wound from the picture of her kissing Phil.

I don't have hard feelings toward her. She was just kissing a hot actor. Whether or not she knew what Phil was up to doesn't matter—I've decided that it doesn't affect me and isn't worth dwelling on. It wasn't Cate kissing Phil, and that's all I care about.

My phone lights up.

With a little trepidation, I lean over to check it.

It's an email from Dr. Wee.

I set down my tea and open it, heart thumping.

Dear Rachel,

We don't care who you are dating or how many magazines you grace the cover of. Let's schedule a check-in next week to discuss your progress.

Regards,
Dr. Natalie Wee

I grin. At least she's direct.

"Good news?" Abby asks.

I nod. "All of that worrying about how dating Cate would affect my career might've been for nothing. I'll have to call my mom later to gently tell her how wrong she was."

This leaves me with the only two opinions that matter: Cate's and my own. I know what my heart wants, and I'm running out of time to find out if she wants me back.

While the crew reels the zip-line's T-bar back up to the crane for another take, I scan for her among the actors. What if she's not even on set? I haven't seen her yet today—it's all been her stunt double.

"When are you going to head down and tell her you love her?" Abby says, watching me.

My heart skips. "When I stop panicking over whether she loves me back."

"Chicken," Abby says.

"It's called self-preservation."

While Abby makes chicken noises, the director shouts from below that this is the last take. There's a distinct noise of disappointment from the neighbors' balconies.

I stand. Where's Cate? Why haven't I seen her?

People have already started taking down the white tents.

"Abby, what if—"

"There," Abby says, pointing.

On the far side of the metal fence, a black SUV rolls up, and Ken steps out, unmistakable in his large build. Cate is striding across the movie set toward him. She's out of her costume and carrying a bag.

I curse. "Abby, she's leaving!"

I pick up my phone and tap her name. The phone rings and rings, but Cate keeps walking, giving no sign that she hears her phone. It must be on silent.

"I double dare you to run after her," Abby says in a saucy tone.

I face her, an exhilarated smile pulling at my lips. "Dare accepted."

As I race inside, Abby follows. "Get that girl, Rachel. I'll see you later. I'm off to use some of our Phil Niles money for a shopping spree. I need new pants."

"Pants?" I say, ramming my feet into my shoes. "When have you ever worn pants?"

She smacks her ass on the way into her bedroom. "Exactly."

I sprint out of the apartment, down the stairs, and out onto the street.

The security guard stands in front of the opening of the metal fence, and as I run toward him, he puts his hands up.

"The set is closed, love."

"I need to see Cate Whitney," I say, pleading.

"Don't we all?" he says with a pointed look to my left.

A horde of fans presses against the metal fence, phones and printed photos in hand, craning for a glimpse of Cate.

"Come on, man." I glance at his name tag. "Ferguson. I was here with her before. Rachel, remember?"

"I know. But even if we weren't wrapping up and in the middle of a shoot, I can't let you in without a badge."

"Did Cate tell you not to let me in?"

Ferguson raises an eyebrow. "Um, no. I'm not supposed to let anyone in. It's nothing personal."

I crane my neck. The SUV is still there, a glimpse of blond hair moving toward it.

Cate is about to leave through the fence. I have seconds to get to her, and running around the perimeter of the set will take way too long.

"Cate!" I shout.

She's too far away. Not even the nearest crew members look up at me, like I'm invisible—just another fan like the group to my left.

"Sean!" I shout, but he's nowhere in sight.

Ferguson gives me a pitying look but doesn't waver.

With a spark of insight, I recall Cate giving me Sean's number when we first met, the day she invited me to visit her on set. I fumble for my phone and press his name in my contacts.

He answers in one ring. "Hello, this is Sean Richards speak—"

"Sean! It's Rachel. I'm outside the fence and I need to talk to Cate. She's about to get into a car with Ken. Can you stop her?"

"I—no—Rachel, I'm really busy right now—"

"Please, Sean. Stop her, or tell Ferguson to let me through."

In the distance, Cate squeezes through a gap in the fence, about to climb into the SUV. I have seconds to get to her.

"I'm packing up Cate's trailer, honey," Sean says, clearly struggling with something. "I've got my arms full of clothes, I haven't eaten or peed in six hours, and I'm a little—"

I curse and end the call.

The crane holding the zip-line is a few strides away on the other side of the fence. At the top, the T-bar sways in the breeze, ready for the final take. Cate's stunt double and a few crew members are walking this way.

An obstacle course of people and equipment clutters the distance between me and Cate.

Get that girl, Rachel.

Going through the set will get me jumped on. Going around the set will take too long. That leaves me with one option: I have to go over the top of it.

Heart thumping, I point at the group of fans. "Hey, is that guy supposed to be climbing the fence?"

The moment Ferguson looks, I bolt through the opening toward the crane.

He catches on immediately, and his footsteps pound behind me. "Dammit. Rachel, stop!"

I climb the steps two at a time, heaving for breath. Ferguson is close behind, his shouts spiking my adrenaline.

I've gone past the point of no return, and this is probably the worst idea of my life. Worse than kissing a woman who has a boyfriend. Worse than drinking everything in an expensive gift basket and then waking up at six a.m. the next day for a flight. Worse than crawling under a table and ending up covered in mustard just in time to meet my celebrity crush.

At the top of the crane, I grab the T-bar. It's cold and provides a good grip. Crap, this is high up. My stomach clenches into a ball.

Ferguson is a step behind me, shouting. "Rachel, don't even think—"

Screaming, I jump off the platform and soar down, flying across the movie set, over the yelling cast and crew.

My body reacts instinctively, drawing fast breaths, every muscle taut and ready for impact. I tuck my knees up as I fly into the pizza place, like Cate's stunt double did, and smack hard into the opposite wall, where an enormous black landing pad engulfs me.

I let go of the bar and collapse to my hands and knees, wheezing for breath.

Okay, that was reckless and dangerous.

But also kind of fun?

I get my feet under me, but I'm shaking too much to stand. Then a hand closes around my arm and hauls me to my feet.

"What the hell are you doing?" a deep voice says.

Heart pounding, I look around to find shocked and horrified faces, including the director, who is the one with his hand around my arm.

"I need to talk to—"

"Somebody get this girl off the set—now!" he shouts, a vein throbbing in his forehead. "Check the zip-line and make sure she didn't compromise it."

Ferguson runs in, swearing. "Rachel, get on the ground and put your arms out!"

Shit, I've really pissed these people off.

"Oh my God, honey, why?" Sean says from somewhere behind me. "Excuse her, everyone. She was born without survival instincts—"

"Wait!" Cate shouts.

The crowd parts, and Cate stands behind them, staring at me, her hands out to stop Ferguson from hauling me away. Despite her perfect makeup, her face is pale, and her eyes are heavy like she hasn't slept. Her shoulders are more slumped than usual, her posture reminding me of the way I looked driving back from camping—defeated, regretful, heartbroken.

I pull free from Ferguson's grip. "Cate."

My heart swells. She's also wearing the pants she got from Rainbow's shop.

There are so many people staring at us. The cast and crew surround us. Ferguson stands like an attack dog waiting for a release command. Sean is covering the lower half of his face with a clipboard, his wide eyes darting between Cate and me.

"Can we talk?" I say, my voice carrying through the clockwork pizza parlor. "I'm not ready to say bye."

My lips go numb as the blood drains from my face in panic.

What if she says no?

Her eyes go glossy and she nods. "I'll meet you at your place in ten minutes?"

Whispers break out around us.

"Okay," I say, my face tingling. "See you soon."

The hold the moment had over us snaps, and Ferguson steps forward to grab me. The cast and crew step into each other to whisper and gossip.

As Ferguson's grip tightens over my upper arm, Ken says, "I can take it from here, man."

He shows up on my other side, leaving Ferguson to let go and step back.

Ken escorts me to the exit. My pulse pounds, making me jittery.

"You're something else, you know that?" he says.

I don't know what to say to that, so I just grimace.

"She's been a wreck," he murmurs. "Just so you know."

I nod, a twist in my gut. "So have I."

Chapter 27
Extreme Beach Walking

I open the door before Cate can knock and stand back to let her inside. She hesitates, then brushes past me, the gentle rub of our arms sending my heart fluttering.

For a long moment, we just look at each other, and I sink into her eyes.

I remember what I wanted to tell her and swallow hard.

Before I can speak, she steps closer. "Rachel, I'm so sorry I didn't trust you. I know you value my privacy. I panicked. It was completely my own issue and so unfair to put you through that."

"Thank you," I say, her apology making my chest tight. "Cate, I—"

"The truth is, I know how much you care about me because that's one of the things I love so much about you. You're genuine and honest, and when I'm with you I feel safer than I ever have. I promise I won't do that to you again. I never want to doubt you—"

"Stop," I say, grabbing her hands. Her words are whirling around in my brain, and I need to get my words out before I forget everything I wanted to tell her. "I'm sorry I ran away from us. I've done a lot of thinking, and I'm going to get a therapist to help me deal with my high school trauma. The only opinions that matter in this relationship are mine and yours. Others can say whatever they want, and I won't let that affect how I feel."

Cate's eyebrows pull down. "Rachel, you don't owe me any apologies. I never should have let you get into that situation with Phil or the tabloids or any of it. I should have protected you."

I shake my head. "It's impossible to protect me from everything—the internet, people with cameras, TV. I need to learn how to deal with that kind of attention. I *want* to."

She studies me, her brow furrowed, like she's trying to gauge how serious I am.

"I'd do anything for you, Cate. Like hide in a changeroom to avoid the paparazzi and then buy a thousand dollars' worth of trinkets and harem pants from a woman named Rainbow."

Cate laughs, that bright, contagious sound that ripples pleasantly through me.

I clear my throat. "What I really wanted to say…"

It's getting hard to speak. I draw a breath. It's like her presence is a vacuum pulling me in, bringing all the air and light in the room to a single point.

"I love you," I say, my heart leaping as the words come out, like I've launched off the zip-line again.

Her lips part like I've surprised her.

Fuck, that wasn't supposed to be a surprise. It was supposed to be inevitable.

She tilts her head. A smile curves her lips as she whispers, "I love you too."

Everything inside me is light, airy, like I'm floating into the sky. "You do?"

"Rachel, of course I do. I've never had this kind of connection with anyone."

I smile. "Me neither."

Suddenly, our relationship is more than just this moment—it's tomorrow and the next day and onward. We have a future. Where will it lead us? What adventures will we have, and where will we end up?

I step into her arms, pulling her into a kiss.

Our lips move against each other, and she's as soft and sweet as ever. Her hands run down my back and over my waist, and she pulls my hips closer. Our bodies fit together as I melt into her.

"Is your roommate about to walk in again?" Cate murmurs.

I shake my head so our noses brush. "She went shopping for pants, so she's going to be a while."

"Good."

She pulls me in firmly, her thigh between my legs.

I run my fingers through her soft hair, over her shoulders, down her bare arms.

"I'm glad you didn't decide to go back to Phil," I whisper.

She wrinkles her nose like the thought repulses her. "Rachel, when you saw that photo of Phil kissing the woman you thought was me, did you think it was real? Did you think we were getting back together?"

I hesitate. "I don't know what I thought. I was confused."

Sadness pulls down her features. "I thought you knew how I felt about you."

"I guess part of me thought our relationship was too good to be true. Like maybe Phil was your true love and I was an experiment."

"An experiment?"

I bite my lip. The word slipped out, but I guess it was my fear from the beginning. Julia hurt me by treating me that way, and maybe I didn't get over that as thoroughly as I thought. "I guess I was projecting my own baggage onto our relationship," I say. "I was afraid you just wanted to try being with a woman and that I was…interchangeable."

"Oh, Rachel. You aren't a fling. I like you for you."

A tingling goes out to my fingers and toes. That is exactly what I wanted to hear. "Okay. That's good—"

She cups my face. "I mean it when I say I love you. I love your brain, your body, your soul."

My breath catches and I nod, words failing me.

We kiss again, and with Cate's hands caressing me and my fingers in her hair, the flutter in my belly is so fierce that it's like we're kissing for the first time. We press closer together, lips moving hungrily. Her gentle touch on my bare waist sends a shiver through me.

Gratitude fills my chest. I wish I'd known on that day I left the campground, miserable and full of self-loathing, that I would meet my soulmate a few hours later. I must be the luckiest person in the world to have the universe bring us together—lucky and a little reckless. What possessed me to sneak onto the set and talk to Cate like that? It was bold, and I could have easily said no to Abby's dare. But I'd done it, and it led me here.

It's like Cate said when we met for drinks: we all end up where we need to be. A string of seemingly insignificant decisions and luck led us to this moment in my kitchen, and I wouldn't trade any of it—even the rough parts.

I graze my fingers down her neck, over her breasts and down the curve of her waist, memorizing her. Her breath hitches, and the sound sends a tendril of heat through me.

"Do you want to spend the night together?" I ask, the words coming out breathy.

She nods. "Maybe you can take me on your favorite uitwaaien route later."

"I would love to. We could also go for a fancy dinner—hand-picked cheese and aged potatoes or whatever."

"Sounds lovely," she whispers into my lips.

I slide my fingers into her hair and back her into the wall. Our kiss is deep, heat licking between us. Before, we were always so frantic, so overcome with passion, but now we know we have time—a future.

Still, we're soon tugging each other's clothes off, and her body against mine is intoxicating, leaving me dizzy.

She runs kisses along my neck and shoulder and moans. "I also love your fingers."

Our hands move between each other's legs and she closes her eyes, leaning her head against the wall. Her knees weaken and she sinks a couple of inches.

The sight of her losing control sends waves of longing through me. With one hand on her waist and the other between her legs, I nestle into the crook of her neck, getting lost in her—the feel of her on my fingers, our sweaty bodies pressed together, her fingers rubbing me faster.

Her breaths quicken. She trembles, and her nails dig into my shoulder. "Rachel…"

"Me too," I say between gasps. "Come with me."

We lock lips in a deep kiss as we climax together, gasping into each other's mouths, our bodies shuddering. It's hard to stay standing, and we use each other and the wall for support as our legs give out.

We lean against each other for a long moment to catch our breaths, and my heart swells to twice its normal size.

I could spend my whole life finding ways to make this woman happy.

We get dressed and go for dinner, and as the sun sets over the Pacific Ocean, we walk hand in hand along the retreating shoreline. I laugh as Cate comes to the jarring realization that the stretch of beach I walk is mostly rocks and barnacles.

"I thought when you said you like walking the beach, you meant barefoot on sand," she says, stepping gingerly.

"Consider my hobby to be Extreme Beach Walking. Wait until you feel how cold the water is."

She looks dubiously at the frothy black waves lapping toward us. "If you splash me or push me in…"

I grab her and she screams, clutching me like she's ready to take me with her.

"I wouldn't," I say, pulling her close.

We kiss, tongues flirting, nipping each other's lower lips. The waves hiss beside us, and the wind whips our clothes and hair.

"Hey, I was thinking," I say, my heart skipping over what I'm about to ask. "We've never taken a selfie together."

"Are you asking me for a photo?" Cate asks, grinning.

"If it's not too much trouble. I'm a big fan of your work."

She laughs.

My pulse is racing, but with Cate at my side, I'm full of hope. I've set up a therapy appointment, and I'm determined to heal. I want my future to include a thousand pictures and videos of Cate and me on all the adventures we're about to have.

The salty breeze plays with a lock of her blond hair, framing her face. The setting sun gives her skin a gorgeous glow beyond anything a makeup artist could do. Her eyes are piercing, ethereal. How did I get so lucky?

I spin her so the shoreline is at our backs. In the distance, the North Shore mountains touch the sky. "Right here."

She holds up her phone, and we snap a photo with the beach and mountains behind us, Cate kissing my cheek, me smiling like I'm the happiest person in the world.

This one is going to be my phone background.

Holding hands, we continue our stroll along the shoreline.

"When do you have to fly home?" I say, asking the question that's been churning inside me. The words come out casual, but my heart beats fast in anticipation of the answer.

Cate hesitates. "My flight is in the morning."

There's a sensation like a boulder dropping into my stomach. "Oh."

"But I can fly back and forth to visit as much as I want...or...I could cancel my flight."

I bite my lip, a grin stretching across my face. "I think you should cancel your flight."

She searches me with those gorgeous, ice-blue eyes, a smile playing at her lips. "You do?"

"Definitely."

"Where would you recommend I search for real estate?"

The breath leaves my lungs, a rush of exhilaration. *Real estate? Like, to buy a home?*

She must see the thought process passing behind my eyes because her smile widens. "I told you I'm tired of LA. In truth, I haven't been happy there for a long time. I've been thinking about moving somewhere a little further from Hollywood, but I never found the right place—or a convincing enough reason."

"What about Josie and Waffles?" I ask, numb.

"I can fly back to see them whenever I want. I'm ready for something new, Rachel."

"So you want to live here?" I say, the words feeling surreal as they pass my lips.

She nods.

"For how long?"

She casts that genuine smile I fell in love with. "From now until forever."

Other Books from Ylva Publishing

www.ylva-publishing.com

Breaking Character
Lee Winter

ISBN: 978-3-96324-113-0
Length: 315 pages (106,000 words)

Life becomes a farcical mess when icy British A-lister Elizabeth and bright LA star Summer try to persuade an eccentric director they're in love to win Elizabeth her dream role—while convincing a gossiping Hollywood they're not. Worse, they're closeted lesbians who don't even know the other is gay.

A lesbian celebrity romance about gaining love, losing masks, and trying to stick to the script.

Just Physical
(The Hollywood series – Book 4)
Jae

ISBN: 978-3-95533-534-2
Length: 271 pages (116,000 words)

After being diagnosed with MS, actress Jill takes herself off the romantic market. On the set of a disaster movie, she meets stunt woman Crash, whose easy smile makes her wish things were different. Despite their growing feelings, Jill is determined to let Crash into her bed, but not her heart. As they start to play with fire on and off camera, will they be able to keep things just physical?

The Wrong McElroy
KL Hughes

ISBN: 978-3-96324-263-2
Length: 176 pages (64,000 words)

When Fiona's best friend, Michael, needs a fake girlfriend for Christmas in Arkansas, Fiona steps up. How hard could one family weekend be, anyway?

That's before she meets his boisterous clan, including Lizzie, Michael's beautiful, charming sister who is so intoxicating that Fiona can barely concentrate.

An amusing lesbian romance about finding unexpected love inside family expectations.

Scissor Link
(The Scissor Link series – Book 1)
Georgette Kaplan

ISBN: 978-3-95533-678-3
Length: 197 pages (72,000 words)

Wendy is in love with Janet Lace. Janet is beautiful, she's intelligent, and she is also Wendy's boss.

Still, a little fantasy never hurt anyone. Or so Wendy thought until Janet got a look at the e-mail she sent. The one about exactly what Wendy would like to do to Janet.

But when Wendy gets called into the boss's office, it might just be her fantasy coming true. If it doesn't get her fired first.

A lighthearted comedy about a kinky office romance.

About Tiana Warner

Tiana Warner is a writer and outdoor enthusiast from British Columbia, Canada. She is best known for her critically acclaimed "Mermaids of Eriana Kwai" trilogy and its comic adaptation. Tiana is a lifelong horseback rider, a former programmer with a Computer Science degree, and a dog mom to a hyperactive rescue mutt named Joey.

CONNECT WITH TIANA

Website: tianawarner.com
Facebook: facebook.com/TianaWarnerAuthor
Twitter: twitter.com/tianawarner
Instagram: instagram.com/tianawarner
TikTok: tiktok.com/@tiana_warner

From Fan to Forever
© 2022 by Tiana Warner

ISBN: 978-3-96324-691-3

Available in e-book and paperback formats.

Published by Ylva Publishing, legal entity of Ylva Verlag, e.Kfr.

Ylva Verlag, e.Kfr.
Owner: Astrid Ohletz
Am Kirschgarten 2
65830 Kriftel
Germany

www.ylva-publishing.com

First edition: 2022

Credits
Edited by Alissa McGowan and Michelle Aguilar
Cover Design and Print Layout by Streetlight Graphics

Printed in Great Britain
by Amazon

85993445R00125